XOXO,

D1545150

the hard truth about

Sunshine

SAWYER BENNETT

Find Sawyer on the web!
www.sawyerbennett.com
www.twitter.com/bennettbooks
www.facebook.com/bennettbooks

Dedication

To that wounded marine with no leg and only half a hand I met in the Orlando airport… your pain made an impression on me. Semper Fi.

Table of Contents

Chapter 1

SOMETIMES I MARVEL at the stupid shit I do. When I was seven, I tried to see how many dandelions I could put up my sister's nose. She was three at the time, and as it turns out, four was the magic number. It took a lot of concentration on my part, especially because she wasn't quite so sure she wanted to participate. But it was only two in each nostril, so I didn't think it was a big deal.

But that wasn't the truly stupid thing I did on that occasion. When she started getting upset that her nose was clogged full of flowers, I tried to pull them out, but dandelions are a lot easier to stuff into closed quarters than to pull them out with clumsy little boy fingers. Apparently, it was a ~~brilliant~~ stupid idea to get my mama's crochet needle to pull them out.

While, technically, I didn't yank her brains out with the hooked end, I wasn't as delicate as I guess I should have been, and there may have been some blood involved. That earned me an ass whippin' from my pa—using his belt, of course—that made it impossible for me to sit down for three full days.

From my ma, I only got the guilt trip. "Christopher James Barlow… I'm so disappointed in you. You could have pulled her brains out."

No, Ma… pretty sure I couldn't have done that.

Then there was the time in high school when some buddies and I thought it would be fun to break into the principal's office at night and super glue every movable object in there to something else. Turns out, not so fun when you get caught.

Or when I was dating Cici Carlan and thought I could also date Kim Flick at the same time, and neither would be the wiser.

Turns out that girls talk.

A lot.

Stupid, stupid shit I get myself into.

Of course, those were just things that were pettily foolish. I've committed far worse idiocies over my life that resulted in ~~bad consequences~~ death and destruction for all involved. Sounds dramatic, but it's completely true.

But today… at twenty-six years of age… I marvel over my latest act of foolishness as I head west on I-40. I'm driving my big black Suburban filled with a misfit crew of people I can barely stand but have committed to spending the next several days with them on the open road.

"Christopher, can you turn the A/C down a bit?" a

timid voice asks from the backseat directly behind me. My eyes cut to my rearview mirror, and I look at Dead Kid's reflection. His hand pulls nervously at the collar of his t-shirt and I can see a thin layer of sweat on his forehead, extending upward to the bald top of his head and across his acne-infested cheeks.

"You going to be sick?" I ask suspiciously as I turn the temperature down before looking back in the mirror to try to determine if that's a tinge of green to his skin.

"No," he assures me, tugging at his collar. "Just hot."

"Tell me if you're going to be sick," I insist, my foot easing off the gas and my eyes going to the passenger-side mirror to see if I can start making my way over to the shoulder of the interstate in case he needs to puke.

He shakes his head and looks at me through the rearview mirror, giving me a reassuring smile that fully reaches his brown eyes, which, admittedly, haven't seemed as dull as they had for the past few weeks. "Not going to be sick."

I let my gaze drift back to the road, accepting his word.

Not going to be sick, but you're definitely going to die. That's a fact, kid.

"Here… barf in this if you have to," Goth Chick says from the backseat, and my eyes cut back to the mirror. She hands him a McDonald's bag that had previously held the sausage biscuits we ate for breakfast.

"I'm not going to puke," he reiterates in a firm voice,

but I notice he takes the bag.

"You better not," Goth Chick warns, her teeth flashing in a grimace made whiter by the black lipstick she's wearing.

"He said he's not sick so leave him alone," a softly lilting voice says from beside me in the front passenger seat.

I have to force myself not to turn my head to look at her. Even a brief glance at Jillian Martel and her droopy blue eyes wouldn't be safe to me, and she's probably the real reason why I think I've made a stupid mistake in taking this trip.

She claims to be suffering from depression because of her condition, but fuck if you'd ever get that from her. Her disposition is as sunny and bright as her golden hair, which I know will be shimmering from the late morning sun that pours in through my glass sunroof overhead if I were to look at her. I'd nicknamed her Sexy Eyes on the day we met and that still holds true today, so it's best I don't look at her.

I don't need the reminder that this girl is the epitome of everything that I am not.

I met this weird-as-hell crew—Sexy Eyes, Goth Chick, and Dead Kid—in a group therapy session where our pit-bull of a leader, Mags Bundy, is desperately trying to facilitate a friendship among us as we work through our issues.

I have little in common with the lot, but there is a

thin thread of commonality that connects me to Dead Kid. He's dying—and I want to die on some occasions—so I guess I'm a bit envious of him. I also have some resonance with Goth Chick. She's bitter, angry at the world, and likes to smoke pot. I'm also bitter, angry at the world, and like to smoke pot.

But I can't find anything in common with Sexy Eyes.

There's an aura of something odd that comes off her. It's her words, her tone of voice. It's the way her eyes crinkle slightly when she smiles, which is the most movement I ever really see from them given her medical condition. The way she looks at you directly and the way her shoulders are always loose and relaxed, displaying an overt confidence in herself and surroundings. Out of all of us, she has a firm acceptance of her fate. Setting her even further apart from this group, she doesn't seem upset about it at all.

In fact, I can't figure out for the life of me why she's even in our support group because Jillian Martel is just in a league all by herself, regardless of her disease.

She actually radiates light.

Happiness.

Joy.

Invincibility regardless of her situation.

She seems filled with so much goddamn delight over life as she knows it that it sort of makes me hate her for it.

But the reason I made a stupid decision and came on

this trip is that I'm as equally intrigued by Jillian Martel as I am repelled by her. My intrigue won out, and I agreed to this ludicrous idea of a group journey so I could be near her.

I agreed because I need to know how she does it.

How she can have such a grim future and still smile as if all is right with her world.

Chapter 2

I PERUSE THE candy selection offered in this convenience store while my SUV is gassing up. I'm looking for my favorites, because junk food is always essential on a road trip. I'll admit… it dredges up some bitter memories because the only road trips I ever really took were with Maria, but I'm not going to let my love of sour gummy worms, corn nuts and white cheddar popcorn be marred by the memory of what we were to each other but are no longer.

"Corn nuts?" I hear Jillian say from behind me as I grab a bag.

"Essential road trip food," I tell her without looking her way. The cheery disposition she wears on her face sometimes hurts my ~~soul~~ eyes, like I'm looking directly at the sun.

"Any good?"

"Yup."

I grab the sour gummy worms and turn my back on Jillian, heading over to the chips aisle in search of popcorn. Her footsteps pad behind me and my shoulders stiffen with unease that she might continue the conversation.

It's painful to me... to make small talk. I'm the world's worst conversationalist and while I know Mags proclaimed this trip was truly for Dead Kid's sake, she was also hoping it would get some of us to open up.

Namely Goth Chick and me.

I've known this group of people for a total of six weeks, since our first weekly group session. I doubt Goth Chick and I have said more than a handful of words to each other or to the group on any given day, and that's fine by me. I got nothing really to say.

My eyes rise up and over the aisle of chips to see Goth Chick herself swiping a pack of gum from an endcap and shoving it into her bra. She doesn't even bother to look around to make sure the cashier isn't watching her, and that's because she truly doesn't give a shit if she gets caught.

She does lift her face to look at me, and we share loathsome stares with each other. Even from ten feet away, I can see her green-brown irises are glazed. If I were to stand next to her, I'd smell a hint of pot, because as soon as we pulled into the gas station, she headed around the back to smoke. I totally would have killed for a hit or two, but I'll be damned if I was going to ask her. Besides, I'd promised Mags I'd be sober if I was driving. I might be a shit most of the time, but I am a man of my word.

Goth Chick's real name is Barb, but her appearance earned her my nickname. Black hair cut in a short, cropped style a bit longer on the top and buzzed on the sides and back. Two rings pierced through her eyebrow, three rings through the middle of her bottom lip, and heavy, hollow ear gauges that a nickel would probably fit through. Tattoos cover both of her arms and clunky, metal rings adorn each finger painted with black polish. Her dark persona is always capped off by dark eyeliner and black lipstick, which makes her pale skin look even whiter. Today, she has on ripped fishnet stockings, combat boots, a black mini skirt, and a tight black t-shirt with the words "Fuck Democracy" across her small chest. No clue what that means, but I suspect she doesn't either. Probably just wearing it for the shock value of dropping a public "F" bomb.

"That was ballsy," Jillian says under her breath, almost reverently, and I realize she's come to stand beside me in the chip aisle. And I can't fucking help myself… I turn to look down at her—since I top her by a good foot—and watch her observing Goth Chick with an amused smile.

"That's second-hand nature to her," I tell her dryly. Goth Chick's a common criminal like me.

"Maybe," Jillian whispers, never turning to look at me but keeping her gaze on the little thief. "But she took that for Connor. He's addicted to gum."

My eyebrows rise… shocked over her proclamation.

How the fuck would Goth Chick even know that? As far as I know, they've never even really conversed as Goth Chick doesn't talk much in group unless it's to make caustic comments about someone else's pain. Maybe Dead Kid mentioned it, and while I've been ignoring much of what goes on in group, perhaps Goth Chick listens.

Still, I have to ask. "How does she know that Dead Kid's addicted gum?"

Jillian turns her head to me slowly. I know enough about her condition from observing her the past few weeks that it is about as fast as she can swivel her head because of muscle weakness. But from the fire in her eyes, I know she would have snapped her attention my way if she could.

"Don't call him that," she snarls at me, and she sounds like an aggrieved tiger.

Well, actually a kitten. Jillian Martel doesn't have it in her to be anything more than that. She's too fucking nice even in her anger.

I should be abashed that what I said was offensive. I know I should feel some measure of guilt.

I feel neither, so I merely shrug, "Why not? He's going to die."

"We're all going to die," she practically hisses at me.

"Yeah," I taunt, leaning my head down toward her so she can hear me clearly. "But he's the most imminent. Would it help if I clarify it and refer to him as Imminent

Dead Kid?"

My crudity causes Jillian to gasp.

Her gasp causes me to smirk.

I don't regret saying that, because I stopped caring what people thought about me a long time ago. I sure as hell don't care what Jillian thinks.

I brace and wait for the backlash, and I brace hard. While Jillian Martel may not have a vicious tongue from what I've come to learn about her, the way in which she castigates is pretty brutal. It's much more sinister than any amount of angry ranting I could ever do. The girl with the mushy heart and Pollyanna attitude will hit me hard in a much different way.

Jillian's eyes, which already have that perpetually softened look due to her disease, round just a tad further and her lips curl slightly in an empathetic sort of smile. She steps into me, laying her hand on my forearm without any regard to the shredded and scarred skin that lays thinly over bone. "I get it."

"Get what?" I grit out, glancing down briefly at where her tanned hand lays against the disfigured remnants of my arm.

"Why you feel the need to be so mean."

"You think I'm mean?" I ask, flashing my teeth at her in a mocking sneer. I'm so much more than mean.

"I think you're full of self-pity and anger, and that makes you feel justified to act like a jerk. I think the only small measure of relief you get from your pain is by making others feel bad or uncomfortable. I think you've all but given up on the potential for good to happen in your life so you're content to be mired in your anger. But please, Christopher, you can level that meanness at me if you want—or Barb, she's tough and can take it. But lay off Connor, okay? His days are numbered, and he doesn't need you throwing that in his face."

She says all of that softly… kindly, without an ounce of derision in her voice.

Rage courses through me over her words—that she would even think to preach to me about how I should conduct my life. And to do it with ~~empathy~~ pity directed at me. It's almost too much to bear, accepting that kind smile she has leveled at me right now.

But even as I open my mouth to lay into her—to let this bitch know she hasn't even begun to see the type of malice I hold within me—I find myself noticing a distinctly uneasy feeling starting to take root in the center of my chest. A dull ache. Perhaps a twinge of regret. Worst yet… an odd fascination over the fact she said there's the potential for good in my life.

That better not be fucking hope I'm feeling. I quashed that son-of-a-bitch emotion months ago, and I'll be damned if I'm going to succumb to that shit again. The fear that I might fall prey to the bright side of life distracts me from my need to put her solidly in her place.

The moment of fury passes as quickly as it slammed into me, and I'm left without a good comeback to throw in her face.

Instead, I take a deep breath, let it out slowly, and decide to give her this one. "Is that all?"

"That would make me happy. If you don't call Connor Dead Kid, I mean," she says with a twinkle in her eye. "For now."

For now? What the hell does that mean?

She wants me to make her happy in the future?

The way Maria looked to me for happiness and security? The way I knew she depended on me, and the way I felt so fucking good because I was responsible for the smile on her face?

Is that what Jillian "Pollyanna" Martel wants from me?

Yeah, that's not going to happen.

With a curt nod, I turn my back on her and walk up to the cash register. From the corner of my eye, I see Jillian walk out the door. She heads toward the gas pump where Goth Chick is pulling the pack of gum out of her bra to hand to ~~Dead Kid~~ Connor. Even from this distance, I can see him blushing and I almost have to suppress a slight urge to smile, but the moment passes.

There's a young girl behind the counter, sporting a red vest with the gas station logo over one breast and a name tag proclaiming her to be "Natalie" on the other. She gives me a flirty smile as I walk toward her, her eyes traveling down me slowly. When she gets to my legs, her shoulders tense, as expected, and when she lifts her gaze back to me, flirtation is gone and sympathy holds the smile in place.

I don't say a word as I place my items on the counter and reach in the back pocket of my cargo shorts for my wallet. She silently rings everything up and doesn't meet my eyes as I slide my credit card through the scanner and she bags my purchases.

I think I'm going to get away without a single word from this girl, but just as she's pushing the bag across the counter toward me, she swallows hard and says, "Um… I just wanted to say thank you for your service."

No secret… the U.S.M.C. t-shirt I'm wearing is a good enough hint I served. What she sees below my waist is another one.

I stare at her a moment, seeing hope in her eyes. Hope that my sacrifice was an honor for me to bear, and that her ability to sleep under a safe blanket of freedom is due solely to my leg that was mangled beyond repair while driving through the Helmand Province. She hopes I will thank her for her kind words, and that I will make her feel better for feeling safe at the expense of my blood and bones.

"Fuck off," I growl at her, actually taking great pleasure in the hurt and mortification on her face before I grab the bag and head out of the store. I take such immense pleasure in her discomfort that I know without a doubt that my shit-stained soul can never be scrubbed clean and salvaged. That I am a man who cannot be redeemed.

While my character as a human being is as foul as they come these days, I didn't always treat people like this. For the first few months after I was released from the hospital, I tried to give a nod of gratitude to anyone who acknowledged my service and sacrifice.

But then it got old.

I mean, really old.

And heavy. The heaviest of burdens weighing down on me like concrete. It made my chest squeeze with anxiety the minute someone would open their mouth to talk to me, and I would start to turn inward upon myself before the words of gratitude could penetrate me. It was as if an entirely different being resided within me, because I would watch almost from a distance, deep within myself, as I started to make up lies to tell people.

"Oh, I wasn't injured in combat. Shark attack."

Or...

"Bad incident with a combine working on my granddaddy's farm."

Or...

"Pissed-off girlfriend. Tried to cut my dick off, but got my leg and fingers instead."

Whatever.

The point being, I was tired of people thanking me for something I hadn't intended to do. I did not intend to get myself blown to pieces. When I signed up to serve my country, I didn't do so out of some deep sense of patriotism, but because it was a way out of a terrible life in the coal mines. My lies started getting more and more outrageous until I finally just ran out. I couldn't come up with one more interesting accident that could have destroyed my body the way it did.

And so, I just started telling people how I really felt. I told them to "fuck off." It truly was the best way to shut the conversation down.

There were no follow-up remarks like, "Oh, wow... a shark? That's amazing."

Or...

"Geez... I thought those combines had safety shut-off features."

Or...

"Is your girlfriend doing prison time, dude? Because she should totally be doing prison time for that."

The "fuck off" line did not invite reciprocal commentary, so it's the method I now employ one-hundred percent of the time to get people to leave me alone in my misery.

It's not where I'm happiest, but it is where I'm most comfortable.

Chapter 3

Six weeks ago…

I TOOK A deep drag off my cigarette.

So deep that the heat seared the skin of my thumb and forefinger, but I ignored it. I'd felt worse pain than that before. With a practiced flick, the glowing butt tumbled end over end into a flower bed of dried-out petunias. For a split second, I waited to see if they'd catch fire. If they did, then I'd get out of that stupid meeting, but, as always, the fates weren't kind to me. I watched as it continued to smoke slightly but caused no damage to the foliage, and so my immediate fate was decided.

I was already ten minutes late to the meeting, a fact I was very much aware of as I stood outside the library entrance while smoking down my Marlboro Red. I knew it wasn't the best way to make a good first impression, and I also knew that failure to attend the meeting would earn my ass a one-way ticket to a forty-five-day jail sentence.

And I still didn't give a fuck.

I mean... so what? I'd bet a jail cell wasn't much different than my shitty five-hundred-square-foot apartment filled with water stains on the ceiling and cockroaches on the walls. The meals were probably better.

It was the same old shit I'd been given the last year and a half.

Fuck you very much for your service to your country. You lost a leg, but here's a shiny new one for you as a consolation prize.

Or...

What the fuck, Marine? We get you have some "issues" following your injuries, but that's nothing that a little mental health tune-up can't help you with.

Now insert a condescending pat on the head as I was handed a bottle of antidepressants along with the directions to the Wake County library where I was supposed to attend group therapy as a means to avoid jail.

I pulled my phone from the pocket on the leg of my cargo shorts. It clanged against the metal of my prosthetic before my stiff fingers could get a good grasp, and I pulled it out. I figured if I was getting ready to sit with a group of depressed losers, I might as well pile the misery on good before I went in there.

The text icon indicated three awaiting messages, and I found it telling that my heart didn't race anymore at the prospect of hearing from Maria. I wanted to hear from her, but I didn't feel as if my existence depended on it anymore, and I supposed that was some progress.

Immediately, I saw what I'd seen for the past four months. Or not seen actually.

Nothing from Maria.

Nothing to have indicated she'd come to her senses and realized she'd made a huge mistake by breaking up with me. Because seriously... who didn't want an incomplete man with an enormously fucked-up head?

There was a text from my brother, Jody. *Leeds River Mine is hiring.*

I deleted the message immediately. It did no good to respond and decline, because it wouldn't stop Jody from trying to get me to come back home to West Virginia and partake in the family tradition of coal mining. I wasn't sure why it was important to him, because my family had made it clear they didn't give a shit what happened to me over there.

Another text was from Ferguson... a dude I served with in Afghanistan. I didn't even bother reading it, but I could imagine what it said. *Thinking of you, buddy. Stay strong. God Bless. Semper Fi. Blah, blah, blah.*

Delete.

Finally, a message from Digger. My drug dealer. *Just scored. B at ur place at 9.*

That one I didn't delete. The prospect of smoking myself into oblivion that night while kicking Digger's ass in *Call of Duty* caused an actual smile to come to my face. Well, I thought it was a smile. I had a two-inch scar running from the left corner of my mouth down to the side of my chin that actually pinched and tugged a bit, which usually meant I was smiling, but without a mirror, I wasn't sure.

Tucking my phone back in my pocket, I entered the library, immediately thankful for the icy blast of air conditioning. It was a blistering ninety-five degrees in Raleigh, North Carolina—a bit high for May—and some people refused to turn on the AC unless it was officially summertime. But these morons would never know what hot was really like until they'd walked around in a scorching desert carrying ninety pounds of gear and weaponry.

Just beyond the circulation desk was a wooden door with a brass plaque beside it on the wall that said "Anderson Reading Room". I didn't bother with a knock, but pushed the door open without preamble. I immediately took in a round circle of chairs facing inward, no more than ten total. At least half of them were empty. A small woman stood from the chair nearest me and waved me in.

"Come in, come in," she said in a distinctly southern voice. She was small… not even five foot. And old. Like older than my grandmama, Kaylene, on my daddy's side who was like sixty and had a rough life complicated by drugs and alcohol. And yet, this woman looked older than that. She had short, cropped hair the color of snowy clouds and deeply lined skin that was more pronounced around the corners of her eyes, lips, and along her neckline. Sparkling blue eyes looked at me with almost a hint of amusement. I knew her name was Mags Bundy from the paperwork I'd received that ordered me here and that she was to be our counselor and facilitator.

"Now that Christopher is here, we can get started," Mags said as she settled into her plastic chair. I found an empty one without anyone immediately to either side and sat. She crossed one small leg over the other, and the hem of her faded jeans pulled up to reveal pink socks with red lips on them. Somehow, that didn't surprise me.

"This is a peer-led support group for anyone suffering from traumatic stress and depression. It's sponsored by the county, so that's your tax dollars hard at work. It's not designed to provide counseling services, but merely to allow a safe place where people can come together to discuss their issues. The reasons we're all here are varied, and we'll get to know each other well. Today, we'll just spend some time with introductions. I'll start first."

I lowered my gaze to the floor and tried to tune out Mags' voice. She was clearly a native of the south as indicated by her accent, but she spoke quickly and with purpose. If I had to describe her in my limited exposure and in just three words, I'd have said, "Tough. Old. Broad."

"I've been leading this group for thirteen years now. It runs every quarter for twelve weekly sessions, an hour each session. I suffer from chronic depression stemming from a long string of woes that have happened to me, starting with my father sexually abusing me for several years and ending with an abusive husband who liked to flick cigarettes at my head for sport."

My shoulders gave a slight jerk and my head tilted up to see Mags staring at me. I could picture the cigarette I had just flicked away not five minutes ago as it tumbled end over end away from me. I imagined doing that again... right now... right at Mags' head. The thought didn't offend me too much, because while yeah... sucked to be diddled by your daddy, that didn't have shit to do with me.

We were apples and oranges.

She had two strong legs and was clearly not feeble in the head. She could have walked away from that shit where as I couldn't even crawl away from my shit. I had to be scraped off the desert floor.

Mags continued to talk about the format of the group. She said something about confidentiality and maybe taking field trips...like we were at summer camp or something. I tuned her out and started looking at my fellow prisoners.

My eyes immediately came to the woman sitting directly across from me. She stared raptly at Mags, shoulders relaxed and her knees pressed primly together. One delicate hand rested on her lap while the other fiddled with a long lock of golden-blonde hair that hung over her shoulder.

Her face was an interesting study. High cheekbones, a sloped nose that tilted upward, and large, almond-shaped eyes that gave her an elfin sort of look. I couldn't tell what color her eyes were because her lids hung a little heavy, almost as if she were drowsy. Actually, it was kind of a sexy look.

Bedroom eyes. That was what they looked like, and I had a sudden longing for Maria that struck me deep in the pit of my stomach. Maria laying on the bed, naked and looking up at me with those heated eyes filled with lust. God, I missed that look. And fuck, I missed sex. And I hated her for taking it away from me.

The blonde's head turned slightly, and she looked directly at me. It was a weird gaze because I expected her eyes to widen a bit when she realized I was staring at her, but her lids still hung low, again giving that slightly drowsy look. My guess was she was drugged out of her mind.

Well, regardless... she had perpetual bedroom eyes and wouldn't be a hardship to look at over the next few months.

My gaze cut away from Sexy Eyes, and I look at the person to her left. Young guy... still in his teens if the acne and protruding Adam's apple were anything to go by. He was skinny and gaunt and bald. Definitely sick. Pale skin and tired eyes that told me he'd had chemo or radiation. I saw plenty of veterans in for cancer treatments while I was rehabbing. I decided to call him Dead Kid, and I quashed the tiny kernel of sympathy that flickered within me because I sometimes imagined going where he was headed, and it didn't seem like a bad option.

Moving on...

That left one other person in the room, and she sat to my left with a chair in between us. I had to crane my neck to look at her, so it was obvious I was staring. Her face tilted to meet my gaze, and we leveled hateful stares at each other. I hadn't noticed it before, but I did now. The distinctive, sour-smoky smell of pot coming off her along with the slightly glazed irises of a creepy green-brown color. She was totally goth looking, covered in piercings and tattoos with a nasty vibe of "I hate everything" coming off her.

She was unique and angry, and that was compelling to me. I wondered if she'd give me a blow job in return for the joint I had stashed in my cargo pocket.

On second thought, she was so angry looking I was afraid she might bite my dick off and I couldn't afford to lose anymore body parts. When the IED exploded under our Humvee, most of the blast got absorbed by the undercarriage of the vehicle. It was ripped and torn steel that cut into my leg, shattered the bones, and took two fingers from my right hand. My tender nuts and dick didn't get a scratch—not that they were doing me much good. My left side was untouched except for a small fragment of debris that caught me on the chin.

"So, let's go around the room and introduce ourselves to each other," Mags said, and I pulled away from the death-glare match I had going on with Goth Chick. "Who would like to start?"

There was utter silence, a few fidgeting moves from everyone, and then Sexy Eyes raised her hand slightly with a small smile. "I will."

"Very brave, Jillian," Mags praised with a beaming smile.

Jillian? Hmmm. Pretty name for a pretty girl. I bet she would not, however, give me a blow job for a joint. She definitely looked too sweet and innocent for that.

"So… um," Jillian stumbled while pushing her hair behind an ear with one hand. "I'm Jillian Martel. I'm here for depression. I've been diagnosed with Kearns-Sayre Syndrome."

Another tuck of her hair back on the opposite side and a brave smile.

"It affects me in a bunch of different ways. I'm going progressively blind. Right now, I have no peripheral vision and things are a bit blurry sometimes… like my vision is streaked with dirt, but that comes and goes."

She paused a moment and let her gaze circle around the room, briefly touching on each of us with a warm and friendly smile before she continued. "Um… because it's a neuromuscular disorder, the muscles in my eyes are paralyzed. It's hard for me to open them all the way, which makes it even more difficult to see."

Huh? So those weren't intentional bedroom eyes, which made more sense. Her overall sweet and demure look should have told me she wasn't "that type of girl". And I could finally see her eyes were blue.

Jillian gave a dismissive wave of her hand and looked back to Mags. "There's some other stuff that goes with this disease. Muscle weakness. Cardiomyopathy. But I'm sure everyone would be bored by it."

Fuck yeah, we'd be bored by it.

I gave an exaggerated mock yawn, which was loud and made it clear I found her story boring. It caused her face to lift slowly until she was looking directly at me. I could tell it was an effort for her to do that small move. Her gaze was impassive, but from what little I'd observed about her in the past twenty seconds, I knew that was because she didn't have any muscle control over her eyes. She couldn't tell me with her eyelids and eyebrows what I saw deep in her irises as they turned to the color of dark denim.

I'd hurt her feelings. Or maybe even pissed her off.

Boo-hoo.

"Well, thank you, Jillian," Mags said to break the awkward silence. When my eyes cut over to her, she gave me a disapproving look. I lifted my right hand, raised my middle finger, and rubbed at the corner of my eye with it while I looked at Mags innocently.

She gave a knowing look right back to me. It said, "I've seen your kind. A dime a dozen. Yeah, you're a badass, but I'll chew you up and spit you out, boy."

I knew at that point not to underestimate that little old lady.

Mags turned away from me, and her gaze swept the group. "Maybe I should take a moment before we continue with introductions to explain why the group dynamic is important. I'll facilitate conversations, and you should all feel free to jump in when you feel like it."

I looked back over at Jillian. She was politely watching Mags, but I could tell her anger at me was completely gone. I was an asshole to her, completely dismissive of her issues, and yet she sat there listening to Mags with a sweet smile on her face and even a bit of eagerness to belong to this group.

God, she was fucking weird and I narrowed my eyes at her.

Regardless of her tragic tale of disease and disability, my gut instinct said she didn't belong in this group. It was for people with "issues" but, more specifically, for people who had a hard time dealing with their "issues." She didn't seem all that upset by her impending blindness and cardio-whatever-the-fuck-she-said-she-had. The emotions vibrating off each person in attendance were tangible, ranging from the most heavy-hearted melancholy to bitter hatred of life.

But not Sexy Eyes.

She seemed to radiate an inner joy that felt completely out of place in this room.

Yeah... she was fucking weird.

Chapter 4

Present day...

WHEN I DROVE the front passenger tire over the IED and it exploded, I didn't feel pain at first.

I remember being aware of screaming, and smoke, and more explosions in the distance that shook the ground, but the sounds were muffled because the detonation caused temporary acoustic trauma to my ears. I looked to the passenger seat where Jelonek had been sitting just ten seconds prior, prattling on about his wife who was due to deliver their first baby any day now. It made me think about Maria, and I wondered how fast she wanted to have kids once we got married. Soon, I had hoped.

One minute, Jelonek had been sitting beside me, chattering away. The next, the passenger seat was gone.

The *entire* passenger side of the Humvee was gone.

Jelonek just… gone.

There was nothing left of him or our conversation except a fine mist of blood that seemed to hang heavy in the air around me. My first involuntary breath in, I sucked the remains of Jelonek into my lungs, tasting the coppery fluid from within and immediately expelling him out in a nasty, hacking cough.

I gagged once... twice... then a spray of vomit hit the steering wheel in front of me, which I vaguely noticed was twisted from the force of the explosion.

Then I felt the pain.

Twelve months in Afghanistan, safely driving my anti-tank, missile-ladened Humvee.

One unfortunate turn where my front tire rolled right over an IED.

Twenty-four hours in a military field hospital to get me stabilized.

Thirty-six hours at Landsthul Regional Medical Center in Germany to prep me for a medical flight to the States.

Thirteen long months at the new Walter Reed National Military Medical Center in Bethesda where doctors spent three months trying to save my mangled leg as it oozed with puss and infection. It was held together by the thin spokes of an external fixator that looked like a giant cage, as if they were afraid my leg would just up and run away from me.

That was the worst three months of my life, and I was actually relieved when they cut that rotting thing off me. It was one of the few times I'd felt happy since the explosion.

Not sure I've felt it since.

I take a deep drag off my cigarette as I lean my elbow on the open window ledge of my Suburban. It's only two years old, has low mileage, and is loaded with nice features. It was one of the first things I bought when I got out of rehab with the money the government handed me along with my discharge papers. The only modification I made to it was having a left-foot accelerator pedal added to it, but that wasn't a permanent device. It merely attached to the right pedal with a bar, so when I pushed on the left gas pedal, it also depressed the right pedal, causing the vehicle to speed up. I could take it off easily if someone with a living right leg wanted to drive my car.

Not that I was going to let anyone drive my car.

It was my vehicle, paid for free and clear, so I smoked in it and made no apologies. But when Jillian made delicate coughing noises but stubbornly refused to roll her window down, I'd conceded and lowered mine. Now her face is turned away, looking out as we travel east on I-64, just a few miles from the campground we're staying at outside of Louisville, Kentucky.

Craning my neck side to side, I hear the bones crack and roll my shoulders to loosen the stiffness. I've driven a little over nine hours total today, and I'm a bit sore. I take another drag off my cigarette, which is down to the filter. With a practiced flick, I shoot it out the window and it arcs away from the Suburban with a trail of embers sparkling in its wake. I roll the window up, mentally telling myself not to call Connor Dead Kid by mistake, and repeat the mantra a few times so it sticks. It's not that I'm afraid of hurting his feelings, but because when I nodded my head at Jillian back in the convenience store a few hours ago, I was making a promise.

And while I'm a man of my word, I'm not promising another damn thing to anyone in this group on this ~~descent into hell~~ trip. I'll do my duty and then I'm done.

Out.

Finished.

This ~~grand adventure~~ lame-ass road trip is purely voluntary, unlike the group counseling. That was non-negotiable, or so the court said, and if I refused to attend the therapy, then I could simply go to jail. But the trip is part of group therapy, and Mags bargained with me to go. She promised I wouldn't have to attend the other group sessions if I went, and that she'd proclaim to the court I had completed their requirements. So I'd weighed a week in a car where no one would try to make me talk against six more weeks of forced therapy.

Seemed like a decent trade-off at the time. It still feels like a good deal because there's no way I'll ever get suckered into letting these people into my life. I have enough crappy shit to deal with without taking on other people's burdens.

We've all got sob stories but none can compare to mine, so I don't care about theirs.

♦

WHEN WE DECIDED as a group to drive across the country, Mags made it immediately clear that she was not going to be accompanying us. She told us she had other duties she couldn't ignore and that we were all adults—except for Connor, but he was almost there and she got permission from his parents for him to do this—and that we would need to make group decisions. I could see the triumphant gleam in her eyes that she would be forcing us to at least talk to plan the trip.

So, we had a few things we all had to agree on.

For instance, in whose vehicle would we travel?

That was easy and I believe my exact words were, "We'll take my Suburban, and no one drives it but me."

I expected a fight, because in the six weeks we'd all been around each other, that's all we did. Well, that's all Goth Chick and I seemed to do. Our specialty was mocking Jillian and Connor when they'd try to have a serious conversation. But no one seemed to mind my demand because they gave me blasé shrugs in response.

So I added on, "I'll also plan the route and decide where we stay."

Yes, I'm a control freak, so sue me.

Connor raised his hand tentatively as we all sat in the therapy group circle, indicating a need to perhaps argue with me about that suggestion. "Um... Christopher, do you think we could maybe stay at campgrounds along the way?"

"Why?" I'd asked, bewildered.

Connor's parents had no qualms about giving him permission to go on this trip, despite him being a few months shy of eighteen. Their kid was dying, so they were going to indulge his every whim. They were also loaded with money and figured he could stay in five-star hotels if he wanted.

"Because I've never been camping before," he said with a sheepish grin. "Our family vacations were a little more refined. It's a bucket-list thing."

I'd snorted, but immediately given in to the kid's wishes. This whole trip was because Connor was dying. It was at the top of his bucket list to travel the country and see the West Coast. Turns out, I love camping and the outdoors. It's one of the things I miss the most about West Virginia.

"Looks like we're camping along the way," I said to the group, looking at each one in turn and daring them to argue.

Goth Chick had said, "I'm not pissing and shitting in the woods."

"Relax," I'd told her with as much condescension as I could muster. "Campgrounds have bathrooms and showers."

It was decided we'd camp a few times along the way, and other nights we'd stay in a hotel.

♦

THE SUN IS hanging very low as we pull into the Bluegrass Campground. I stop at the main office, just inside the entrance gates, and try not to limp too badly as I walk inside to secure a spot. While I've never tried to diminish the obviousness of my disability, it still makes me feel less than a full man when I can't walk with the smoothest of gaits. But the long hours of driving have made me stiff and sore, and I just can't fucking help myself as my first few steps are more like lurches until I get my bearings and work the kinks out.

I pay an extra ten bucks for a place that sits on a creek that cuts an "S" shape through the middle of the campground. As soon as I get back behind the driver's wheel, I tell the others what their share of the cost is, including the groceries I had bought just before we arrived here. In another five minutes, I'm backing the Suburban up into the spot so that my tailgate faces the bubbling water that flows over rocks and a rotted tree trunk caught near the bank.

This is our first night, capping off the first day of our trip. We've been on the road for nine hours and by my estimate, if we bust our ass, we can make it to our ultimate destination in three more days. Let Connor have his peep at the Pacific Ocean and then hightail it back east so I can be done with these freaks.

I pull bags out of the back of the SUV. To my surprise, everyone had packed light as I'd suggested. When we picked Connor up at his house early this morning, his father had helped lug out a massive tent bag that looked brand spanking new. Connor told me with a red face, "Um... I didn't own a tent so my dad bought one. It's pretty big, but Jillian will share it with me as she doesn't have a tent either."

I had shrugged because I didn't give a fuck who slept where. Didn't even care that Goth Chick told me she was sleeping in the backseat of my Suburban, and equally didn't care that she brought her own pillow when I picked her up at her apartment.

Now, they all line up to accept their stuff. I throw Connor's large tent to the ground beside me and tell him gruffly while pointing to a spot, "I'll help you set that up in a minute if you take it over there."

I then hand him his duffle, a high-speed Under Armour bag that presumably holds his clothes and medicines, and a rolled-up sleeping bag that smells as new as his tent. Goth Chick accepts a large backpack from me that has stickers all over it that say things like "Acid—the ultimate high" and "Bite me, bitch". I also pull out a knotted pillowcase that she had thrown in there this morning that looks to be stuffed with clothes. She grumbles something at me, not a thank you for sure. I actually think she said "moron," but whatever.

And finally, Jillian's standing there, looking at me with those pretty blue eyes that are now the color of dark denim since the sun is setting and her back is to it. I turn away from her quickly because half the time, I'm afraid I won't be able to break eye contact with her, and pull out her rolled sleeping bag. Unlike the others, hers appears well used. I wouldn't have taken her for someone who likes camping, but I put that immediately out of my mind. I don't care what her background is.

"Thank you," she says sweetly as I hand it to her. I ignore her and turn back to the vehicle to pull her bag out, which is also duffle shaped, and is bright pink with black canvas trim.

"Christopher," she says from behind me, and her tone is soft and secretive. Almost embarrassed sounding.

"What?" I say gruffly as I wheel around on her.

"Um… I sort of left my wallet at my house," she says, her eyes dropping to the ground where her foot kicks at the grass. And yeah… her feet are pretty too. She's wearing flip-flops that have clear crystals on the straps and her toenails are painted pale pink. "And um… I don't have any money on me."

"You're fucking kidding, right?" I ask in unamused amazement, because that's a colossally stupid thing to do.

She gives me a sheepish smile. "I'm sorry. I'm normally an organized person. I had it laying there on my bed along with all my other stuff I'd set out to pack, and I don't know… I must have just overlooked it or something. I'll pay you back for gas and the campground fees as soon as we get back if that's okay."

"Why didn't you say something when you first realized you'd forgotten it? We could have turned back."

Her eyes cut away from me. "I didn't realize until it was too late."

"Wait a minute," I say, my eyes narrowing on her as my brain replays the various stops we made on our trek from North Carolina to Kentucky. "Have you eaten anything today?"

Because now I remember she didn't order anything for breakfast when we stopped at McDonald's a few hours into our trip. And she didn't buy anything at that gas station where she lit into me for calling Connor *Dead Kid*, although everyone else got a sandwich and some chips. I didn't pay any attention then, but I remember that now.

"Have you?" I ask again. "Eaten?"

She shakes her head and hastily says, "I'm good. I packed some protein bars to snack on."

"And what?" I sneer at her. "You plan to ration them out over the entire trip?"

Her face flames red as she snaps at me, "No."

I cock an eyebrow at her.

"Okay, fine... I haven't exactly decided what to do, but I don't need a lot. I'll figure it out."

"Jesus fucking Christ, you're a mess," I tell her as I turn back and grab her pink duffle. I push it on her and she grabs it, looking at me with those half-mast eyes. I don't hold the annoyance from my voice. "I'll pay your expenses and feed you. Keep track of what you owe me and you can pay me when we get back."

She nods at me hesitantly, but I push past her before she can utter a word of thanks. I honestly cannot ~~handle~~ accept gratitude from her right now.

Chapter 5

N OT A KID but just a few short months of legally being an adult, Connor suffers from alveolar rhabdomyosarcoma. He had to repeat it three times in group before anyone could understand what he was saying. It apparently started as a tumor in his hand. He'd been through surgery, chemo, and radiation, but it came back with a nasty vengeance and spread to other parts of his body.

He summed it up nicely on that first day we all met in group, "They just can't kill it. The doctors are optimistic that I have about six months."

Hence the nickname of Dead Kid.

I have to mentally keep repeating the name Connor in my head the entire time I set up our campsite, afraid I'll inadvertently call him Dead Kid and earn another lecture from Jillian that will be rooted in pity rather than just generalized disgust. I set up his tent, which is roughly the size of the Taj Mahal, all while he watches with ~~doomed~~ keen eyes. I suspect tomorrow night he'll want to try to put it up himself.

After building a fire, I set up the propane cooktop so I can fix an easy meal of hot dogs with roasted potatoes and onions while I sip on a beer. Goth Chick slunk off into the woods, presumably to smoke a joint, while the others hang out by the campfire. Connor has a smile on his face a mile wide, barely able to contain his joy over sleeping in the great outdoors, eating food cooked ~~over an open campfire~~ on a propane stove, and hanging out with ~~rejects~~ friends around a toasty fire as the sky turns a brilliant shade of orange-pink when the sun starts to dip below the western horizon.

We eat in silence, mainly because we're starving—particularly Goth Chick when she comes back. She eats half a bag of potato chips that I'm sure are a product of the munchies, and then Jillian insists on washing the dishes in a portable tub I had brought along that stores the eating utensils and doubles as a wash bin.

The sky is dark as ink now and because of cloud cover, the stars can't be seen. It's getting late, but no one seems interested in crawling into their sleeping bags and going to sleep. Connor is enjoying campfire talk too much, and Jillian and he just prattle on, mainly about literature as they both share a love of Herman Melville. I smoke a cigarette and listen to them talk. Goth Chick also listens, but not as intently. She's laying on her back on top of our site's picnic table, staring at the night sky. When I think I can't handle another minute of the discussion of *Moby Dick*, and I realize Jillian looks even more beautiful in the firelight, I grab my duffle and head to the low-slung cinderblock building that houses men and women's showers and bathrooms, one on each side.

After taking a piss and brushing my teeth, I grab a quick shower. It's precarious given the lack of ~~handicap~~ stability railing. I take my prosthesis and liner off, lay them against the wall as far from the spray as I can so they won't get wet, and manage to get cleaned up with one hand balancing on the wall and the other working soap all over me.

By the time I get back to the campsite, the fire has dropped low and I can hear Connor talking in a somber voice. I get ready to chastise them for not adding wood when he leans over in his chair, grabs a few logs from the small cord I'd purchased at the main office when we checked in, and places it in the center where it causes the fire to flare upward.

I throw my duffle in the back of the Suburban, grab another beer from the small cooler there, and head back to my folding canvas chair that sits to the right of Connor and across the fire from Jillian.

When I take my seat, I hear Connor say with a humorless laugh, "…and so we started going to church on Sundays. My parents would sit there… eyes all scrunched so tight… hands clasped, and just praying their asses off for a miracle."

He gives a slight cough. In a roughened voice, he murmurs, "Praying that I won't die."

I want to roll my eyes and tell the kid that praying never works. I want him to pass along to his parents that they're on a fool's errand and their time is better served spending what precious Sunday mornings they have left by doing something fun and meaningful with their son. I want to take him by the shoulders, look him directly in the eyes, and tell him I know from personal experience that there is no God. That there's nothing up above us but clouds, and sky, and atmosphere. That past that, there's only empty space—not an omniscient deity that loves all of us poor, worthless humans down here on earth.

We are all alone and that's the truth. I know this because I can't begin to remember all the times I called out to God to ease my suffering, but the pain only got worse. Or I beseeched him to just let me die, and yet my body just wouldn't quit working. Months and months of agony. Torturous pain while they tried to heal my shattered leg. Brutal, vicious, unrelenting misery while infection raged through my leg and puss seeped out of the open wounds, and they would cut chunks of skin and flesh away, hoping to stay ahead of the rot, but they never could. Pain so terrible it made me crazy. I would rant and sometimes piss myself until, finally, I was begging the doctors to cut my leg off.

Yeah... that request was honored.

God may not have listened to me, but the doctors did.

"Many people turn to prayer when they are at their lowest. Some people find great solace in it," Jillian tells Connor, validating his parents' futile efforts. Goth Chick ignores us and stares at the sky. ~~Dead Kid~~ Connor bobs his head in understanding.

I, however, snort with derision. It's loud and obnoxious and there's no doubt by anyone in our pathetic group that I find the concept ludicrous.

"Tell your parents there is no God," I tell Connor as I look him directly in the eye. "He can't save you."

I keep my eyes pinned on him, refusing to give him an ounce of empathy because I don't have any.

I'm all dried up.

"Shut up," the soft voice of Jillian says, floating sweetly across the crackling fire. I don't want to look at her because I think I might go fucking ballistic if she shoots that poor, misunderstood Christopher ~~truth~~ Barlow shit at me.

But I'm almost knocked backward when she shows me a side to Jillian Martel I've never seen before. Rather than try to sling happy, optimistic shit my way, she lets me have it good.

"Who in the hell are you to judge Connor or his family?" she yells at me with narrowed eyes. I wonder how much of a chore on her paralyzed muscles it is for her to glower at me like that. "What gives you the right?"

I vaguely notice Goth Chick sit straight up from her supine position on the picnic table and look at Jillian with surprise.

I open my mouth to tell her all about freedom of speech, but she rolls right over me. "You might have had some serious injuries, and I'm sorry for it, but it doesn't give you the right to be an asshole to others. I bet if you spent as much time seeking positivity as you do reveling in negativity, you'd feel a hell of a lot better about yourself. But since you seem to like being a jackass, and it sort of suits this whole "bitter-wounded-warrior-who-feels-betrayed-by-everyone vibe" you've got going on, I'm guessing you don't have the backbone or the fortitude to be anything more than what you are right now. It's pathetic really."

"Damn," Goth Chick says under her breath with a taunting voice. "You just got your ass handed to you."

I can actually feel my ears turn hot as I flush with anger and embarrassment. The last person who talked to me like that ended up in the hospital with a broken jaw, and I ended up in a support group to avoid an assault conviction. Now, I clearly can't ~~kiss~~ knock the righteous condemnation off Jillian's face because I'd never hit a woman, but my tongue is way sharper than hers can ever hope to be in this lifetime. I intend to draw tears from those pretty, lazy eyes.

I open my mouth to give back as good as I just got—and then some—when Connor says, "I get where Christopher's coming from."

He shoots an apologetic look over to Jillian because

he undermined her and says, "No offense, Jillian. But I mean... I get it. Christopher lost a leg, probably came close to dying from it. You're losing your eyesight, and nothing can be done to stop it. I'm dying and can't be saved. If there is a God, why do these things happen to people? So I get his pessimism, and I respect it."

"Hey kid," I snarl at him, even though I feel myself deflating because he fucking hit the nail on the head. "I don't need you to defend me."

"I'm not defending you," he says earnestly with a sober look my way. "Jillian's right... you're an asshole. I'm just saying I get why you said what you did."

"But you shouldn't be an asshole to us," Jillian says softly, and while I know I'm an asshole and it's never bothered me before to be such a creature, her gentle admonishment punches me deep in the gut. She's no longer glaring at me and her voice is dove-like. Almost as if she's imploring me to consider her words. "You should be nicer. We're here to help each other, and we have several days we must spend together. You should be nicer because you're stuck here with us, so make the best of it."

"But he doesn't want to be here," Goth Chick pipes up, and we turn to look at the woman who has hardly had anything to say. "Being forced to do something against your will tends to make you churlish."

"Bitch-like," I say in agreement, because she can be a total bitch most times.

"Right," she affirms before flipping me off with a

sneer lest I forget we are not friends.

"No one is here against their will," Jillian says pragmatically, and all heads turn back her way. She looks around at each of us, making pointed eye contact although it's still the lethargic look that hampers her facial expressions by disease.

"I beg to differ. I'm not here by choice," I tell her as I slouch back down in my seat.

"Technically, you are here by choice," Goth Chick says as she turns on the picnic table to prop her booted feet on the bench.

"Wrong," I say with a bored voice. "The court made me come."

"No," she argues emphatically, and I can't help the tiny, miniscule, barely perceptible tinge of respect I feel that she's standing up to me with reasoned argument versus an illogical rant because she's a bitch. "I'm sure there was a choice to be made. Group or jail. You could have chosen jail. In fact, it would have been a valid choice. But you chose to come to group, and you also chose to come on this trip."

"Well, yeah," I respond with a nonchalant shrug. "When you put it that way, sure… I made the choice to keep my freedom in exchange for group therapy, but—"

"And I seem to remember last week… you said you didn't have anything to contribute," she throws at me with her chin tilted aggressively high. "In fact, you even said to leave you the fuck alone as we were ironing out the details of the trip. But you sure seem to have a lot to say now."

"Mags said this would happen," Jillian says in a smooth voice, and my gaze slides over to her where I try not to get sidetracked by the dancing lights and shadows the fire casts upon her face. "She said we'd learn something from each other because our circumstances are all unique. She said it would become clearer the more time we spend together what things we have in common, and which we can use to draw strength from."

"We have nothing in common," I sneer, still mightily incensed any of these fucktards could even think to compare their misery to mine.

And no… I swear I absolutely do not want to kiss Jillian right now because she looks so goddamned perfect sitting on the other side of the fire, even though she's saying things ~~I don't want to hear~~ that must make some sort of sense to her.

"You're wrong," Goth Chick says to me. Everyone sort of jerks with surprise that she's actually got more to share. "There's one thing we all share with each other."

"Yeah… what's that?" I ask, my tone laced heavy with sarcasm.

She raises her eyes to mine. For a split second, I don't see the bristling anger she always seems to have bubbling just beneath the surface of her muddy-green eyes. Instead, they look weary, old, and wise.

So wise that I feel compelled to listen, but I'll never

admit it to her or any of these freaks.

"Each of us here," Goth Chick says with a sweep of her arm around the fire. "Each one of us hates our life. It's a burden to us. It's unfair. It's nothing but misery and torment, and we're pissed we're the ones who have to suffer it. Maybe not to the same degree, and not for the same reasons, but it's the absolute tie that binds every one of us."

I wait for her words to bounce off me, for my trademark lip curl of condescension to spring forth. Instead, her words barrel into me with the force of a grenade launcher. They actually have a ring of familiar truth because I know I'm at the height of my anger and bitterness when I see just how great other people have it. I want to slap their sunny smiles off their faces, and I want them to come down to my level where they can wallow around in the sludge of desolation with me. I want everyone to feel as bad as I do, because it's unfair that I can't seem to feel better on my own.

So maybe Goth Chick has it a little bit right.

Except for Jillian. I don't think she hates her life the way I do.

Surging out of my chair, I totter for a second until I get my balance. "Well, that was enlightening, Dr. Phil. Maybe you should get a job counseling depressed people everywhere. I'm sure your bubbly disposition would be a hit with others."

She doesn't respond, picking at her nails with her

shoulders hunched over protectively, indicating she's clearly done with this conversation as well.

Fine by me.

I walk past her toward my Suburban because I have a pill with my name on it just begging to be swallowed, pretending I don't care that I feel Jillian's eyes burning into my retreating back.

Chapter 6

A S I HEAD from the campground bathrooms back to our site, I realize I'm not as cranky this morning as I thought I'd be, given the fact I didn't sleep well. Had nothing to do with camping in general. I had a good tent, a decent sleeping bag, and level ground. It was a bit too warm last night, so I'd left my tent flaps open to allow some breeze. This, unfortunately, let in noise that would have otherwise been filtered had I kept it closed.

I would have been able to sleep but for Jillian's soft voice as she talked to Connor for what seemed like hours after they entered that huge tent to go to sleep. It had three areas separated by internal flaps, but when I set it up yesterday, I noted with interest that Jillian and Connor laid their sleeping bags right next to each other in the middle section.

Oh, I didn't think there was any fucking around going on. From the very first group session, Jillian established herself as Connor's "older sister he never had" and became his protector of sorts. She was always there to come to his defense should Barb or I lash out at him during the rare times we talked.

Incidentally, I'd decided this morning I should probably call Goth Chick by her real name of Barb, only to avoid Jillian's sanctimonious wrath should I slip up. Self-preservation and all that.

Last night, I listened to Jillian and Connor talk about everything from music to movies to politics. Even about Connor's impending death. There was a different tone in his voice because his guard was totally down with Jillian. I suspect he puts on a braver-than-normal face in group because he's a dude and we don't like feeling vulnerable. But last night, he pulled no punches with her.

"I obsess about every little symptom that crops up," he had told her when she asked how he was doing. "Afraid it means the end is coming or something. Sometimes I can't sleep at all because I'll obsess about something stupid like having the sniffles or something."

If he'd told that to me, my response would have been to "suck it up" and deal with it, because that's all the fuck I've been told since I lost my leg. But Jillian has far more empathy than I ever could, and she did nothing more than validate him.

"I can totally imagine feeling that way," she said softly. "Fear of the unknown is one of the greatest fears of all in my opinion."

"But it's taking away from enjoying what time I have left," he'd returned to her. His voice floated through my tent with surprising grit, and I almost smiled into the dark over his fierce determination. "I don't like being controlled like that."

Jillian had given a soft laugh, and I could even imagine her ruffling his hair if he had any. "Then don't let those emotions control you. Have those feelings, acknowledge what they are, recognize them for what they're worth, and then let them go. Turn your attention to that next great thing you want to accomplish."

Fuck, she made it all sound so simple. It's not the first time I've heard those words. I've had other counselors tell me with great care and consolation that it's okay to feel angry, it's okay to hate my circumstances, and that one day, things will look better. I sneered at every single one of those people who would dare make such a prediction when they sat there whole and hardy.

But Jillian isn't whole or hardy. She's delicate, fragile, and going blind.

And yet, she has that unfettered optimism that seems impossibly real.

At any rate, I shamelessly listened to their entire conversation, mainly because I couldn't sleep and it took my mind off my own problems. But also, I liked the sound of Jillian's voice. I'd tried to just concentrate on that rather than on the content of their discussions. I'd finally fallen asleep to the sound of it.

♦

THE NEXT MORNING, I find Jillian and Connor sitting at

the picnic table on opposite sides of each other. Barb sits in the back seat of my Suburban with the door open. She's turned sideways, feet planted on the running board, her head bent over as she picks at her nail polish.

Jillian gives me a dazzling smile, which is surprising given I was a total ass last night. "Good morning. Sleep well?"

"Yup." The lie comes easily, but I'm not about to tell her I eavesdropped last night. I make my way to the large cooler and pull out the carton of eggs and package of bacon I'd bought yesterday.

"Can I help with breakfast?" she asks, swinging her legs over the bench and standing.

"Sure." I push the eggs and bacon at her. "Be my guest."

At that, I take the seat on the bench she just vacated, waiting to see what she does.

There's no surprise when she gives me a cheery smile and turns to the propane stove I've got sitting on the folding utility table. She bends over and squints at the knob on the front, then turns it to the left as indicated while hitting the ignitor button.

Nothing happens.

I watch as she hits the button a few more times before turning the knob back to off. Jillian turns to me while slowly raising her eyebrows up in silent question. "What am I doing wrong?"

"Turn on the gas," I tell her.

"Well, damn," she mutters as she turns to the small tank and does exactly as I instructed. Within seconds, she has the stove lit and puts the battered old camping skillet I have over the blue flame to heat.

"So what's our goal today? Where are we headed?" Connor asks, looking to me since I'd planned the route we'd take.

"Kansas City, Missouri," I tell him as I keep one eye on Jillian as she cooks. She seems confident, so I don't worry about it too much. "Figured we'd catch a Royals' baseball game."

"Really?" Connor asks with excitement, his eyes practically bugging out of his head as if I'd given him the goddamn cure to cancer or something. "Seeing a professional baseball game is on my bucket list, but it was sort of a low priority."

"You have an actual bucket list of things you want to do before you die?" I ask, because I'd conjured up a bucket list myself when I was in the hospital and hovering on the brink of death. During the few lucid moments I had, I vowed that if I survived, I'd do grand and glorious things like travel the world to climb the highest mountains and shit like that. Such a fucking waste of energy to have even thought that way.

"Well, I've always had a list of things I wanted to do in life before I knew I had cancer." I take a quick peek at Jillian and see she's listening intently. "But it's been narrowed down quite a bit since this last round of chemo wasn't effective."

This is the first time I've conversed with Connor about his impending death, and it's not as awkward as I thought it would be. I'll never admit it to him, but I've been a bit impressed at his level of maturity and grace given that he's not even technically an adult yet.

"What else is on your list?" Jillian asks as she flips the bacon she's got going in the pan. My gaze slides over to Barb. Her head is now raised as she listens to the conversation, although she looks bored by it.

"Let's see," Connor says. "Obviously, one is seeing the Pacific Ocean, which is the biggest so I can say I've traveled across the country. But I'd also like to eat something really adventurous—like cow tongue—and I'd like to do something really scary… like bungee jumping or skydiving."

Jillian laughs in delight. "I bet we could find those things along the way. The bigger cities will have restaurants with weird cuisine, and we'll Google a place where you can maybe do a tandem jump."

"I'll do that with you," I add in, because I'd totally love to skydive. Bungee jumping is out because of the leg straps. Hate to have my leg pop off and freak everyone out.

"What else is on that list?" Jillian asks, still working the bacon over and I can see it turning a nice, crispy brown. I love crispy bacon and have to say, I'm glad she's taking the extra time with it.

"Hmm," Connor says, placing his chin in the palm of his hand as he ponders. His eyes immediately light up with a mischievous glow. "I know… I've always wanted to go egging."

"Egging?" Jillian asks curiously.

"Yeah, you know… where you go and throw eggs at people's houses," Connor says as he sits up straighter and turns to me. "You ever done that?"

"Yup," I tell him. "Rite of passage where I come from."

"You seriously throw eggs at people's houses?" Jillian asks with a dumbfounded look on her face.

"You've never heard of that?" I ask her, surprised she's clueless about what we're talking about.

"No," she answers in disdain. "That's awful and mean."

"It's what kids do," I say dismissively.

"He's not a kid," she says with a maternal glare toward Connor.

He just grins back at her. "Come on, Jillian. I'm dying. It's a simple bucket-list request."

"We're doing it," I say with determination as I slap my hand on the picnic table. "Tonight… after the baseball game. I'll take you egging."

"I'll go too," Barb says, and we turn to look at her in surprise.

She hops out of the Suburban, closes the door, and stomps her way over to us. Ripped camo shorts, her black combat boots, and a white tank top with no bra on underneath is her outfit of choice today. Her nipples poke out, but they do nothing for me. The angry goth vibe isn't appealing in the slightest.

Not that I wouldn't say no to a blow job. I could take one of those from just about any woman.

But with a quick look at Connor, I see his eyes glued to Barb's chest. I'd bet a hundred dollars that Connor's a virgin, and I wonder if losing that virginity is on his bucket list. Maybe we can find him a hooker or something along the way.

Barb walks behind Connor and takes a seat on the bench to his right. Connor looks back to Jillian as she places the bacon on a plastic camp plate covered with paper towels. "You've got to come too, Jillian."

"Egging?" Her tone is completely disapproving, but there's a tiny smile playing on her face.

"Yes! Say you'll come," the kid practically begs.

"Fine," she says with a long, scornful sigh. "But I'm not throwing eggs."

"Goody two-shoes," I mutter automatically, and I actually jerk in surprise over my own tone of voice. Normally, that would have come out contemptuous and scathing. Instead, it was light and teasing, and… what the fuck am I doing?

I'm actually fucking smiling at Jillian as I fucking joke around with her!

What. The. Fuck?

"I am not a goody two-shoes," she throws back at me with a glare, but I can hear the humor in her voice. She abruptly changes the subject. "Everyone good with scrambled eggs?"

A chorus of "yups" and head nods occur around the picnic table, and Jillian pulls out a plastic bowl and starts cracking the eggs in it.

"What's on your bucket list, Jillian?" Connor asks. "You know… before you go blind."

Jillian doesn't look over at us but stays focused on her task. Her eyes and facial muscles remains lax, but there's a tiny bit of wistfulness in her expression. "I'd like to see amazing things. I'm excited to see the sun set on the Pacific. I've seen it rise my whole life in the east, but I want to watch it drop into the water. The Eiffel tower. I wish I could go to the top of the Eiffel Tower and see all of Paris. Or even the Taj Mahal. Or the Northern Lights."

"Think you'll get to do any of those?" Connor asks her. "Other than the sunset thing."

Jillian shakes her head. "Nah. I don't have that type of money and besides, my—"

She stops abruptly, and I can tell she was on the brink of sharing something she didn't want us to know about her. Instead, she surprises the hell out of me when she looks straight at Barb and says, "I'd like to get high at least once. That's on my bucket list too. I want to do it before I go blind, because I've heard it can cause paranoia, and I don't want that occurring without the ability to see. That would totally wig me out."

I can't help it. I bust out laughing, and Connor starts laughing right behind me. Sweet, innocent goody-two-shoes Jillian wants to smoke a joint.

She doesn't even bother to look at us. Instead, she keeps those lazy eyes on Barb. "Can I? Smoke one with you?"

I hear a cell phone ringing and pin it coming right from Jillian. She pulls it out of her pocket with one hand while the other holds an eggshell, looks at the screen, and then hits the button to send it to voice mail. Shoving it back in her pocket, she continues to break the remaining eggs into the bowl, and doesn't press Barb for an answer as to whether she'll let Jillian get high with her. But if she won't, I'll score something and give her that bucket-list wish.

It's silent for a moment until Barb says firmly, "I want to piss on a grave outside of Tulsa."

We stare at her with wide eyes and open mouths.

Although, it's to Jillian that she looks. "It's a bucket-list thing."

"Then we'll do it," Jillian says with a smile and nod of her head. She turns to me to ask my permission, but her tone says she expects me to agree with her. "We can budget that into the trip. Right, Christopher?"

Goddamn it.

That's going to add an entire extra day onto this

craziness of a trip.

One more day than what I'd planned to spend with these losers, yet I'll have to admit... I'm not as angry as I could be.

Chapter 7

Two weeks ago…

"**I** HAD A sister who died," Jillian said in a quiet voice. Connor made a sound of distress and reached out to squeeze her shoulder. Those two had become thick as thieves during our group sessions, which wasn't surprising since the two of them did eighty percent of the talking.

The other twenty percent was either me or Barb lashing out with derision because we were both assholes, and it was the only way we apparently knew how to deal with our pain.

Mags had taken to ignoring us when we did that, as had Jillian if the scorn was leveled at her. But the minute Barb or I directed something at Connor, her claws would come out and she'd lay into us. This would embarrass Connor greatly as Jillian never even gave him the opportunity to stand up for himself, but she couldn't see that. She was too busy trying to put Barb and me into our places.

"What happened to her?" Mags asked softly.

I kept my head tucked down, staring at the tile floor, but I listened. I always listened when Jillian talked because she sounded harmonious, even otherworldly at times, with her sweet voice and cheerful disposition. There was no one in my world like that, and the oddity of it fascinated me.

"It was almost five years ago," Jillian said as she looked at Mags, one hand coming up to cross over her chest and pat Connor's hand at her shoulder in acknowledgment of his support. "We were vacationing in Emerald Isle, and she got caught in a rip current and drowned."

"I'm so sorry," Mags crooned at Jillian. "That had to be tough."

I'd looked up just in time to see Jillian nod in acknowledgment with a brave smile. "My parents took it really hard. They are still having a hard time with it."

"But what about you?" Mags pushed at her.

With a hard shake of her head, Jillian insisted, "It was worse on them than me. I mean, I loved Kelly and we were close, but she was their daughter. A parent isn't supposed to lose a child."

Connor bobbed his head in agreement at that.

"I understand that," Mags said in a deliberate voice. "But how did *you* grieve?"

"Silently," Jillian admitted. "Most of the time I had to bolster my parents."

"Almost like you became the parent," Mags observed.

Barb let out a slight yawn beside me, and I had no clue if she was bored or just drowsy from drugs, but I kept my gaze on Jillian.

She shrugged. "I guess."

Connor pulled his hand from Jillian's shoulder, but I saw him give her another squeeze before doing so. "I have to do that with my parents sometimes. You know… put on the brave, happy face so they don't worry about me being scared."

Parents could be an interesting dynamic in any family.

It seemed Jillian's were mired in grief and couldn't see past it.

Connor's parents, who admittedly were trying hard to make his remaining months as normal as could be, were forcing their kid to hide his true feelings because he loved them so much.

And my parents?

They were pieces of shit.

They came to visit me in the hospital one time when I got transferred from Landstuhl to Walter Reed. They took one look at me, and I could see the naked fear on their faces. Fear of a son on the verge of death with whom they weren't overly close to begin with. Fear of him dying, and, just as pronounced, fear of him living. I was sure I looked terrifying with tubes coming out of me all over the place. My mangled leg had been wrapped in heavy gauze oozing with blood because none of the surgeries to try to piece it back together were done overseas. My hand had been operated on to close the wounds after losing my last two fingers, and my ma had just fixated her stare there. She couldn't look at my leg or my face, but she could look at my bandaged hand.

They never came back after that.

Not for the entire thirteen months I was in the hospital and the rehab facility.

They sent cards, but I had the nurses throw them away without opening them.

Hank, my brother, had visited me a few times over the course of my recovery. He'd always say that Ma and Pa missed me, laying out every excuse in the book why they couldn't make the trip. But I knew those were all lies. They'd already written me off.

"Barb," Mags said loudly. From the corner of my eye, I could see Barb sort of jerk in her seat at being called out. For the most part, the two of us were left alone, but occasionally, Mags would try to force us to participate. "What do you think of that role reversal?

"What?" she asked aggressively.

"When the child has to take care of the parents," Mags prompted her.

"I think most people are douches and shouldn't be allowed to procreate," she'd said with a sneer.

Now that was interesting. Pretty much what I thought about my parents, but I hadn't voiced that out loud. Seemed like Barb and I had something in common besides a love of grass.

"Is that your experience?" Mags asked her very quiet-ly... almost like she was tentatively reaching out to a wild animal.

Barb's eyes glittered with hostility as she replied through gritted teeth. "You know it is."

I supposed that was true. Mags had all our files and the reasons we were in group therapy. She knew each of our backgrounds and used her knowledge to gently poke at the important stuff. Apparently, she decided to poke a bear that day.

"Why don't you share with us?" Mags bluntly sug-gested, all pretense at geniality swept aside.

Barb gave a shrill laugh. "What? You think sharing's going to make me feel better or something?"

"It might," Mags offered.

Barb gave a bark of a laugh this time, full of skepti-cism and ire, and I half expected her to storm out of the room. To my surprise, though, she leaned forward in her chair and pinned her eyes hard onto Mags. Her voice went so quiet I had to strain to hear it, but the malice I heard caused a shudder to run up my spine.

"Fine," she said in that eerie voice. "You want me to talk about how my uncle abused me from the time I was about eleven until I was sixteen? How he would sneak into my room at night and just help himself to a little bit of Barb? Or would you rather me focus on the parental unit, because that was what you wanted to know originally, right?"

It was almost as if all the oxygen had been sucked out of the room. This was the most Barb had ever spoken, and I could tell with a brief glance that Jillian and Connor were terrified at the prospect of what she might reveal. I was ghoulishly intrigued to know what her issues were and why she was in group. Only Mags seemed calm, and she just gave Barb an encouraging nod of her head.

"Well, my parents failed miserably to protect me," Barb murmured, but with no less hatred in her voice for them. "They refused to believe that dear Uncle James would ever do such a thing. After all, he was such an upstanding member of the community. And when they refused to believe me, I gave up on caring about anything."

"You're very angry at your parents," Mags said, sounding supportive to show Barb it was okay to feel that way.

No shit, Dick Tracy.

"I wasn't angry at them then," Barb admitted, her voice now losing some of the heat. "I was sad, and letdown, and completely alone. The anger came later."

"Would you like to share that?" Mags asked, skirting around what I thought was going to be even more of a bombshell than what Barb just laid on us.

Barb shrugged and got that bored look on her face. I recognized it for what it was... her walls were going back up. To my surprise though, she went ahead and shared in a detached, impersonal tone. "One day, I came into the kitchen. My mom was laughing with my dad as she cooked dinner. They were sipping wine and gave me bright smiles when I came in. My mom asked how my day was, and I told her point blank I wanted to kill myself. You know what she said to me?"

"What did she say to you?" Mags asked to push her forward.

"She told me to stop being so dramatic," Barb choked out, almost as if she couldn't believe her mom had said those words. "So you know what I did?"

Mags just inclined her head, never letting her gaze waver from Barb. This conversation was really between the two of them, but Mags was very much aware that there were three other people listening intently.

"I picked up the butcher knife from the counter. My mom had just cut some onions with it, and I placed it on my wrist. I had every intention of showing my parents just how dramatic I could be."

I could see it happening as Barb laid it out for us. I'd thought there weren't any parents out there worse than mine, but I'd been wrong. At least mine had just slipped away quietly. Barb's had actually mocked her pain.

Her voice gentled, went almost childlike. "My mom told me to stop being a drama queen and to put the knife down. And I remember asking her in total disbelief, 'You don't think I'm serious, do you?'

Barb stared hard at Mags but she was talking to all of us. "My mom just rolled her eyes at me and said, 'I think you're just looking for attention.'"

She gave a half laugh, not really like she found humor at what her mother said, but almost in disbelief that a parent could be that heartless to their child who held a knife to their wrist.

"What did you do then?" Mags asked in a firmer tone than what she'd been using. I knew she could sense Barb slipping away and wanted her to finish what she started.

"I cut my motherfucking veins open and bled all over her pretty, white-tiled kitchen," Barb said gleefully, and I know it was a moment of deep vindication for her.

Jillian gasped, visible tears in her eyes. Mags gave Barb an encouraging smile, but Barb was done. She'd shared more than she'd ever intended, bringing up all sorts of feelings I was sure she'd rather kept deeply buried. With a quick heave out of her chair, Barb stomped out of the therapy room, slamming the door behind her. She didn't come back for the rest of the session.

Mags, Jillian, and Connor talked about what they'd just heard discussing ways they could be sensitive to Barb's issues when she returned. I quickly tuned that out because Barb hadn't said a damn thing that would make me treat her any differently. She was still a bitch, and yeah... rightfully so, but the reasons for it weren't my concern. As I'd said… got my own fucking problems.

But I was quite fascinated with her suicide attempt. I wanted to ask her more about it—try to understand the depth of darkness she had to have been in to make that decision.

Because I'd thought about it quite a bit. Granted, I thought about it most when I was in the hospital and then rehab, but since then, I'd continued to consider the option.

Except I wouldn't use a knife.

I'd use a gun.

Single bullet to the side of my head was how I'd do it.

Chapter 8

Present day...

S INCE IT SEEMS I can't say no to Jillian, we're headed
to Tulsa. It will end up adding more than a day. I
figured that out quick enough when I pulled out the map
after breakfast as Barb and Connor washed dishes.

My original plan had been to head due west from
Louisville, straight through to St. Louis and into Kansas
City. From there, the interstate went straight to Denver,
our next big stop. It was the most direct route to the
West Coast, and I chose it as the fastest way to get to our
destination.

But now because Barb wants to piss on someone's
grave—still not sure if that's a metaphorical pissing or a
literal one—we're heading southwest toward Tulsa.
When I looked at the space between Tulsa and Denver,
I'd cursed out loud to see there was no real direct route
to cut back northwest once Barb emptied her bladder.
We'd either have to travel a little further southwest
before cutting up to Denver, or we'd have to backtrack
into Kansas. Either way, it would be another twelve

hours of driving time.

After a few hours of driving, we decide to stop somewhere on the other side of St. Louis to eat lunch. I find a barbeque joint off I-44 that everyone agrees on, because why not enjoy something original and unique to the place? It's really kind of funny, but through all the shit I've been through… from the surgeries and rehab and total depression manifested in extremely rageful fits and the resulting melancholy from them, my appetite had never suffered. I'd eaten heartily before I'd gotten blown to bits, and I still do the same now. I'm lucky I'm tall and have good metabolism because I certainly don't work out the way I did when I was active duty. I'm fortunate that nothing has settled around my midsection yet.

In the Marine Corps, I was a buff dude. My friends and I spent a lot of time in the gym lifting, and Maria certainly made it clear she liked the six-pack abs and bicep guns I'd created from hard work. Since my injury, that muscle definition is long gone, but at least I'm not fat yet.

I'm sure that's coming though as evidenced by the fact I order ribs, brisket and pulled pork along with French fries, coleslaw, and banana pudding.

We eat quickly and head back to the car. It isn't long before Barb and Connor are sound asleep in the backseat, each of their heads resting against their respective passenger windows. We drove through a heavy rainfall after leaving the restaurant, and between the pattering on the roof and the swish of the wipers, it was enough to put anyone out.

It's since calmed to only a sprinkle, and the sky in front of us looks to be clearing of the gray clouds. I take a quick peek at Connor through the rearview mirror, noting he actually looks pretty good today. Maybe it's the excitement of going egging or something. Or maybe it's because the remainder of the poison from his last round of chemo has exited his body.

Jillian has assumed the role of the front passenger again. She's named herself the assistant navigator and uses a paper map to ensure we're getting off at the right exits, despite the fact I have the travel directions programmed into my phone and some female voice telling me when to turn.

Truth be told, I like Jillian's voice better. It's sweet, lilting, and light on the ears.

Right now, she's got her bare feet on my dashboard, legs slightly bent as she plays on her phone. I'd be dead not to notice how gorgeous those legs are. Tan and perfect in every way. Even her feet are fucking pretty. She's got on a pair of white shorts that come to mid-thigh and a Carolina Tarheels t-shirt. Her long, wavy hair is pulled into some kind of messy concoction on top of her head, and she's just fucking stunning.

"How much of a dork do I look in these?" she asks out of the blue, and I turn my head to look at her briefly before giving my attention to the road again.

"Dork?" I ask in confusion. I notice the rain has completely stopped, so I turn my wipers off.

"Yeah, these glasses," she explains.

I give another quick look and can't help but chuckle. She looks like a complete dork wearing black plastic frames with lenses as thick as Coke bottles to help her failing eyes, which are hugely magnified when she looks at me. In the Marine Corps, we called those "beat me, fuck me" glasses.

"I look like a dork, right?" she asks with a smile.

Turning my gaze back to the road., I have to admit, "Yeah… a bit of a dork. But those thick lenses really make the blue of your eyes stand out."

She doesn't say anything for a moment, and then her sweet voice floats across the cab to my ears, "Christopher Barlow… that's the absolute nicest thing I've ever heard you say."

The skin around the left side of my mouth pinches, indicating an involuntary smile has come to my mouth as it's pulling at the scar there. Still, I tell her, "Well, don't expect it too often. Haven't you figured out I'm an asshole?"

I reach into the center console and grab my Marlboro Reds in an easy pinch between my thumb and the two remaining fingers I have of my right hand. Such an easy task now, but fuck if it didn't take me weeks to learn how to pick shit up with a hand that was missing the ring and pinky finger. I tap the pack opening against my left hand as it rests on the top of the steering wheel, my eyes dropping to my right arm for a moment.

Even after almost eighteen months, the damage to my arm sickens me. I have no clue what did it, but I assume a piece of sheered metal, possibly the floorboard or something blowing upward. Almost the entire muscle from elbow to wrist on the top of my forearm shredded so badly that most of it couldn't be salvaged. They were able to repair and connect the remaining thin shreds of tendon and muscle with thousands of micro-sutures, and then they grafted skin from my left hip over the top. It's grotesque. It looks as if there's a long concavity running down my forearm with my radius and ulna bones standing out in stark relief. The transplanted skin is shiny with some puckering around the edges, but the missing muscle is what makes it look so hideous. I'm self-conscious about it, no doubt, but not enough to wear long sleeves. It's high summer and hot as fuck outside. Besides… no one here I'm trying to impress.

Not really.

"Must you do that?" Jillian drawls out in a dramatic voice.

"Do what?" I ask as I pull a cigarette out and put it between my lips.

"Smoke in the car," she says.

I already knew what she meant, but I like playing dense at times because I know it irritates her and, for some reason, I like to irritate her.

"I'll roll the window down," I tell her, the cigarette bobbing in my mouth.

"I can still smell it."

"Roll your window down too," I suggest.

"It sticks to your clothes, and you smell like smoke all the time," she says.

When I turn my head to look at her, I'm surprised her facial muscles are strong enough to maneuver a cocked eyebrow at me. Those muscles aren't overly bothered by her disease because it arches quite high.

"It's not attractive at all," she sniffs.

Turning my head so I can take a quick peek at the road, I ensure I'm straight and then look back to her. "Not attractive?"

As the cigarette bobs in my mouth, I feel utterly ridiculous. I'm a grown-ass man, and I'm talking to this beautiful creature with a nasty cigarette hanging from my lips.

I turn to look at the road, but with my right hand, I take the cigarette out of my mouth. With a sigh, I throw it down into the center console and ask with irritation, "Are you happy?"

"Extremely," she says. "You should just quit, you know."

"Don't want to," I mutter.

"Bet you can't," she says with challenge. "I think it's an easy crutch for you."

"It's an addiction," I contradict her.

"But one that can be beaten, no doubt," she says. "With the right willpower. And Christopher, I look at all you've overcome and I think you have amazing willpower."

I don't dare look at her, with those coke-bottle-magnified eyes looking at me ~~sexily~~ earnestly. What could she possibly know about what it's taken to get me where I am today?

Still, I haven't forgotten she said smoking wasn't attractive, and that sort of implies that I could possibly be attractive if I didn't smoke.

That's an interesting thought, because I haven't given two seconds to ponder how women view me in a very long time. After Maria dumped me because she couldn't accept I wasn't a full man anymore, I had no intentions of ever getting involved with someone again. One-night stands, hookups, prostitutes… that is all I'll ever do, because I can't worry about how a woman truly thinks I look.

I know I'm a good-looking guy in the face—that's not ego talking. And Maria was smoking hot. But my face is scarred now, my arm is mangled, and my leg… well, it's gone. How could any of that be attractive?

"Let's make a bet that you can't go the entire trip without smoking," Jillian says, and my head snaps her way briefly.

I roll my eyes and look back to the road, wanting

that cigarette I just threw into the console now more than ever. "Like what kind of bet?"

"I don't know," she responds flippantly. "We'll come up with something good."

I think about it a moment, wondering if I should I take her bait. She's challenging me to do something hard. I've been smoking for over a year now, starting shortly after I entered rehab. It was something to do to pass the time. I don't want to quit because I don't give a shit about my health, and yeah… she's right… it's a bit of a crutch.

But I can't let go of what she said about willpower, and that has more of an effect on me than anything. "Let me clarify something," I say to her. "The bet would just be smoking cigarettes. Not pot, right?"

"Right," she says, and I find it hilarious she's not turned off by me smoking dope. Maybe the goody two-shoes isn't so goody after all.

"Okay," I say resoundingly. "I won't smoke the rest of the trip."

"And what do you want if you win?" she asks.

"Nothing," I tell her. "I don't need any incentive. If I say I'll do something, I'll do it."

She beams a smile at me. "Willpower."

"Willpower," I agree. I fucking have it in spades, and it's the only thing that got me through months of grueling agony during my recovery. Granted, it's wavered here and there, but it has held mostly strong.

Let's put it this way... I haven't put a bullet in my brain yet.

Jillian gives a laugh, and it's full of delight and joy. "Oh, Christopher... I just feel it. I think this trip is going to be amazing."

I give her another look. She's got her head tilted slightly, staring out at the rushing scenery as we book it down the interstate. There's a serene smile on her face, a relaxed and happy set to her posture. Those coke-bottle glasses are the only testament that she's not perfect.

Without those, no one would know she's going blind. Or that her heart could stop working at any moment. Jillian wears a smile on her face almost all the time, unless she hears something sad, then she's sad too. But I've never seen her down. I've never seen her angry about her condition. In fact, she always talks about it with such earnest optimism that it's almost phony.

In group about four weeks ago, Jillian showed up late. She apologized and said it was because she'd had a rough night. She'd had to go to the emergency room for an irregular heartbeat. Turned out, they'd done some crazy-ass shit and shocked it back into rhythm. Yet, there she was in group the next day, laughing about it and certainly downplaying it.

When Mags had tentatively asked her if she should be at home resting, Jillian gave an impatient wave of her hand and an impish grin. "Plenty of time for resting when the heart finally gives out on me. I'm fine, so stop worrying."

And that was a prime example of the Jillian Martel I'd gotten to know from a distance the last several weeks. She took her disease in stride, seemingly wasn't depressed about it, and always looked for the best in every single situation.

"How do you do it?" I blurt out, and I can sense her shift in her seat to face me.

"Do what?" she asks, and I don't bother looking at her. I can imagine her pretty face, the soft smile, and those magnified eyes as she patiently waits for me to explain.

"Stay so cheerily optimistic all the time. It's like nothing gets you down, and honestly... I can't even understand why you're in our group."

"Maybe I'm there because the rest of you need a dose of my cheeriness to help you along," she teases.

I snort. "Seriously, you're going blind, and you could have a heart attack in the next thirty seconds and die. How in the fuck doesn't that get you down? How can you not be mad at God or your lot in life or destiny or fate? Why aren't you railing against all those forces that dealt you these shitty cards?"

Jillian shifts back in her seat. With stolen peeks, I can see as she lays her head against the headrest. She closes her eyes as a serene smile settles on her mouth. At the same time, the clouds seem to peel away from each other and a bright blast of sunshine filters down to earth. I grab my sunglasses from above my visor and put them on.

"I love when the sun comes out after a dark rain," Jillian murmurs, her eyes still closed. "How it just brightens everything."

Something squeezes in the center of my chest, and it has to do with the reverence in her voice as she talks about the sunlight. Maybe someone with as sunny an outlook on life has a special affinity for the sun or something. I think the squeezing sensation I feel is sadness for Jillian that she'll lose that one day.

It's the first time since I'd been injured that I felt empathy for another human being, and I have to be honest… it ~~fucking freaks me out~~ shakes me up a bit. My entire being is so filled up with anger and bitterness that I don't have room to worry about anyone else. Yet, in this moment, I can't deny that I wish Jillian didn't have to go through this.

I give a slight cough to clear my throat. "I bet you're going to miss the sunshine when you finally go blind."

She lifts her head, and I give her a short glance. Her head is tilted as if she doesn't understand my question. "I'm not following you."

I sweep my hand out in front of me, indicating the beautiful golden scenery before us. "Aren't there going to be things you'll miss? Doesn't it bother you at all that it will be gone and you won't be able to enjoy it anymore?"

Of course, I'm also thinking of my leg right now, but

the same concept applies to Jillian and her impending blindness.

Jillian merely gives a tinkling laugh and sits up straight in her seat, pulling her feet off the dashboard. She turns on one hip so she's facing me, and while I can't make eye contact with her, I give occasional glances at her as she talks.

"Christopher, I'm going to tell you a hard truth I had to learn, and maybe you'll understand where I'm coming from." She takes a deep breath, blinks those heavy eyes once, and continues. "I won't miss the sun because it's not going anywhere. It will always be there for me, continue to bestow its magnificence upon me until the end of my days. I might not be able to see it, but I can feel it. I can feel the warmth that caresses my skin on a late spring day and the tingle on my skin when I start to get a sunburn in high summer. When I go blind, I'll merely open my other senses. I'll smell the flowers that the sun helps to grow, and I'll taste the vegetables from my mom's garden that thrive because of the sunlight. It's not going anywhere, only my ability to perceive it in a certain way is, and I can easily make accommodations."

I want to disbelieve every word within that pretty speech. It's almost like she's been given a pack of lies from someone that she's regurgitating out to me, and now she wants me to drink the Kool-Aid.

But no, that's not it. Deep down... I hear it in her voice. She truly believes that her blindness isn't a loss, but merely an opportunity to change her perception about the world.

I realize in a moment of stunning clarity that she is truly at peace with what's happened to her, and what will happen to her, and because of that, she can focus on the positive.

What I don't understand is how someone gets to be that way. Me, in particular—how do I let go of the nasty feelings that seem to permeate my very soul? How do I look at my stump and not get filled with self-loathing for driving over that IED in the first place? How do I let the anger go, especially when it's on a constant low simmer deep in my belly, just waiting to explode?

I know none of these answers. Up until about thirty seconds ago, I had no clue where to find them. Clearly group counseling isn't working. Neither are the antidepressants or the self-medicating with dope and prescription pills. The most those things do are let me exist, and they probably prevent me from taking a gun to my head.

But can I move past that?

Can I have more?

A small flicker of hope flares in my heart, and while my instinct is to crush it down, I let it burn a little brighter. The feeling isn't all that unpleasant, although by the hammering of my pulse, I can tell it scares the shit out of me to believe in something like happiness and peace.

I think the answer to those questions is sitting in the passenger seat beside me. Jillian makes me want to believe in the possibility of happiness, and I vow to myself that I'm going to have her show me how it's done.

Chapter 9

TURNS OUT THE grave Barb wants to piss on is in a small town by the name of Vinita, Oklahoma. She's been closemouthed about whose grave it is and why she wants to pee on it, but none of us have bothered asking either. We figure she'll either tell us or she won't, and if she does, I suppose we'll listen. Regardless, it's a bucket-list item for her, so we're indulging it.

Jillian and Connor will be empathetic, whatever it is, and I'll be jaundiced and want to begrudge her the right to feel pain when mine is overwhelming at times. At least, I think that's how I'll be.

Actually, I'm not sure since my talk with Jillian in the car today while the others slept. I've thought a lot about her words, and her meaning is quite simple. It's nothing more than finding the good in a situation and appreciating it with such passion that it makes up for the loss of other things. It's redirecting.

Refocusing.

Accepting.

Moving on.

All the things I've not even been able to start to comprehend since I got out of the hospital. I don't understand how she's been able to do it, but I can't stop wondering.

What makes her stronger than me?

Maybe things would have been different if I'd had supportive parents who were by my side. Or if Maria had stayed with me, proclaiming to love me with or without both legs. Or the big question I keep asking myself from time to time, which is wouldn't it just be easier if I ended my miserable existence? I look behind me, and the days are dark. I look ahead, and the days are bleak. I struggle to see even a tiny glint of the sunshine that Jillian feels such an affinity for, and I wonder if I have the willpower… the fortitude… to seek it out.

I think the mere fact I'm analyzing my choices has got to be a good thing, though.

Right?

We check into a budget motel, guys in one room and the girls in another. This was Jillian's idea, and I suspect it's because she wants to try to get to know Barb a bit. I also think it's because Barb is getting ready to face a demon tonight, and Jillian is worried.

We eat a quick dinner at McDonald's, solely for Connor's benefit. While his parents seem cool beyond all reason, they're apparently health-food nuts. Conner's life has been mostly tofu and carrots or some shit like that. His goal on this trip is to eat as much junk food as possible, and frankly, the kid is so damn skinny he could use the extra pounds he might put on.

The game plan for tonight is simple and as soon as the sun sets, we're heading to the cemetery. However, we're first stopping at a grocery store and loading up on three dozen eggs… one for me, one for Connor, and one for Barb. Jillian is still steadfastly refusing to actively participate, although she's going to go and watch us. Disdainfully, I'm sure. After Barb does her pissing thing, we'll seek out a good neighborhood that isn't too well lit and has plenty of side yards with no fences. That way, if we're pursued, we can run through easily. Getting caught and having to escape is half the excitement of doing this.

It's an odd mixture of things that we're doing tonight, but I've come to learn that this trip is nothing like I thought it was going to be.

◆

I REMEMBER THE first day in group as I was assessing everyone, some things were quite clear.

Jillian really didn't belong there.

Connor was clearly physically ill and dying.

And Barb had established herself as an anti-social right off the bat. When asked to introduce herself, she merely snapped at Mags, "I'm Barb. I have a bad habit of trying to kill myself. Apparently, I suck at it. I'm here by court order, but don't expect me to say a fucking thing else."

My eyes had dropped down to Barb's wrists where lines of scars were obvious and so I knew a blade was her choice of weapon long before she told us the story of her mother daring her to do it.

That memory is on my mind when we get to the cemetery. Night has completely settled in, and it's quite dark. Light poles stretch periodically down the winding road that meanders through the plots, but I let Barb direct where we need to go.

Finally, she tells me to stop, and I do, shutting off the engine and plunging us into darkness as the nearest lamppost is a good fifty yards behind us.

Barb snags her backpack and opens the passenger door, but Jillian stops her by asking, "You want us to come with you?"

"I don't give a fuck," Barb says before jumping out and slamming the door behind her.

Without any hesitation, Jillian and Connor scramble out of the Suburban. With a sigh, I follow behind them. I have no clue what the fuck is fixing to happen, and I'm probably not equipped if a meltdown occurs. I've got a joint in my cargo pants, and I should probably just set my ass on a gravestone and watch everything unfurl while getting high.

Barb pulls a flashlight out of her backpack and cuts across three rows of graves until she finds the one she's looking for. She paces down ten more plots and stops, shining her flashlight on a simple, rectangular headstone with the words *James Canton* and the years that spanned his life carved into it. Looks like he died when he was forty-seven.

"Is this your uncle who molested you?" Jillian asks quietly as she comes to stand beside Barb. I'm stunned that Jillian would ask her that point blank. Mags was the only one who pushed Barb to share.

To my further surprise, Barb nods as she stares at the grave. "Yeah. He died about six months ago in prison."

"For what he did to you?" Jillian asks. Connor and I stay back a few feet, silently listening.

Barb nods again. "After I cut myself in my parents' kitchen, I was committed to a hospital. I told my shrink the truth about what my uncle was doing to me, and he involved the police since I was a minor. Of course, my parents—well, mostly my mom since he was her brother—still refused to believe it. But I proved them wrong eventually."

"How?" Jillian whispered.

"Because I gave birth to his son five months later. DNA proved he was the father, so he was arrested for diddling his niece and sent to prison."

"Jesus," Connor mutters, and I have to admit… that's some fucking wild news she's laying on us. A tiny pulse of sympathy for Barb starts to unfurl within me.

Jillian puts her hand on Barb's shoulder. She flinches slightly but doesn't move. "He died in prison. Fucking pneumonia if you can believe it, which was far easier than he deserved."

I didn't think she'd go for it, but Jillian was not to be daunted by an uncomfortable subject. Just like Mags would have done if she were here, Jillian gives her a gentle push. "And the baby?"

Barb's words are completely flat, toneless... absolutely emotionless. If I had to pick a color for her words, I'd call them gray. "I gave him up for adoption. I wasn't in any shape to care for him. All I wanted to do was die."

"That was very brave of you," Jillian says softly.

There's a few moments of silence as Barb and Jillian stare at the headstone, while Connor and I stare at them, before Barb drops her backpack to the side of the grave and hands the flashlight to Jillian.

"Well, let's get this over with, shall we?" Barb says as she starts to unbutton her faded jeans.

Connor immediately turns around, but I don't. I know Barb doesn't care, and I can't see shit anyway as she's facing us and her shirt hangs low enough to cover her private parts. Jillian also watches as Barb pushes her jeans and underwear down, squats right over the top of the grave, and starts to pee. She lets out a steady stream that hisses and makes a splattering noise on the dirt and sparse grass. It goes for a long time, and when she's completely empty, she straightens and efficiently pulls her pants back up.

"You can turn around now, kid," I mutter to Connor, and he does.

"Feel better?" I ask Barb, because honestly... for someone as volatile as Barb, peeing on a grave is kind of lame in my opinion.

"Not quite yet." Her voice has a tinge of what I'd call mischievous malice.

Bending over, she grabs her backpack, turns toward Jillian to shine the flashlight into it, and then she pulls out a hammer. When she looks up, I can see an evil glint in her eye from the glow of the flashlight.

"What are you going to do?" Connor asks fearfully. He takes a step back, because really... why is she carrying around a hammer? I think he truly believes Barb may try to kill us or something.

But not me. I just silently watch as she turns to the headstone and swings the pronged end of the hammer right at her uncle's name. Chips of concrete go flying, as this isn't any type of fancy marble stone. She swings the hammer again and again, hitting at the name and the dates, until they are completely obliterated from the tombstone. She doesn't try to gouge deep, just enough to erase the engraved grooves. It takes her several well-aimed strikes, but when she's finished—chest heaving from the exertion and sweat running down her face—her tone is unnaturally light, "There... *now* I feel better."

Barb then coughs up a huge glob of spit and sends it flying at the mangled headstone. "Now you're nothing," she whispers with a smile on her face as her loogie slides down the front of the marker.

She watches it a moment before turning to us. Jillian has the flashlight aimed at her, but only at chest height so she's not blinded. Still, there's enough light that I can see a wide smile on Barb's face.

It's filled with vindication, joy, and accomplishment. Many would think this to have been a very cathartic event for her, but I know enough about that deep type of despair to realize there's probably no way she can ever shake that shit off completely.

Chapter 10

THE NEIGHBORHOOD IS perfect. Square lots that back up to one another, little to no fencing, and pretty much set in a grid pattern that will make navigation easy. I left my Suburban parked five blocks away, and we'll stay a good two blocks away from it in our pursuits tonight. The sidewalks are lined with large trees that help to filter out the streetlights, and the only real problem with exposure is from porch lights. Luckily for us, we won't be getting that close to the houses.

"Okay, there's an etiquette to egging," I tell the group as we squat down behind a bush at the edge of our first target's yard. I can't squat down as far as the others because of my prosthesis, but I can get low enough that I'm part of the tight circle we've formed. Jillian on my left, Barb to my right, and Connor opposite of me. He looks at me with earnest dedication, as if I'm teaching him how to perform open-heart surgery.

"First," I continue. "No houses that are completely dark. There's no risk in that, which means there's no fun in that. Try to aim for windows or storm doors, particularly ones where the occupants might be standing near. It helps to scare the shit out of them."

Connor nods in understanding, committing this rule to memory. Barb rolls her eyes and Jillian tries to look censuring, but I can see the amusement in the tilt of her lips.

"Second... we all throw together on my count. Once your egg makes contact with the structure, we run to our next designated point."

"Why do you get to count?" Jillian asks.

"Be quiet," I tell her with a stern look. "You're not participating so you have no say."

She giggles in response and Christ... I like that sound. My scar pinches, which means I'm smiling, and I give into it.

Turning back to Connor, I make sure he understands the most important rule. "Finally, don't panic if you're pursued. Ditch the rest of the eggs if you can without being seen. If you're caught, deny everything."

Connor swallows hard but nods again, his eyes starting to sparkle with excitement.

"Are we ready?" I ask the group.

"Yes," Connor and Barb say together, palming the egg they'd pulled from their respective cartons. We're all traveling light right now... nothing but a carton in one hand and a single egg in the other. Jillian's holding onto the Suburban's keys, but I noted she put on tennis shoes tonight in case we have to run. I guess she's running with us, even though she's not participating.

"Okay, our first target is this house," I say as I nod over my left shoulder to the small brick house on the other side of the bush. I do a quick scan of the street, see no one around and no cars coming, and then complete my instructions. "There's a woman at the window washing dishes. Try to aim there."

Connor, Barb, and I all stand from our squatting positions and cock our arms back. Jillian gives a long-suffering sigh, but stands as well.

"And on three... two... one," I murmur to my squad. "Go!"

The three of us throw the eggs, mine and Connor's hitting the kitchen window. Barb's hit just to the right of it on the brick, but the splatting egg was so startling the woman washing dishes shrieks in fear and ducks down low out of sight, I'm sure thinking she was being shot at or something.

Snickering, I turn and take off running down the darkened sidewalk. I'd worn my running blade tonight, which is a special carbon-fiber reinforced polymer prosthetic that helps with spring and balance. I'd received this through the Veteran's Administration along with my C-leg prosthetic, but I hardly ever use it. Haven't been that into running since my injury.

But tonight, as I find I'm able to move fairly quickly for a dude with only one leg, I feel a surge of adrenaline and perhaps personal challenge rise within me. Why am I not running again? I was good at it when I was in the Marine Corps, sometimes running five to eight miles, several times a week.

Connor, Barb, and Jillian all run behind me, any of the three probably able to overtake me with nominal effort, but they don't. Instead, they follow me down one block, and south down another two where I scout out another house. By the time the woman washing dishes figures out what hit her house, she won't be able to find us.

Now, she might call the cops and that does up the risk factor a bit, so I intend for us to unload our cartons quickly.

"Okay," I say, dismayed at how out of breath I am from that run. I really need to start exercising again, and, of course, the smoking hasn't helped. But proudly, I haven't had a cigarette since Jillian laid down her challenge. I was jonesing for one when we were at the cemetery, but right now, I'm high on adrenaline and fun and have no desire for a smoke. "Next target is that house, then see the other one three down across the street? With the white truck in the driveway? We're going to hit that as we're running by."

"Got it," Connor says. Barb doesn't respond, but she pulls two eggs out of her carton and Connor follows suit. Jillian just smirks and shakes her head, amused by how juvenile we are.

I get two eggs out and tuck my carton under my left

arm, holding one egg in that hand. I'm right-hand dominant, so I take the other egg easily between the three digits remaining on that hand and count my group down again. Cocking my arm, I murmur, "In three... two—"

"Hey," a deep man's voice filled with anger comes from behind us. "You fucking kids hit my house with eggs?"

I don't even bother looking over my shoulder. I just drop the eggs, grabbing Jillian's wrist with what's left of my right hand. She doesn't hesitate, actually sliding her hand down and clasping her palm to mine.

We take off running down the side of the house we were getting ready to egg, right into their dark backyard. I think Barb and Connor took off down the block toward our next targeted house, and I can hear the man call out again, "Stop, you little bastards."

A quick look over my shoulder as I run with Jillian in tow, and I can see we're not being pursued. Just as we hit the back of the house of the yard we're cutting through, a floodlight goes on and that makes me run faster. I go deep into the backyard, beyond the harsh glare of the floodlight, where a line of tall bushes mark the property boundary, and then pull Jillian behind a thick one that can hide us. The light doesn't touch out here, but it filters in enough through the leaves that I can see Jillian beside me as she peers through the branches.

I listen intently, but can't hear anything except for

the sound of our heavy breathing. It's not that we ran far but because that dude scared the shit out of us.

"Damn, that was close," I whisper as my heart rate starts to slow down.

Jillian lets out a nervous laugh and then claps a hand over her mouth. I look down at her, her face speckled with light and the shadows of leaves, but I can see her eyes shining with excitement and humor. She releases my mangled hand but before I can even think that I might miss her touch, she turns into me and puts both hands on my chest.

She peers up at me and her voice is girlish, almost giddy. Her expression bears the mark of someone loving the thrill of adventure. "Christopher... that was the scariest but most fun thing I've ever done."

I take in her words, but they don't really resonate. And that's because my brain is going into meltdown over the fact that Jillian has pressed in closer to me and her palms are warm against my chest. I can see a flickering in her eyes, and I don't know what it means.

I haven't been this close to a woman in a long goddamn time, and I'm just not sure what it fucking means.

Before I can rationalize, reason with my sanity, or talk myself out of it, I bring my left hand up to Jillian's face, pressing my palm to her cheek. I don't want her to feel the lumpy skin or gnarled bones of my damaged hand against her skin.

Her eyelids, which are always perpetually droopy,

drop just a little lower and her lips curve into a smile. Still not sure what any of this means, I watch as her gaze slowly slides down and focuses on my mouth.

Or is it my scar she's looking at?

What in the fuck does she want and what in the fuck do I do?

"Christopher," Jillian whispers, and then she takes all the uncertainty away. "Are you going to kiss me?"

I'd like to tell you I have no hesitation, but a million reasons why I shouldn't hit me all at once. I'm deformed, half a man, a total asshole, and she's way too good for the likes of me. I'm bitter, angry, a lame-ass loser who can't seem to get over my bad circumstances, and I don't deserve to kiss one of the bravest people I've met who's facing some serious medical shit.

"Maybe I should say," Jillian murmurs, "that I'd like you to kiss me."

Those doubts still remain and I'm ~~hesitant~~ scared as fuck, but they're overwhelmingly overshadowed by a sudden and complete desire to give Jillian just what she asked for.

So I bend down and touch my lips to hers very gently, with some uncertainty in myself, but mostly because I want this to be good for her.

Jillian sighs contentedly into my mouth, and my head spins.

It's the first time I've kissed a woman in... well, fuck... almost two and a half years if the total time I was deployed before I was injured is counted, along with the time since then. Maria was the last woman I'd kissed.

Made love to.

Loved.

It's been so damn long, and I don't remember it being like this.

I don't remember it being so stirring, and I'm not talking about my dick.

I'm talking about something much deeper than that.

"Once I catch you little assholes..." a man's voice filters through the night air again. I can hear multiple sets of feet pounding the concrete sidewalk to the right of us. I pull back from Jillian and turn my head toward the sound.

"He's going after Barb and Connor," Jillian says fearfully as her hands grasp onto my t-shirt reflexively.

"I know," I growl in frustration as I drop my hand from her face and pull away from her, heading into the next yard. Jillian follows behind me, and we cut through one more additional yard before we're at the other side of the block. Across the street, I can see Barb and Connor huddled behind some garbage cans at the curb, and a big, burly dude stomping toward them but not actually seeing where they are.

When the man is five paces from the cans, Barb decides to flee and takes off running. Connor stands up, but he hesitated too long. The man grabs him by the back of his shirt collar. "I got you, you little fucker."

Without thinking, I break into a trot toward them, Jillian right behind me. But to my surprise, Barb comes to a skidding halt and whips back around.

She's closest to the man holding Connor and charges at him like a little mini-bull. He doesn't see her coming though, concentrating on holding Connor, who is squirming like a snake as he tries to break the man's grasp.

"Leave him alone," Barb yells as she pushes the man right in the chest. He doesn't budge an inch, turning a face blazing with anger at Barb before he makes a grab for her shirt too.

She's quick, though, and jumps backward.

"Let him go," I call out to the man as I approach him aggressively... hand and a half bunched into fists and long, springy steps from my running blade.

The man turns his head to look at me, and I watch as he braces for my attack. We're about the same height, but he's got probably forty pounds of muscle that I don't by the looks of it.

Guess that doesn't matter since he's got a hold of Connor.

Guess it also doesn't matter that I've already been convicted of assault, which is what landed me in group therapy and led me to this exact moment.

"Wait a minute," Jillian cries out. She rushes past me in a blur, positioning herself between my enemy and me. She holds both hands out, one palm facing each of us.

"Please… don't fight."

"I don't want to fight," the man growls. "But you assholes egged my house a few blocks over and someone's going to go clean that shit up or I'm calling the cops."

"We didn't do it," Barb tells the man with a glare, spouting the party line like I told her.

Deny, deny, deny. Good job, Barb.

"I just saw you with the eggs," the man yells in frustration. "You dropped them and ran."

"Doesn't mean we threw them," Barb insists as she crosses her arms over her chest defensively, her eyes flicking over to Connor. The kid is now sort of hanging in the man's grasp like a limp ragdoll, his pitiful amount of energy expended.

"You threw them," the man returns confidently. With a big, meaty hand that moves to Connor's neck, he turns and starts marching him down the sidewalk. "This one's going to clean it up. You three can come if you want."

"Please let him go," Jillian implores as she runs to catch up to the man, laying a hand lightly on his free arm. Barb and I follow along. "He's sick."

The man stops and looks at Jillian. "Sick?"

"Cancer," Jillian says softly. "Alveolar rhabdomyosarcoma. He's terminal."

The man immediately releases Connor and turns to look at him with a shrewd eye. "That true?"

"Yes, sir," Connor says. "And I'm sorry. It was a

bucket-list thing—"

"I threw the eggs," I say loudly, talking right over Connor. "I'll clean your house up."

The man looks at me again, and this time his gaze travels down, pinning on my prosthetic. When his gaze lifts back to mine, there's an even harder glint in them that goes beyond mere frustration at some hoodlums egging his house.

"You in the military?" he asks.

This catches me totally off guard as there's nothing about me to indicate I was a marine. I'm wearing an old West Virginia Mountaineers t-shirt and my hair is longish, hanging an inch or so past my ears and collar.

"Marine Corps," I say.

"Army," he answers gruffly. "Lost a lot of good friends over there."

I don't respond because I don't want to bond with this turd who thinks we have some affinity because we were both in the military. He came back with all his parts as far as I can tell. He stares at me a moment longer before turning to Jillian.

"What is this?" he asks as he waves his hand in a sweeping gesture to include our entire motley group. He can see at a glance we don't belong together, but he's keen enough to know there's some bond there.

"We're all in group therapy together," Jillian explains, and I think she lays it on a little thick to be honest. "I'm going progressively blind, Connor's dying,

Barb keeps trying to die, and well… Christopher lost part of his leg and hand. We're taking a cross-country trip so Connor can see the Pacific Ocean before he… well, you know…"

The man's eyes round in sympathy and fuck if I don't even see a sheen of tears forming. Most people would have called bullshit on our story, even though it's true, but he's apparently bought it hook, line, and sinker.

"How old are you kids?" the guy asks.

Jillian provides the information, because she apparently pays attention to everything in group. "I'm twenty-one, Christopher is twenty-six, Barb is twenty-four, and Connor is eighteen."

I'm surprised by her little white lie about Connor, but it was smart to do so he wouldn't ask questions why a minor was with us.

"I'm Keith," the guy says, then gives a chuckle. "You scared the shit out of Cammie, my wife. You all come back to my house, you can rinse the eggs off, and we'll have a beer."

"Really?" Connor asks in complete stunned amazement that this is even going down like this. I'm half suspecting he wanted to be arrested or something, which would be a much cooler accomplishment for his bucket list.

"Yeah," Keith says in resignation. "You can even have a beer too, seeing as you're dying and all."

"Cool," Connor says, and then he starts to follow

Keith as he leads the way back to his house.

This trip is definitely nothing like I thought it would be.

Chapter 11

A S WE WALK back to the house, Keith and Connor keep up a running dialogue. While I know he was pissed as hell we egged his house, I can see he's highly intrigued by our group. And I'll also have to just go with my hunch he's a guy with a good heart, because most people would certainly not invite a bunch of criminal twerps into their home for a beer.

Barb follows right behind Keith and Connor. Jillian and I take up the rear, walking awkwardly side by side.

We went from a heart-pounding but brief kiss to cleaning eggs off a brick house. I'm not sure where we stand. Was Jillian just caught up in the exhilaration of the moment, perhaps the thrill of being chased and caught causing her to be daring and reckless? Or did she really want me to kiss her?

Without warning, preamble, or a head's-up, Jillian quietly slips her hand into mine. I'm completely shocked and nearly stumble. Because she's walking on my right, she has to take my deformed hand and I fucking hate it.

Hate it because I don't want to gross her out, and

hate it because half the remaining skin around the area where I lost my fingers is numb and I can't really feel her skin against mine.

But mostly I'm embarrassed and ashamed, and I actually pull my hand back a little with the intention of moving around her so she can hold my left hand.

I'm ~~thwarted~~ rewarded when Jillian's hand tightens around the half that's left of mine, and she murmurs one word. "Don't."

Don't pull away.
Don't be scared.
Don't be ashamed.
Just don't.

I try to calm my stammering heart, try to push down all my self-conscious thoughts, and try like hell to just be in the moment. It's hard because I've not let myself be in a moment in a long time. I've kept myself so sheltered from the real world that human touch feels foreign to me.

I'm not sure if I like it or not, but I don't pull my hand away.

When we reach Keith's house, he says, "Come on inside. I'll introduce you to Cammie."

We follow him in, and I wonder just how pissed Cammie is going to be at us. She's waiting for us in the living room as we enter, taking in the entire group with an eyebrow cocked high and her arms crossed defensively over her chest. Whereas Keith is built like a mountain,

Cammie is the opposite. Small, petite, and delicate looking.

"Caught them," Keith says as he jerks his thumb over his shoulder at us. "They're going to clean up the mess. After that, we're going to have a beer."

Cammie's eyebrow cocks higher. "I already cleaned it up. Got the garden hose out and sprayed it off before it could dry."

"Huh?" Keith says, scratching his head. "Well… what should we do with them? Can't have my beer without penance."

Connor snickers, causing Cammie's eyes to drift over to him. They immediately fill with sympathy as she takes him in, meaning she recognizes he's sick.

"Well," she says with a mischievous smile at Connor as she uncrosses her arms. Pointing to the kitchen, she says, "You can finish cleaning up my kitchen. Then we'll be square."

"Deal," Connor says, accepting quickly, and Cammie's expression warms even further.

Okay, so I am going to have to admit it… Keith and Cammie may be two of the ~~coolest~~ weirdest people I've ever met.

◆

"SO EGGING HOUSES was seriously on your bucket list?" Cammie asks Connor as we sit outside on their deck. It's small, and there's only a table with four chairs around it.

Cammie, Connor, Jillian, and Barb are at the table, while Keith and I lean back against the deck railing.

Connor shrugs. "I've been sick for such a long time, so there was a lot of fun growing-up stuff I missed out on."

"Well, we're honored you chose our house," Cammie says jokingly and holds her beer up to Connor.

He taps his can to hers with a sheepish grin. "I won't ever forget this."

"We want to thank you for how cool you and Keith have been about this," Jillian says. Her back is to me, but I can imagine the apologetic expression on her face. We had dropped hands as we walked into Keith's house. Since then, she's barely looked at me.

"How long ago did that happen?" Keith asks quietly from beside me, and this does not offend me the way the "thank you for your sacrifice" does.

I turn my head, and his head nods down to my leg. "Little over a year and a half ago."

Keith turns around and rests his elbows on the edge of the deck rail, holding his beer can in one hand. It's a move that says, "Let's talk a bit more privately," so I turn to face the railing and mimic the way he leans over it. I'd already finished my beer and declined a second one offered by Keith since I'm driving. While I'm sure I'd be fine driving with two beers, I don't want to worry ~~Jillian~~ the others about whether I'm impaired.

I'm vaguely aware of Jillian telling Cammie more

about our group and how we came to be on this trip together, but I tune it out when Keith says, "Lost my best friend over there."

"Sorry, man," I mumble, because really… what else can I say?

Hey, your best friend is lucky compared to me.

"Yeah, I've been diagnosed with that PTSD shit," Keith continues as he stares out into the darkened backyard, and now I feel awkward. This is some personal shit, and I get enough of that from my cronies sitting at the table behind me. "They say I have survivor's guilt."

Now, I'd been thinking Keith was a pretty cool guy up until now. He gave us a pass for egging his house and invited us in with amazing hospitality. But fuck if I want him to ruin all that goodwill he'd built up by telling me he's got fucking survivor's guilt. He has no goddamn clue how lucky he is.

Still, I manage to keep my voice level when I ask, "How can you feel guilty about being alive and uninjured?"

Keith turns to look at me. "I'm thinking you and I went into the military for different reasons. I was a third-generation Army man. It was ingrained in me from the day I was born that it was my duty to die for my country if I was called to war."

"You're fucking kidding me," is all I can respond with, because no one should have that death wish over them.

"Well, that might be a bit dramatic, but it's still true. I've never wanted anything else than to go into the Army and serve my country. It was an honor when I got deployed. It was an honor to serve with the men and women who sacrificed their lives or their limbs."

"Yeah, well, it wasn't a sacrifice I signed up for," I mutter as I grip my hands into fists, the urge to smoke hitting me with a painful, addictive crush for the first time since I told Jillian I wouldn't.

Keith doesn't try to argue with me, but instead asks, "Why did you join?"

I shrug. "I thought it would be a better life than working in the coal mines like everyone else in my family."

"Regretting that now, aren't you?" he asks.

I want to tell him "fuck yes." If I'd just stayed home and worked in the mines like everyone else, I'd still be alive, and whole, and married to Maria by now. But something holds me back from answering so quickly with that sentiment.

In fact, I can't answer at all, and I don't know why.

"Maybe you're right where you're supposed to be," Keith says softly as he gives a slight nod over his shoulder. "I saw you and your girl together. Wouldn't have met her unless you went to group therapy, and you wouldn't have gone to group therapy if you hadn't got your leg blown off, right?"

Well, yeah... of course. But I'm not sure meeting

Jillian is ultimately a good thing. While I'm intrigued and fascinated by her, I can't tell if she's really what I need or want. And she is in no way "my girl."

Because if she is, then I'll have to have a serious attitude adjustment and I'm not sure I'm ready for the type of work that would take. There's something easy in my solitary, angry world, and fuck if it makes me a loser in every way, but I'm a bit afraid to give that up.

I don't want to talk about Jillian with this stranger. We may have just shared a beer together, but I don't know him. Despite the fact he served, he doesn't know me. Not about to spill any fantasies I may or may not have about Jillian, especially because I don't know if it's right to have them.

But I am curious about one thing, and Keith is just the guy to ask, "The army being your life and all... I suppose you like it when people thank you for your service?"

Keith shrugs. "Well, yeah... I mean, it's nice for the recognition, but it's not why I joined."

My head drops, and I look down to the mangled remnant of my right hand. It's my dominant hand still, even though it's half a hand. Lifting my head, I turn to look at him. "I fucking hate it. I hate strangers giving me that look of sympathy, coming up to me wanting to shake hands. They reach their right hand out, showing how brave and unafraid they are of my deformities, as if they're doing me a favor by trying to normalize me. And

Christ… when they say how sorry they are for my losses, and that they feel safer at night because of my sacrifice, I want to knock their heads clean off their shoulders. Their words do nothing but rub my nose in this shithole of a life I've fallen into."

Staring at me with raised eyebrows, Keith says, "Dude, that's a lot of anger right there."

"It's why I'm in group therapy," I say dryly, turning to look back out into the dark.

"You *should* be thanked," Keith says, and I whip my head back to frown at him.

"What?"

"You should be thanked," Keith repeats. "It *was* a sacrifice."

"Bullshit," I growl at him, and then lean in a little closer. "Losing my leg and my hand didn't do one damn thing to help a single individual American."

Reaching out, Keith puts a hand on my shoulder and squeezes. It's a fatherly move, although he can't be more than ten years older than me at the most. "That's because it's not about you. It's about the collective whole. Your unit as a team. Your group effort in the war. Our military's effort to stabilize the region. You were just a single casualty, but it was a risk you were aware of and took when you joined up. When the risk got you, it became a sacrifice whether you want it or not."

"I don't want it," I reply lamely.

"Fuck, who would?" he returns as he pulls his hand

from my shoulder. "Not going to ask if you want my advice because you'll say no, so I'm just going to give it. I suggest you get your head out of your ass and look at the good you've got around you. Otherwise, you are in for a long and miserable existence."

He's right. I didn't want his advice, but I had no choice but to listen.

And the pitiful thing is, I know he's right. I've told myself over and over again to just get over my issues. Be strong. Man up. Figure a way past this. I've known for months that if I don't get my shit together, then the rest of my life will indeed be miserable.

And that's why I think about killing myself sometimes. Because I don't want to live in misery for the rest of my days. I don't have enough willpower to survive it despite the fact Jillian seems to think I'm brimming with it.

Chapter 12

Four weeks ago...

"**I**'D LIKE TO propose an idea to the group," Jillian said as she sat up straighter in her chair, looking only at Mags. She did that because she already knew that Barb and I didn't care, and that whatever it was, Connor would already be on board.

"What's that?" Mags asked with interest.

"Last week, we talked a lot about Connor dying and how he started to prioritize what was important to him," she said carefully, turning to give a reassuring smile to Connor. He looked back at her with glowing affection. Those two had become very close, very fast. "And there are things he obviously wants to do before we lose him, so I thought maybe we could provide some of that for him."

Interesting that she'd said "before *we*" lose him. As if this was a group of friends or family, and that his death would be a blow to us. Personally, I didn't care if, when, or where the kid died. It had nothing to do with me.

Still, I watched Jillian carefully. The first two weeks,

I'd kept my stare firmly planted on the industrial gray carpet of our meeting room, but during the last two sessions, I found myself unable to tear my gaze from her. While it was nice to just listen to her voice, when paired with her face and those eyes, well… it was just nicer to get the entire package.

"What did you have in mind?" Mags asked, one thin leg crossed over the other, revealing white socks with Sylvester and Tweety on them.

Jillian hesitated, and I knew in that moment that she was going to ask for something impossible. She took in a deep breath, let it out, and forged ahead. "Connor has never seen the West Coast. He wants to see the Pacific Ocean before he dies, and I know that's a huge and monumental trip, but maybe we could go as a group and do some other things along the way."

She never even paused for a breath. It was as if her speech was rehearsed.

"Mags, you're always saying that we need to interact more, and well… that's just not been happening very well here."

At that point, she shot a look—and by that I meant turned her head slowly—toward Barb and me before she looked back to Mags. "I thought maybe a trip like that would… I don't know… bring us closer. It's a crazy idea, for sure, but I think we'd get a lot more out of that than just sitting in this room and talking about the same things over and over again."

When she finished, she let out a sigh of relief, as if it had taken all her courage to throw that out there.

"I'm not sure that's really doable," Mags said in a kind but firm tone. "Connor is a minor—"

"His parents already said he could do it," Jillian butted in.

Mags did nothing more than give a small smile and an understanding nod. I'd listened enough in group these last several weeks to know that Connor's parents pretty much indulged his every wish. Not in a spoil-the-kid kind of way, but so they could make his remaining life as wonderful as possible. I was slightly surprised they'd let him go on a trip that would take several days, as it would be that many days they wouldn't have to spend with him, but again... I'd gotten the impression he could do whatever he wanted.

"What do you think, Christopher?" Mags asked me.

"Not interested," I muttered as I looked back down at the floor.

"Why not?" she pushed at me.

Hmmm... why not?

Because I wasn't sure I could be in close quarters with Jillian for several days. The hour and a half each week was brutal enough. I'd pretty much hated her that first week even though I thought she was hot, but the more I listened to her, the more intrigued I became.

For weeks, I'd listened to her soft voice with that very slight southern twang. Even though she was from North

Carolina and further south than me, I had more of a redneck accent than she did. But her voice was light and melodic... almost musical. And then there was that fucking smile. She always had it. Coupled with the lazy eyes, it was sexy.

But that smile made no sense to me.

Jillian was a person who seemed to always be happy and content. She was maternally affectionate with Connor, joked around with Mags, and even tried a few times to stir some conversation with Barb and me. She was filled with optimism, which meant she really didn't belong in this group, and I thought everyone else in this room was a dumbass for not recognizing that.

But more importantly, and what also boggled my mind, was that Jillian never talked about "her" fears. As far as I could tell, she wasn't afraid of dying. She'd accepted she was going blind and even joked about it. She'd even said one day that she was thankful for the twenty years of sight she'd had, because that made her far luckier than those who were born blind.

I swear to God she was like fucking Snow White... all tra-lah-lah, skipping through the forest and singing to the birds. I hated it and because I'm a sick fuck, I wanted to see more of it at the same time.

"Christopher," Mags said, and it broke me out of my thoughts. "Why aren't you interested? I'd make it worth your time by giving you credit for a few sessions if you went."

Oh, I was interested all right. Too interested in Jillian's voice, her hair, her eyes, her smell, and her fucking outlook on life, but the problem was that I didn't want to be interested. There were too many dangers and pitfalls to let myself go down that path.

"What's the point?" I asked snidely. "He's gonna die. Seeing the ocean ain't gonna help that."

I expected someone to chastise me for my crudeness. To my surprise, Jillian leaned forward in her chair, tilted her chin up so she could see me a little better because of her droopy eyes, and said, "Come on, Christopher. Where's your sense of adventure?"

A bolt of anger jolted through me, and I glared at her fiercely. "I lost it when I got my leg blown off."

She wasn't repentant or put in her place. Merely giving me a look of disappointment, she said just one word to me. "Typical."

"Typical?" I growled at her.

"Typical," she said simply. "You hide away from everything. And it's okay… I get you feel safer that way. You haven't participated hardly at all, so I guess what I really mean is that your refusal to consider the trip is just typical of you."

A genuine flush of embarrassment swept through me. At that, I was even more embarrassed because she probably saw my face go red. "You know nothing about me," I snarled.

"Exactly," was all she said back.

And then it hit me.

Jillian wanted to know more about me.

Me.

Oh, I didn't think she designed the trip just for that. Her heart was ~~always poking where it didn't belong~~ in the right place and she was definitely doing this for Connor, but she *was* baiting me to go on this trip.

She actually *wanted* me to go.

Could I do it? Could I sit in the same car with her for hundreds of miles and smell her, listen to her... try to figure her out?

I didn't want to look like a pussy who would easily give in, so I left myself an out to try to hold on to my man card. "Okay... fine. I'll go if Barb goes."

Because no way in hell would she be interested in this type of thing.

I turned to look at Barb, confident she'd save me from myself.

She just shrugged with the same half-angry, half-bored expression she always wore and said, "Sure. I don't have anything better to do."

Aww, Christ. I was screwed.

Chapter 13

I T'S ALMOST MIDNIGHT by the time we head back to the hotel from our evening's adventure. We left after Jillian and Connor gave Keith and Cammie hard hugs and promises to keep in touch. It seems new friendships were formed. I'd shaken Keith's hand, but I know we'll never talk again. Gave a polite nod to Cammie and thanked her for the beer, but never did apologize for egging her house.

Barb had just muttered, "Later," as we walked out.

The ride back to the motel is silent. There's no conversation because a worn-out Connor fell asleep with his head resting against the window, Barb doesn't talk much anyway, and things are still very awkward between Jillian and me. We haven't spoken or touched since we entered Keith's house. Of course, my first and most pitiful thought is that it was all a mistake.

Were we just totally caught up in the moment when it came to that kiss? Or what about her holding my hand with such affection? I imagine it was because she was grateful to me for stepping in to rescue Connor? Because I was willing to go to the mat for that kid, and she loves him like a kid brother.

That's all it was, right?

Our motel is one of those cheap strip buildings with a long row of units to the left and right of the main office. There's a pool off to the side that's empty and moldy looking. The rooms are so old that they have actual antique-looking keys to open the room doors, and they smell musty.

Our rooms are next to each other, our stuff already brought in before we'd left for dinner and the cemetery. When I park the Suburban in front of my room, Barb's tone is surprisingly gentle when she says, "Connor... wake up."

I look in the rearview mirror to see her nudging his shoulder. His head pops up, and he blinks his eyes at her before wiping a tiny bit of drool off his chin. Barb actually gives what I think might be a smile as I saw the very corners of her mouth curl upward maybe an eighth of an inch.

We all exit the Suburban. Connor starts toward our room, and Barb walks to hers as she pulls a room key out. Just as she's unlocking the door, Jillian meets me at the front of the Suburban and says, "Christopher... can I talk to you a moment out here?"

Barb looks over her shoulder, her eyebrows raised in surprise for a moment before she heads inside and closes the door. A tiny thrill runs through me. I'm not sure if it's fear or excitement over what Jillian wants from me, but I just nod my head at her and toss the room key to Connor. He makes a move to grab it and misses. The key clatters to the concrete walkway in front of the door. He gives me a sheepish grin, bends over to pick it up, and goes into our room.

I turn to Jillian and try to appear cool, shoving my hands into the pockets of my shorts. "What's up?"

"I want to talk about that kiss," she says outright, but even her bluntness has a melodic ring to it.

I shrug. "No biggie. I'm sure it was just—"

"I'd like to do that again," she says softly, but the impact of her words slam into me hard.

"You what?" My voice is harsh and disbelieving. "Why?"

Jillian smiles, and it's the one she's given me a few times before so I recognize it. It's the smile of under-standing... as if she knows what drives the words that come out of my mouth, even if I don't.

She takes two steps and comes toe to toe with me. I punch my hands further into my pockets as I look down at her. She does her classic chin lift so she can see me better under those droopy eyelids. Without shame, hesitation, or second thoughts, she puts a hand right in the center of my chest where I know she can feel the mad gallop of my heartbeat.

"I'd like you to kiss me again," she says sweetly. "The

last one wasn't long enough."

"I don't understand," I mutter, because I'm convinced—absofuckinglutely convinced—that this is wrong and I'm being played somehow.

Jillian tilts her head as her eyebrows draw inward. "What's not to understand? I like you. I really liked our first kiss. I want to do it again, so I'm asking. Unless you found it lacking, of course."

I ignore the "lacking" comment and focus on the source of my apprehension. "You like me?"

She rolls her eyes at me. It's a slow effort because of her condition, but I get the message. My question was apparently stupid.

"Yes, I like you," she says in exasperation.

My eyes narrow at her. "Why?"

Jillian tilts her head back and laughs, and when she looks back at me under the slight weight of her eyelids, the blue of her eyes is sparkling with amusement. "Well, because you're hot, of course. My vision might be bad, but I can still see that."

Okay, that's just bullshit.

And it's like she read my mind, because she steps in just a bit closer to me and murmurs, "And don't think for a moment your injuries take away from your hotness."

"Bullsh—"

"I mean… you're an asshole. A hot asshole and it's weird I'm attracted to that. But let's be honest, you're not *that* good of an asshole."

Now I'm confused. "Huh?"

"You're a bit inconsistent to be honest," she says with a cute shrug and a slow bat of her eyelashes. "You say mean things to deflect, but it's really kind of obvious. You internalize, and I'm sure you've got a million reasons to do so. You never talk about what happened to you or how you feel about it, and you clearly don't want to. So you do asshole-like things to push people away. Like I said... totally obvious."

"What does that have to do with liking me?" I ask in a low voice, but before she can answer me, her phone starts ringing. She pushes a hand into her back pocket and deftly hits the button that sends the call to voice mail.

Jillian is a popular person, apparently, because her phone rings a lot even though she never answers it. Connor asked her about it once, but she just said, "I like texting better than talking."

Made sense to me because I'm the same way.

Jillian smoothly continues, the ringing of the phone already dismissed and forgotten. "My theory is that because you're not that great at the whole asshole thing, you probably weren't always that way. And I'd like to find out more about the real Christopher Barlow. But until you choose to do that, I'll just stick with the 'you're hot' reason why I want to kiss you and go with that."

A bubbling sensation forms inside my throat, way

down low. It roils, surges upward, and feels completely foreign as it bursts free from my mouth.

It's a laugh.

A completely take-me-by-surprise laugh that I had no intention of giving, and frankly, I didn't think I had it in me to give. But goddamn, she's funny and sweet, and she makes me think there could possibly be hope for me.

Jillian grins back at me.

"Christ," I mutter as my left hand slides out of my pocket and wraps around the back of her neck where I grip her gently. "You're like a blaze of bright sunshine that the fucking darkest sunglasses can't repel."

She gives me a pouty look. "That's a compliment, right?"

I answer her with that kiss she asked for because in this moment, Jillian forgives me for being an asshole and she thinks I'm hot. I've been a risk-averse kind of guy for the last few years, but right now, I'm thinking she's a sure bet.

For the kiss, I mean.

When our lips first touch, my entire body relaxes for a moment as if this is the most natural thing in the world. Then Jillian boldly opens her mouth to touch her tongue to mine, and my entire body tightens. My fingers dig slightly into her neck, and I have to suppress the groan that wants to tear free. Jillian sighs into my mouth, her tongue rolling against mine. A breathy, dreamy, satisfied sound that makes me feel every bit a man.

It's the best fucking kiss I can remember, which means it's time to pull away. I end the kiss with a soft brush of my lips against hers. I end it because that was about as perfect as it can get, and I don't want anything else to mar that right now.

I stare down at her as she slowly opens her eyes, a wistful curve to her lips. When she focuses on me, she says, "That was good."

"It was." My admission is reluctant because it would be so much easier if the kiss had been bad.

Jillian rubs her thumb along my breastbone before stepping away from me. "I hope we do that again. Good night, Christopher."

I stand there silently and watch her as she goes to her room. She gives a knock on the door without looking back at me, and Barb opens it within a few seconds. Jillian disappears inside, and I am more confused than ever.

When I walk to the room I'm sharing with Connor, I see he's left the deadbolt engaged so the door remains slightly cracked open. When I enter, I see him on the bed closest to the bathroom, surfing on his phone.

He looks over at me and gives me a sly grin.

"What?" I ask defensively, wondering if he was watching out the window or something.

Connor shakes his head. "Nothing."

"Damn right, nothing," I mutter as I pull my toiletry kit out of my bag.

I walk past his bed toward the bathroom, but his words stop me dead. "She really likes you."

My head whips to look at him. "What makes you say that?"

"Because she told me."

"She did?" I ask dubiously.

"Yeah," he returns with a confident nod of his head. "Totally."

I still don't really understand why. I know she said the whole "hot" thing, and she alluded to me not really being an asshole, but now I find out she's told Connor she likes me.

Maybe there's some truth to it.

Maybe I'm just a way to pass her time.

In an unprecedented burst of candor, I tell Connor an absolute lie that should be hard truth. "I don't think I'm interested."

"Why?" His eyebrows are up high, the expression on his face incredulous. "She's amazing."

Apparently, now that I've staked my position to Connor, I feel the need to defend it. "I've been burned before. Not interested in going there again."

"Burned? How?"

I give a sigh and brush my fingers through my hair. "Long story short, I had a girlfriend who dumped me when I came back with parts of me left in the desert."

Connor winces, but I give him the rest.

"My parents never came to see me during my recovery; it was too much on them. I'm not keen on facing the whole potential for abandonment again."

Propping up on his elbow, Connor levels me with a solemn look. "Christopher, I don't think them abandoning you had anything to do with your injuries. I think it had everything to do with the fact that they're the assholes. They're the ones who are deficient and weak—the ones who are broken."

"Maybe so," I say in agreement. "But it's sort of left me with trust issues."

It's a sympathetic look that Connor gives me. "And anger issues. No wonder you're an asshole. I totally understand it now though."

I can't help the snicker that pops out. For some reason, Connor's got me relaxed, so I admit, "Besides... someone like Jillian is too good for the likes of me."

"She's not like that," Connor insists. "She doesn't look at you as broken or less than anything."

"I don't mean that," I say with a shake of my head. The minute Jillian grabbed my deformed hand, I knew she saw past the scars. "I mean, my baggage is too heavy. My issues are too dark. I'd drag her down so fast that her light would be extinguished."

"Or," Connor suggests, "her light is so bright it will drive away your darkness."

I make a non-committal noise. It's a nice thought, but I'd be a fool to hope it's true.

Chapter 14

I HAD OUR cross-country route all planned. My preference had been to drive straight across from Raleigh to Los Angeles, which could be done in roughly thirty-five hours. Connor, however, had wanted to see a specific part of the Pacific Ocean, a placed called Cannon Beach in Oregon. This added ten hours onto my original plan as we had to cut up northwest. Then I made a deviation so Barb could piss on her abusive uncle's grave.

That's fine. Back on track and headed to Denver.

Granted, we could do this trip a lot faster with continuous driving, but I don't trust anyone else to drive my vehicle. Jillian can't see, Connor is just too inexperienced, and Barb would likely drive us off a cliff. I have to settle with driving nine to ten hours a day or more and stretching the trip by a few days.

To help compensate for this extra time on the road, my plan today is to drive hard to make it to Denver by dinnertime, which is why I insisted we leave at six this morning.

Things are never that easy though. Jillian throws a

monkey wrench at me, which is something I actually think she derives pleasure in doing. As I'm rearranging some stuff in the rear of my SUV, waiting on the others to come out of the rooms, Jillian suddenly appears at the tailgate.

"Good morning," she says hesitantly.

I turn to look at her. With a sigh, I ask in a long, drawled-out tone, "What do you want?"

I'd come to recognize that look on her face when she was going to ask for something that she was pretty sure she wouldn't get. It was the same look on her face when she proposed this trip, and when she told me she had forgotten her wallet and needed to borrow money.

"Can we make a change to the route again?" she asks quickly, and I try not to focus on her lips as she talks. Reminds me too much of our kisses. "It's really not that much out of the way. Maybe an additional five hours of driving time, but we can make that up."

With a cocked eyebrow, I stand straight and fold my arms across my chest. "Where to?"

"Yellowstone," she practically gushes. "Connor would love to see Yellowstone, and I Googled it… the difference we lose by not going to Boise after Denver is really only about five hours."

"For fuck's sake, Jillian," I say sarcastically. "It won't add just five hours onto the trip. It will add an entire day once we get there because you don't just look at the sign at the front of the park and leave. You have to drive around and see shit."

"I know," she pleads with me. "But come on, Christopher. He's dying. Why can't you give another day of your time to make this happen?"

Just two days ago, my answer would have been, "Because I don't give a fuck he's dying."

But today, I'm apparently a slightly different man as I find myself nodding in acquiescence without any real hesitation. "Okay, fine."

After Denver, we're headed to Yellowstone.

Because not only has the little twerp grown on me, but shamefully, so has Jillian. I think about those two kisses and what more could potentially come from that, knowing deep down, I'm not put out one bit by spending extra time on the road. I've finally given in to the notion that this trip might not be so bad after all.

"How many more times are you going to use that "he's dying" thing when you want something?" I ask her with a mock glare. "Because that will get old at some point."

Jillian laughs, and it's warm and husky. It makes my entire body flush with tingles. "Maybe I'll have to figure out some other inducement to offer you then."

Yeah, I could get on board with that.

◆

WE'RE CRUISING NORTH to Denver where we'll be going further north into Wyoming rather than west to Boise, but whatever. An extra day or five isn't going to matter in the grand scheme of things. I'm committed to this trip now.

Since I'm not smoking, the windows are up and the air conditioning is blasting. We're into our sixth round of *21 Questions*.

"Is it a person?" I ask.

Jillian says, "No. That's one."

"A place?" Connor says from the back.

"No. That's two," Jillian responds as her fingers drum against her thigh to music playing on low volume. Good song too... *Somebody Told Me* by The Killers. As the driver, I get sole choice of the music. I have my iPhone plugged into the auxiliary audio so I can play what I want.

Back to my turn as Barb isn't playing. She has her earbuds in, bopping to some unknown song as she looks out the window. "An object?"

"Yes," Jillian admits slowly. "Three questions down."

"Bigger than a house?" Connor guesses.

"Yes," she says, now sounding nervous. "That's four."

"In the United States?" I try to narrow it down.

"Yes," she mutters. "Five."

"The Empire State Building," Connor says from the back.

"Damn it," Jillian grumbles as she slouches down in her seat and crosses her arms over her chest. "How can you make such lucky guesses?"

I chuckle because the kid is really good at this game. It's probably just luck, which is weird because I'd call him anything but lucky given his circumstances.

"Want to play again?" Connor asks.

"No," Jillian and I say in unison. Turning, we grin at each other. The game kind of sucks, but it's to keep Connor busy so he doesn't gab about inane things.

One thing I've realized about Connor during this road trip, especially now that he seems to be feeling better than that first day, is that he needs something to do. He can't just sit quietly and look at the scenery. He practically buzzes with energy, and maybe that's his body's way of compensating for all the things he has to accomplish before he dies.

"Hey, Barb," Connor says, and I glance into the rearview mirror as he leans toward her to nudge her arm.

Barb pulls out the earbud that's closest to Connor, not even glaring at him which is strange but I'll count as progress on her end. She just lifts her eyebrows and asks, "What's up?"

"What are you listening to?" he asks.

My eyes flick back to Barb through the mirror as she growls, "None of your business," before she stuffs the bud back in.

Undaunted and perhaps feeling more secure that Barb won't slit his throat since she actually tried to save him from Keith last night, I watch as Connor grins mischievously and pulls the earbud out. He quickly leans closer before Barb can even object and puts it up to his ear.

My eyes go back and forth between the road and the mirror to see what happens.

"You little fucker," Barb snarls as she pulls the bud back from him. "Give me that."

Connor's face goes slack with awe as he stares at Barb with big eyes. "Whoa. You listen to Taylor Swift?"

This gets Jillian's attention, and she actually undoes her seatbelt to turn all the way around in her seat to look at them.

"She listens to Taylor Swift?" Jillian asks with astonishment.

"Yeah," Connor says as if he's seen the Second Coming of Christ.

"What song was it?"

"*Shake It Off.*"

Jillian's head nods up and down. "Excellent choice."

I have no clue what the fuck they're talking about. I mean, I know who Taylor Swift is but I can't say I've ever listened to one of her songs. I prefer rock and grunge.

Another flick of my eyes to the mirror and I see Barb glaring at Jillian, which is why she can't react when Connor grabs her iPhone, deftly pulling the plug to the earbuds out. He hands the phone to Jillian and says, "Plug it in. Let's all sing it."

"Goddamn it," Barb snarls as she makes a lunge for the phone, but Jillian's quick. She flips around in her seat, pulls the cord out of my phone without asking for permission, and plugs Barb's in. When she gives the screen a tap, the beginning notes of a song starts.

Jillian reaches forward, turning the volume knob way up, and my car fills with nasty-ass pop music. But I let it go because of three things. Connor's bouncing in his seat and singing, Jillian's turned halfway in hers, grinning back at Connor as she shakes her shoulders back and forth to the beat, but most importantly because Barb is now slouched down in her seat, arms crossed over her chest, with the sourest look on her face.

My scar pinches. I don't even bother fighting the smile that comes to my face as I turn my attention back to the road and let Jillian and Connor have their moment.

"Come on, Barb," I hear Connor yell above the music. "Sing it with us."

My eyes flick quickly to the mirror long enough to see Connor give Barb's shoulder a slight push to get her to move.

Back to the road, back to the mirror.

"Please, Barb," Connor practically whines as he pushes at her. "It's on my bucket list... to have you sing with me. And I'm *dying*."

God, he's ruthless. I wince as I look to the road. When I glance at Jillian, she looks back at me with amusement over Connor's tactics. I quickly flick my eyes back to the mirror. That was a low blow and for a moment I don't think Barb is moved.

She glares at Connor, and then miraculously, she gives a roll of her eyes and a huge sigh. Turning to look at Jillian she says, "Crank it louder. My singing voice sucks."

"Awesome," Connor shouts as Jillian turns that hideous song up.

And before I know it, all three of them are singing and bopping in their seats to the song.

But I keep cruising,
Can't stop, won't stop moving

I drive and let them have their fun, keeping most of my attention on the road but sneaking glances at Jillian since she's the best thing to look at. And yes, the smile stays on my face and I don't begrudge it.

My eyes flick to the mirror to look at Barb again, as she's the odd duck here, and I find her staring back at me. She must know I'm smiling because I'm sure she can see my eyes crinkled in the mirror's reflection. She flips me off but not before she smirks and looks out the window as she continues to sing along with Jillian and Connor.

Chapter 15

I T'S DARK BY the time I pull the Suburban up to our campsite on the western side of Denver. I'd left here with Barb about an hour ago after I'd built a quick fire and left instructions with Jillian and Connor on how to keep it going. I also told them to try to put their tent up, but I'd help them when I got back if they couldn't.

Then I told Barb to get in the car, and we took off to the nearest pot dispensary, which I'd Googled before we left. Without a Colorado driver's license, a person twenty-one or older could purchase seven grams. I brought her so we could get double, giving us close to thirty joints. I thought I'd be saddened to purchase from a legal dispensary because that goes against the whole anti-establishment, criminal thing I got going on, but I was actually glad.

Glad I'm in a state that legalized pot, so we can get Jillian high tonight.

As my headlights sweep across our campsite, I'm pleased to see that Connor and Jillian were able to get their huge-ass tent set up. Connor had watched me carefully the first time I'd put it up, assisting when he could. He's a pretty bright dude so I guess I shouldn't be too surprised he figured it out on his own. The fire is still going strong, and I see they're working on my tent.

Awesome.

Barb and I exit my SUV. The ride to and from the dispensary was without conversation. Barb had put her earbuds in but before she secured them, I'd asked, "Want me to put some Taylor Swift on?"

She growled back at me. "Bite me."

I'd laughed, played some Alice in Chains, and we'd made the trip in companionable silence.

I go to the rear of my car and open the tailgate, pulling my duffle bag out. I also grab the two bags of groceries from a quick stop we'd made at a small market up the road. I bought as much junk food as I could because if we're smoking tonight, we're going to get the munchies.

"Need any help?" Connor asks as he rounds the back of my vehicle.

I push the groceries at him as well as my duffle bag. "Yeah… take these. I'll grab the cooler."

I'd stocked that with beer and ice at the store. I intended to get smashed tonight.

We dine on hot dogs roasted over the fire, the conversation pretty much carried between Jillian and Connor. As per usual, Barb and I don't offer much, but it's different for me this time. I usually don't participate because I'm pissed at being strong armed to do so. But tonight, I just ~~endured~~ enjoyed listening as Jillian and Connor exhibit the easy-going friendship they've developed. No clue what Barb is thinking, but rather than sequester herself away from us, she's stayed seated at the picnic table long after she took her last bite of hot dog.

I drain the rest of the beer in my can and crush it in my right hand. Despite being light two fingers, it's pretty strong and that's due to the months of rehab I endured. Standing up from the bench, I ask, "Anyone want another beer?"

"I do," Connor says.

"Me," Barb mutters.

"Me too," Jillian adds, and I wonder what type of drinker she usually is. She doesn't look like a beer type of girl, yet she'd drained hers almost as quickly as I had during dinner.

I grab beers from the cooler and take a quick look around at the other campsites. The one on our left is empty. To our right, there's a two-man tent setup but I've yet to see people there. There's a family of four on the other side of that with two preteen-looking kids.

I have a scant moment of turmoil, but then squash it. I'd read the law on where dope can legally be smoked as it was posted in the dispensary, and we're in a private campground on our private spot we paid for. We're good to go. So what if the kids happen to look over and get a peek of us getting stoned?

It will be a life lesson their parents can explain to them.

After distributing the beers around the table, I pull out the plastic bag of marijuana and some rolling papers.

"What's that?" Jillian asks from across the table.

I roll my eyes at her. I only told them that Barb and I were going grocery shopping when we left, but surely she knows what pot looks like.

"Oregano," I tell her dead-panned.

"What for?" she asks, slowly blinking her eyes.

"To get you high," I tell her with a sly smile, and her mouth forms into a little "o" of understanding. "Figured the perfect time to do that was while we were in a state where it was legal. That will hopefully take care of any paranoia you might have about getting in trouble."

"Well, I'm not sure now's the best time—" Jillian starts to say, but Barb cuts her off.

"You said it was a bucket-list thing, and we're doing bucket-list things on this trip. So you *are* getting high."

"Yeah," Jillian says quietly, giving Connor a motherly look. "But Connor's not even eighteen—"

"You're not in charge of me, Jillian," Connor snaps at her, and I turn to look at him in surprise. That's the first time he's ever lashed out at her for her overprotectiveness. "I'm pretty sure if I get arrested for underage consumption of marijuana, my parents aren't going to be too pissed off given my time table."

Jillian's face flushes and she lowers her eyes to where her hands are clasped on the table. "I'm sorry. I'm just being paranoid before we even start, I guess."

"It will be fine," I assure her as I start to roll a joint. "There's hardly anyone around."

"When did you start smoking pot, Christopher?" Connor asks from my left.

I don't take my eyes from my task, but I answer him. "I smoked some in high school. After I got out of inpatient rehab, I moved to a halfway house for disabled veterans who were independent enough to get out of the hospital, but still needed intensive outpatient rehab. My roommate there smoked a lot, and I had him score for me as well. A lot of veteran's self-medicate that way."

"Is that what you call it?" Jillian asks softly. "Self-medicating?"

"Well, none of the pills the doctors gave me were working, so yeah... why not?"

I lick the edge of the paper, finish my roll, and stick it in my lips. Pulling my lighter out of my pocket, I stare at Jillian as I strike the flame and bring it to the end. One short suck to get it going, then a longer inhale to pull the smoke deep into my lungs, where I hold it. Pulling the joint from my mouth, I hand it across the table to Jillian.

She takes it from me, stares at it as if it's dangerous, then looks back to me with those lazy, sexy eyes. I exhale the smoke from my lungs and nod down to her hand.

"Go on. It won't hurt, I promise."

"Bucket list," Barb mutters from Jillian's side to remind her she asked for this.

"Here goes nothing," Jillian murmurs and brings it to her lips. I watch her carefully because I know this is the first time smoke has probably touched her lungs since she's so averse to my cigarettes. She sucks on the end, the cherry flame brightens, and then inhales. It immediately puffs back out of her mouth as she starts to cough, holding the joint out to the side so Barb can take it.

Jillian hacks with her hand covering her mouth, tears filling her eyes.

"It will get easier," I tell her with a wink. She looks across the table at me, blinking her eyes at a sloth's pace to dispel the wetness. "Next time, just pull a little into your mouth. Once it's in, then inhale it. Don't try to take it directly down."

She nods and gives another cough.

Barb takes a long hit, then passes it to Connor. He takes the advice I just gave Jillian, sucking it in like a pro, and fuck... I'm kind of proud of him.

When it comes back to me, Jillian asks, "How long before I start to feel something?"

♦

One hour and another round of hot dogs later...

JILLIAN IS LAUGHING uncontrollably. It started out as a

snicker, which erupted into a snort and then turned into a cackle. Then came the deep belly laugh, followed by wheezing.

I hold out the second joint of the night to her, but she shakes her head and gasps, "I can't do anymore. I'm dying as it is."

And that's almost true. She's been laughing her ass off at almost everything since she felt the first effects. Connor has too, for that matter. Barb and I are just mellow, although I've found myself chuckling more and more.

I take another hit off the joint and offer it to Barb. She takes it without hesitation. I'm betting her ~~tolerance~~ dependence for the stuff is higher than mine because I'm pretty sure she smokes it daily.

"Connor," Jillian says with a slap of her hand on the table. "Did I tell you that I told Christopher he was hot?"

My jaw drops slightly, gaze shooting over to Barb for a brief moment. She looks at Jillian with interest before taking a deep drag on the joint.

"But he didn't believe me, I think," Jillian says in exasperation. She throws her hands up as if she's confused and says, "I don't get it though. He absolutely stumps me."

There's a moment of silence before Jillian's eyes slide guiltily to mine.

I lean across the table and murmur in a low voice, "Did you just use the word 'stump' in reference to me?"

She winces slightly and swallows hard. Her brows draw inward and her lips purse and for a moment, I think she might cry. But then she slaps her hand on the table again as a laugh bursts through her closed lips, making a *pppfffffbbbbtttt* sound.

She starts laughing hysterically, gasping as she sucks in air. "I'm so sorry. I didn't mean to say 'stump'."

But she doesn't quit laughing, leaning so far over the side of the bench I'm afraid she might fall off. It takes no more than three seconds for my scar to pull and my lips to peel back in a grin.

And then, I start laughing too.

♦

Two hours, a bag of Doritos, a bag of Cheetos, and a can of Pringles later…

MARCY PLAYGROUND'S *Sex and Candy* is playing on my iPhone that I'd set into the center of the table, and I take the last hit off the third joint of the evening before I drop the paper end to the ground. Pushing the heel of my tennis shoe over it, I ensure it's snuffed. We're all mellow right now. Even Barb looks relaxed, which is strange because I don't ever recall seeing her that way. Gone is the permanent scowl. She's actually got a slight smile on her lips, although her eyes are barely open because she's so stoned.

"Hey, Barb?" Connor asks, his voice slightly thick

from the pot, beer, or the combination of both.

"What?" she says, opening her eyes up more to focus on him.

"Do you still talk to your parents?" he asks softly, and the air goes still over his bold question.

In any other circumstance, Barb would probably tell him to go fuck himself or viciously stomp off, but she merely says, "Nope. They're dead."

"Dead?" Jillian asks.

"Killed in a house fire," Barb says without an ounce of remorse or pain in her voice. In fact, it almost sounds like triumph.

Jillian gasps, her hand coming to her chest. "You didn't...?"

"For fuck's sake," Barb says with a half laugh, half growl directed at Jillian. "I'm suicidal, not homicidal."

I can't help but snicker at the obvious relief on Jillian's face that there isn't a murderer sitting at our table.

"I left home after I gave the baby up," Barb reveals to us, and there's the pain I know that's a driving force. "Never went back."

"Jesus," Connor whispers.

"You know the funny thing?" Barb says, but I don't think any of us will laugh at what she says. "I'd have died too if I was still living with them. How ironic is that? I wanted to die, and they did it so fucking easily."

"Do you still want to die?" Jillian asks, and that question right there completely kills what was left my mellow mood.

Barb actually gives a genuine smile in return as she nods. "Every damn day."

None of us know what to say, so silence envelopes the table.

And then… in a voice that's barely audible, Barb adds, "But I also want to live every damn day too. I'm just not sure which I want more."

Chapter 16

Fourteen months ago…

"HEY, PEANUT," I said as I answered the phone. That was my nickname for Maria because she was so tiny compared to my six-three height. I liked that about her… how small and vulnerable she seemed. It made me feel more like a man as her protector.

Silence.

Then an awkward clearing of the throat.

"Listen… Christopher… we need to talk," she said tentatively.

And I heard *it*.

Instantaneously, my skin prickled with hyper awareness. I knew… just knew by the tone of her voice, what was coming. And I wasn't about to make it easy on her. "Well, that's exactly what we're doing… talking. You called me after all."

She laughed nervously, and I could almost envision her chewing on her bottom lip, which was what she did when she was anxious. "About us," she added.

"What *us*?" I asked, because I needed her to get to

the point. I'd had enough long and drawn out pain in my life, and I didn't need any more of that shit. I needed her to admit that in her mind, there wasn't an "us" anymore. I'd heard what she hadn't said clearly through the phone. I'd been suspecting it, but now I heard it for sure.

"I'm seeing someone else," she said in a quavering voice filled with regret.

Now *that* I wasn't expecting. "What the holy-ever-loving fucking kind of shit is that?" I yelled through the phone.

I thought I'd known what was coming. A breakup. A sob story about how she couldn't deal with my gross stump of a leg and my mangled arm and hand. I figured she was disgusted and didn't want to be burdened with a cripple, but never in my wildest, fearful imagination had I thought she'd cheat on me before she came to that final realization.

I just didn't think she had it in her to do *that*.

"I'm sorry," she wailed in misery. And then she proceeded to lay it all out. "I was lonely. You've been gone for so long, and Kellan—"

"Fuck me," I roared. "You're seeing Kellan Fucking Meister? He's a fucking jackass who's so stupid he can't string a coherent sentence together. He's got a unibrow for Christ's sake, Maria. I'm pretty sure he's inbred."

"Just stop it," she cried out. "I love him, and he's asked me to marry him."

And all the air was just sucked out of my lungs. A sharp, piercing stab of pain rocketed through my gut, and I massaged my stomach in an attempt to alleviate it.

Maria Alvarez and I had gone to high school together, but we didn't date back then. I was from Cascade, West Virginia, a tiny, unincorporated town near the East Crescent Mine where my father and four older brothers all worked. My sister, Sharon, was married to a miner. Maria, two years younger than me, was also from Cascade. Her father Jorge—a second-generation Mexican immigrant—worked in the same mine. Tansy, Maria's mom, was born and raised in Cascade, where her father and brothers also worked in the mine.

You see the pattern?

Everyone worked in the mines because if you lived in rural West Virginia, that was about the only chance you had to make a decent living. But Maria and I had bigger dreams that didn't involve lungs soaked with coal dust and perpetual grime embedded into the top layer of your skin. My way out was the Marine Corps.

Maria's way out was with me.

After I finished boot camp at Parris Island, I was stationed with Combat Logistics Battalion 6 at Camp Lejeune where I became a support marine in Motor Transport. I eventually became a motor transport operator. While I was qualified to drive seven-ton transporters or fuel and water rigs, I actually drove a HMMWV—pronounced Humvee, or as some juvenile boys would giggle at the name when they were younger, Hummers—during my first deployment to Afghanistan. My vehicle was modified to carry a TOW anti-tank missile system, and I never failed to get a jolt of pure adrenaline rush whenever it was fired. During long convoys, I'd be awake sometimes in forty-to-fifty-hour stretches with nothing but ten-minute cat naps to rest my eyes, always constantly on the lookout for a potential ambush and stressed I might drive over an IED. Exhaustion such as I'd never known, yet when it was time to put the TOW into effect, I'd almost become alive with exhilaration. TOW stood for "tube-launched, optically tracked, wire guided," and it could launch a warhead that would hit a target over two and a half miles away. It was a thing of beauty, and I was proud to be a part of it.

I loved my career with the Marine Corps. I made great friends, saw plenty of action, and definitely didn't have any problems with getting girls. The Corps was an escape for me—a way to get out of a dreadful life that had been planned for me since I was born. I didn't join for any sense of patriotic duty or to avenge those who died on 9/11. I didn't have grandiose ideas that I could actually do something to stop terrorism. No, I joined the military for the sole reason that it would get me far away from West Virginia and would be a decent career for me. Fortunately, the military suited me very well and I made the rank of sergeant about halfway through year four of my six-year enlistment. I was twenty-two years old.

It was also around this time that I made a quick trip home to Cascade as a high school buddy was getting married. At the reception, I reconnected with Maria. She had been waitressing since graduation and was still living with her parents. We got very, very drunk at the reception. One thing led to another in the backseat of my car. To my surprise, at age twenty, she still had her virginity intact. Being drunk and horny, I popped her cherry.

Of course, it was immediate love for both of us. Maria left Cascade and moved to North Carolina to be with me. We got a tiny apartment just off base and played house together. I thought it was the most awesome thing in the world.

I was a marine with a hot girlfriend all my buddies lusted after.

I came home every night to a great meal and even better sex after.

Maria attended beauty school and got her license. I re-upped my enlistment and signed on for another three years. All was good and I was seriously considering popping *the* question to her. I didn't have a dime to my name because we were young, stupid, and didn't save anything. I would have to finance a tiny engagement ring for probably ten years, but I was convinced it was the right time. She was the one for me—I was sure of it.

But then, orders came in that my unit was being

deployed to Afghanistan. It was my second tour, and I was prepared for it. It was my job, nothing more and nothing less.

I hesitated about proposing, unsure if I should hold off until I got back. There were pros and cons to both, but I was a cheap son of a bitch and ultimately decided not to spend the money on a ring at that time. I did, however, commit myself to proposing as soon as I returned.

And, yeah… things didn't go quite as I planned.

During my time back in the States, after the initial round of surgeries to try to piece my leg back together again, things were hazy for a while. I was on such high levels of pain medication, so drugged out of my mind, I probably wouldn't have recognized Maria if she had come to visit those first few weeks.

Not that it mattered because she didn't come to visit me.

At all.

She called… I had a vague recollection of that. Sometimes two or three times a day. I slurred most of my words, and she'd cry sometimes, but she always told me she loved me. I loved her back, but I wasn't sure if I ever told her that.

I didn't start to get fully lucid until they took my leg. My tibia and fibula were shattered and my femur broken in two places, held together by the external fixator, which was nothing more than a huge metal cage around my entire leg with pins attached to the outer edges and drilled down into my bones to hold them together. Portions of my flesh and muscle had been sheared off by jagged steel. My wounds oozed from infection, and a wound VAC constantly ran trying to suck the poison from my body. The pain of just sitting still was horrendous. When physical therapy moved me into my cardiac chair each day, trying to make sense of the mess of tangled wires and tubes coming out of me, I would sometimes scream in agony and jab desperately at my pain button for some measure of relief. Eventually, they had to give me an epidural just to give me the ability to get some rest during those early days.

If anyone had felt just a mere instant of what I was feeling, they would have been begging just like I had for them to cut my leg off.

I didn't have to beg overly hard though, because the doctors knew what I did. There was no saving it. So, the leg came off and with that the pain drastically lessened. When the pain lessened, they cut back on my pain meds. Once my stump was healed, I was immediately fit for a prosthesis. My amputation was above the knee. After several different sockets that had to be continually recast as my swelling decreased, I was finally fit for a C-Leg, which was just about as close to a bionic leg as you could get. Then came months of therapy… physical and occupational.

It was more grueling than anything I had ever been

through before. The therapists at Walter Reed were tough sons of bitches. They didn't ever let up on me, constantly driving me to continually improve, get stronger, and succeed on my prosthesis. The C-Leg was some high-speed tech shit with sensors in the foot and ankle area that transmit data about my gait to a hydraulic system in the knee, which then helped to swing my leg forward. I had to learn to walk again—forward, backward, sideways, up steps, across rough terrains, and over curbs. At every therapy session, I was drenched in sweat and my stump would throb from the exertion. It was some amazing shit. I was happy because I wasn't suffering the type of pain I was in before, but I was still an amputee.

Physically, I was better after the amputation, but I was not happy with my situation. Most thought I should revel in joy that I was alive, but I was too bitter and angry to care.

It seemed that I had fallen into one big cesspool of shit. My days became darker and darker. I was faced with being a cripple for the rest of my life. My military career was down the drain. I had nightmares about the explosion, reliving the pain and memories of the blood and bits of bone that were splattered everywhere inside the remnants of the vehicle. Maria's calls started dwindling until I was lucky if she called once a week. Most humiliating of all was the constant stream of visitors who came through Walter Reed to thank the wounded for their service to their country. Congressman, senators, movie stars, professional athletes, comedians. Every day, there was someone there who wanted to take my hand, give it a hearty shake, and expected me to smile back in gratitude for their compliments. Our therapy room was actually four glass walls with a raised walkway that bordered one side. These visiting dignitaries would come through on a tour and watch all of us poor bastards as we stumbled around on our prosthetics, their faces pressed up against the glass with morbid interest. It was a great way to raise donations.

It had been toward the end of my rehab when I invented my patented "fuck off" response and tried it out on an unsuspecting country music star. She'd been all of eighteen years old, bright eyed and idealistic. I wiped that off her face in a nanosecond. My therapist yelled at me, but I told her to "fuck off" too. I'd actually gotten a measure of joy from the hurt look on that girl's face. I wanted her to hurt as badly as I was hurting, but I knew that wasn't going to happen so I'd have to be satisfied with what I got.

Probably the worst thing to happen to me throughout it all was the lack of familial support those first critical months. Outside of that brief visit from my parents, which sent them running for the hills of West Virginia once they got a look at their mess of a son, there was no one else from my family that had an interest in supporting me through my recovery. This was true despite the fact the government actually had a program where they would pay a family member or close support friend to stay with me as a nonmedical attendant through my rehab, believing that emotional support was as important as the physical when it came to recovery. This person would receive a salary. In return, they'd provide me with companionship, get me to and from appointments, help with meals, manage medications, and assist with my activities of daily living. However, no one in my family had been interested, because that would mean walking away from the mines where they seemed to be tied down with balls and chains around their ankles. Hell, even my unemployed cousin, Lem, didn't jump when offered a paying job, preferring to sit in his sardine-can trailer and eat canned hot sausages while collecting food stamps. Instead, I had nurses who did everything for me with looks of pity on their faces that no one cared enough about me to come.

My only hope had been Maria, but now she was telling me she was in love with someone else?

"And this has nothing to do with the fact that I'm not a full man, right?" I asked bitterly, hating myself as the words poured out of me—making me feel weak and pathetic. I thought it convenient she decided to lay this on me right after my leg came off. Maybe she'd been holding out hope I'd return home with it.

"It has nothing to do with your injuries," she hissed at me. She sounded so vehement I almost believed her.

"It's just that it's been almost two and a half years since I've seen you—"

"You could have come here, Maria." I rolled right over her. "It's not even a four-hour drive. You could have visited me. Fuck, you could have moved here and we could have been together."

"No," she exclaimed indignantly. "You couldn't just expect me to leave my family, my job—"

"You did when you moved to North Carolina with me," I reminded her.

"But D.C. isn't the same. It's so big. The crime rate... and... and I'd be stuck..." She trailed off, realizing her bumbling faux pas.

"You'd be stuck caring for me," I finished for her quietly.

Another long pause but there was no denial. She took a deep breath. "I'm sorry, Christopher. I didn't want to hurt you."

"I'm not hurt," I murmured into the phone.

Because the fight had run out of me. Suddenly, I felt as weak as a baby—no energy left to even have a strong emotion. I leaned back against the pillows in my hospital bed, my right hand coming down to let my three stiff and scarred fingers scratch absently around the edge of my prosthetic socket. I had essentially been abandoned. The government was kicking me out of the military after rehab. None of my family cared I'd been in a hospital for months. The one person I'd thought loved me had been fucking around behind my back.

I didn't say anything else to Maria. I simply pressed the disconnect button and laid my phone down. As I tried to calculate when I was due for my next round of pain meds and for the first time in my life, I seriously contemplated suicide.

Chapter 17

Present day...

I EMERGE FROM my tent into the early morning light, stand to my full height, and stretch. My alarm had just gone off, and I've never been one to repetitively hit the snooze button. When it was time to get up, it was time to get up. And, as always... I want to get an early start. I guess that's left over from my military days.

While I rotate my right leg to make sure my prosthesis has a good seal, my hand strays down with a thought to scratching my balls, but it freezes before it makes it past my waist.

Jillian's already up and sitting at the picnic table with her back to me. She's obviously been up a while as her long hair is damp. She also has a Styrofoam cup of what I'm betting is coffee on the table.

I take a few steps toward her. She raises her head, turning to look at me. Those nerdy-as-hell glasses are on her face, blue eyes as large as a bug's. "Good morning."

"You're up early," I note. Nodding down to her coffee, I ask, "Where'd you get that?"

Jillian nods toward the community building near the front of the small campground. "They have complimentary coffee in there."

I don't bother to look in that direction, noticing she's reading a book. A big book with glossy, colorful pages.

"I'm going to go take a pi—" I stop mid-sentence and change my direction. "Use the bathroom… you want some more coffee when I come back?"

"Sure," she says brightly. "Cream and sugar."

"How much sugar?"

"Enough to make it sweet."

I roll my eyes and turn away from her. After I make short work of taking a long piss, I wash my hands. Looking into the mirror above the sink, I'm slightly startled to see a man looking back at me. One I don't recognize. The brown hair I wear a little too long all over and my brown eyes are the same as always. I didn't shave yesterday, so my stubble is dark. The scar on my chin looks the same, standing out pale against the whiskers.

But the expression on my face is different. It's loose and relaxed. Normally, spiteful eyes stare back at me, condemning me for being so stupid as to drive over an IED, for believing in love, and for even continuing to live in the first place.

Shaking my head, I try not to think of the ways I might have changed over the past few weeks, or even the past few days. Instead, I seek out and find the coffee, making Jillian another cup with hopefully enough sugar. I pour a black cup for me and head back to the camp.

No sign of Connor and Barb, and yet, I don't automatically think to rouse them so we can get on the road. Instead, I see Jillian sitting alone, looking beautifully untouchable as always, and I decide to let the others sleep in a little bit.

Setting her coffee down, I boldly take the seat next to her. I'm still far enough away that we aren't touching.

"Thanks," she says as she picks up her other cup of coffee and drains the remains.

"No problem," I tell her before taking a small sip of my own. It's fucking awful, but I swallow it down, needing the caffeine. "What are you reading?"

Jillian turns her head and smiles. "It's an art book."

My eyes stray down and take in a colorful painting on each page with some text below, presumably describing the art piece. I look back at Jillian with raised eyebrows.

"I was an art history major in college," she says simply, and my body sort of flinches with the realization that I didn't know she'd gone to college. In fact, I don't know much about her personally at all as she's always the one commiserating in group rather than complaining.

"Where did you go to school?"

"University of North Carolina," she says with a shrug. "Kind of a wasteful degree for someone going blind, but I still love to look at art while I can."

A wave of sadness washes through me. What surprises me is that it's not for me. It's for Jillian, and that's something to take note of. I haven't felt true sympathy for anyone in a long time, and it kind of freaks me out a bit because it feels so foreign.

In fact, it really doesn't feel good at all.

To distance myself from trying to analyze my emotions, I lean over and look at the painting on the right-hand page. It's of a hayfield being hand harvested by what I assume are some type of itinerant workers, but I can't be sure. The overall look is golden as it's mostly various shades of yellow caused by the sun glinting down on the field. The workers are bent over, and I can almost feel the strain in their backs as they cut the hay by hand with sickles.

"That's depressing," I find myself saying irritably. I've never in my life looked at a piece of art and analyzed it, but that's actually the first word that comes to mind. I see men with their backs breaking from toil, and that just sucks.

"I find it invigorating… hopeful," Jillian counters in her sweet, rose-colored voice. "See the way the light touches so many aspects in the painting? Look here at this man… it's along his forehead to illustrate the sheen of sweat from working in the fields. The way the back of this person's neck is red from a sunburn. Or even here, how some of the petals on the flowers are almost spotlighted from the sun. It reminds us that nothing can hide from it."

Her words make me feel weird. They're classic Jillian, wanting to see the best in everything. I've fallen prey to that lately, but it's not my inherent being. It annoys me that I'm fascinated by this woman who only looks at things through a cheery filter. It annoys me because it makes me feel bad for feeling bad about myself. This in turn makes me defensive... a bit combative.

With an exaggerated sigh, I tell her, "They're indentured servants, stuck in a field working for peanuts. Do you think they recognize all that beauty? No, they're concentrating on the hollow hunger in their bellies and the pains in their lower back from bending all day to harvest. You romanticize things, sunshine. Time to face reality."

Yes, please face reality and stop making me hope. Face it so I know the straws you're making me want to grasp at are really nothing but pipe dreams.

Jillian doesn't react to me calling her sunshine, but she makes those muscles around her eyes tighten into a narrowed gaze as she continues. "Sure, if you concentrate on the story you seem to think is being told—that's your prerogative, of course. But if you look past that to the setting... to the vibrancy of color, the expressions on their faces, then maybe you'll think they're not servants at all. Maybe this is their land and they take great pride in a successful harvest that will bring sustenance to their family."

My eyes drop to the book again. I study the painting for a moment, tilting my head as I try to see it from her perspective.

And I can't.

I can't because I don't want to.

I want to be able to see things true to my nature, not how others want me to see.

I don't want the dangers that Jillian presents to me, because my carefully ordered world will be thrown into chaos if I give into unfettered belief that the world is full of happiness and joy, just waiting for me to tap into it and suck it out like juice from a ripe piece of fruit.

"Sorry, blondie," I finally drawl out, and her spine automatically stiffens from my tone. She knows I'm not going to be kind, and she braces. "But it's not just your eyes that are fucked up. I don't for one minute buy into this rainbows and sunshine you have seemingly shooting out your ass. I think it's a wasted attempt for you to feel a little better about your own fucked-up situation, but trust me when I say... you're not doing yourself any favors by ignoring reality. And honestly... your continual sunny disposition is fucking grating on my nerves."

The minute the words are out, I feel bad about freeing them. But I can't take them back, because I don't even know how to apologize for being an asshole really. So I just stare at her, mentally preparing for her comeback.

Jillian's face is expressionless for a moment, but then

she leans toward me so she can look me directly in the eye. Up close and magnified through those glasses, the color of her eyes reminds me of tropical waters. She swings her leg under the table and taps her foot against my prosthetic leg.

"So typical, Ahab," she says softly, and I honestly can't tell if she's teasing me, mocking me, or just showing me she doesn't care that I'm missing a leg. "I really can't imagine what you've been through, and that's mainly your fault since you won't talk about it, but I bet it was horrific. I'm even betting you didn't have a good support system when you were injured and had to cope on your own. It's why you don't trust us, and that's understandable. I even get the need you have to make others feel bad... totally understandable."

She pauses, takes a deep breath, and then gives me an encouraging smile that pisses me off and makes me feel gleeful all at the same time.

"But," she tells me with a gentle voice, "I'm here to tell you that you really can't say anything to me that will cause me to quit trying to get you to open up. The others might get tired of your shit and give up, but I won't. I kind of like the challenge you present to me, actually."

Doesn't she know when to quit? Why won't she give up on me?

"God... you're fucking weird," I tell her with a grimace. Or is that a grin? "No one can possibly be that fucking right with the world."

Jillian just laughs at me and turns back to her book. Even though she's not looking at me, her words are pointed and direct. "Stick with me, and I'll make you right with it too."

Fuck, it itches.

That annoying prickle of both guilt and intrigue that Jillian Martel has instituted under my skin.

I'm pissed there's guilt, which came immediately on the heels of mocking her impending blindness. My first goddamn bout of guilt, and I have no clue why I'm feeling it. I've been insulated in a bubble of complete disrespect of all of humanity for so long that I didn't realize how powerfully horrid shame would feel for potentially hurting her feelings.

My guilt, however, is eased a bit by the fact that I seemingly *can't* hurt her feelings. I mocked her and her interpretation of a stupid painting—yet, she tells me she understands my pain. Hell, in that moment, she forgave my rudeness.

I want to pull my hair out and scream at her to just leave me the fuck alone. Not to make promises that she can make me right with the world. I can't dare to want that. Even though from the moment I laid eyes on her, Jillian Martel has definitely made me want... want...

For the first time, she just makes me want.

Her.

Sex.

Laughter.

Happiness.

Brighter days.

Shaking my head, I rub my hand over my face. It makes no sense. Of all the things that just ran through my head—all my wants and desires—how in the ever-loving fuck was my leg not listed at the top? It's the one thing I've bemoaned the loss of ever since I gave the go ahead to cut it off. It's been the fuel for my bitterness and the main source of my rage. Losing my leg, which caused me to lose my girl and my career... it's been the very heart and soul of why I'm so miserable. I don't need any goddamn shrinks to tell me that.

So how, in just the past ten minutes, has Jillian gone from intriguing me, to irritating the shit out of me, to making me feel terrible about myself, to making me want things I didn't ever consider as important.

Her.

Sex.

Laughter.

Happiness.

For fuck's sake... a new leg will make me happy, right?

Right?

Fucking wrong, my brain screams at me. *It's gone. Let it go. Get the fuck over it.*

That's all easy enough to think to myself, but living that as a truth rather than a farce is practically impossible. Especially since I've been conditioning myself for months to hate everything about the way my life has turned out.

But what if…

I mean, Jillian seems to…

She clearly has found some peace.

No, I can't. I can't even consider that there are other possibilities out there, because that would mean opening myself up to hope, and that in turn would mean opening myself up to failure and hurt.

Not even going there.

Chapter 18

A FTER MAPPING IT out, it was going to be an almost ten-hour drive from Denver to the south entrance of Yellowstone. I didn't open it up for discussion with the group. I just made the decision to go to Jackson, Wyoming, which sits on the edge of the Bridger Teton National Forest. The national park abuts up against Yellowstone to the south, and we'll have an easier time getting a campsite there.

I'd given in to the fact that this was adding on an extra day. Truth be told, I'd always wanted to see Yellowstone. My family was so poor that our family vacations were nothing more than a few days at a local campground to do some fishing. And I use the term "vacation" loosely. We didn't do things together as a group when we did go, and my pa pretty much stayed drunk the entire time and would rant and bellow at my ma. The only good thing I got from it was a love of camping and fishing, and I'm eager to do some of that in Yellowstone. Because Connor has started to grow on me and I've become invested in his bucket list, I'm eager to teach him how to fly fish.

We're on the road no more than an hour when I get a phone call. When I glance at the phone in the center console, I see Mags' name. I had promised I'd keep her updated on our travels, and I had done so each day with a text. I have no clue why she's calling, but I ignore it. I'm not much of a phone talker.

It's unusually quiet inside the Suburban this morning. Normally, Jillian and Connor are chattering, making comments about the wide and varied scenery we pass or just talking about stupid shit—gossip about a pop star or pictures of a famous actor kissing someone who was not his wife. But this morning, Connor is in the back playing on his phone, while Jillian is bent over her art book that's resting on her lap, turning the pages slowly as she peruses the various paintings and sculptures. As usual, Barb is listening to music through her earbuds and staring out the passenger window as the world rolls by.

I'll admit there's a niggling kernel of guilt for the way I treated Jillian earlier. My temper is an issue, and my inability to process negative feelings is an even bigger one. Jillian took it full in the face from me. While she didn't even flinch under my harsh words—in fact, she offered me gentle words in return—I'm regretting it.

Already today, Jillian has provoked two very strong emotions within me that I don't normally feel.

Sympathy and regret.

The sympathy merely caused a heavy feeling in my

chest, but the regret?

That sort of slices like razor blades within me.

It's her fault I'm feeling this way to begin with, yet… part of me welcomes that pain. It's either going to be a potent reminder that if I give in to Jillian and the hope she inspires, I'll be in for a world of hurt as I acclimate. Or it's going to push me away from her, which may just be the very best thing for me.

My phone rings again. With another glance down, I see it's Mags again. She's been satisfied with my text updates over the last few days, and now she's calling twice in a row? A prickle at the back of my neck alerts me to the fact that whatever she's calling about is probably important.

I reach down, connect the call with a tap of my finger, then pull the phone to my ear. "Hey."

"Hey, Christopher," she says, and I can tell by tight tone in her voice that something is most definitely wrong. "Listen… Jillian is with you, right?"

I turn to my right, confirming that Jillian is most definitely with me before I say, "Yeah… why?"

Mags doesn't respond to me. Instead, I hear her tell someone else, "She's fine. She's with the group."

My eyebrows furrow inward. "What's going on?"

Mags' voice sounds relieved as she tells me, "Apparently, Jillian didn't discuss with her parents that she was going on the trip. She just left a short note, and she won't answer their calls. She's texted them once to say she's fine, but nothing after that. They just showed up at my office wanting to know if I knew anything. They're about ready to go to the police."

I turn again to look at Jillian, completely unsuspecting of the apparent firestorm she's set into motion. "Well, she's fine, sitting next to me in the car. We're headed to Yellowstone."

At this, Jillian raises her head, turning to look at me. I make a quick decision and take the exit from the interstate that is right before me, having to slam the brakes hard to make it. One of Jillian's hands goes to the dashboard to steady herself, the other grabs at the book that starts to slide.

From the back, Connor says, "What the hell?"

From the exit ramp, I pull onto the gravel shoulder and bring the vehicle to a hard stop. Mags' voice is my ear. "Her parents want to talk to her. Will you give her the phone?"

I don't hesitate. "Yeah... sure."

I hold the phone out to Jillian, my voice hard as granite when I say, "Your parents want to talk to you."

Her shoulders stiffen and her eyes cloud with wariness. She looks at the phone like it's a bomb, but she takes it from me.

"I'm going to step out for some privacy," Jillian murmurs as her hand goes to the door, the other clutching my phone with white knuckles.

"I'd kind of like to hear what you have to say," I

growl at her, furious she lied to her parents and, in turn, lied to us.

She doesn't respond, only jumps out of the car.

I mutter, "Oh, fuck no, you don't," as I bolt out of my door.

I hear the other two doors open, Connor and Barb scrambling out. I round the front of the SUV and stalk after Jillian as she walks up the shoulder of the exit ramp with the phone to her ear.

When I reach her, I catch her side of the conversation. She sounds pissed. "…but I couldn't tell you. You wouldn't have let me come. I left you a note. I've texted I'm fine. Why can't you just accept that? Instead, you drag Mags into this and now the group?"

Jillian is silent. I trot past her, turn, and block her from walking any further. She stops but won't look in my eyes. Barb and Connor approach slowly behind her, having no clue what's going on.

With a heavy sigh, Jillian says in a tired voice, "I can't take it anymore. Just because Kelly died doesn't mean I'm going to."

She listens to whoever is on the other end of the line… her mom… dad… both, not sure. But whatever they are saying produces a reaction. Jillian's shoulders square and her spine elongates, turning ramrod straight. She lifts her face, and those blue eyes are blazing. While she stares directly at me, I can tell the fury on her face is for whomever is talking to her.

When they stop, her voice is calm but deadly serious. "No. I don't accept that. I'll never accept it. So listen to me when I say this… I'm not coming back. You can't make me because I'm an adult. You'll just have to sit there and be thankful I'll send you text updates to let you know how I'm doing. When I get back, we can talk about how things need to change, but I'm done being your prisoner."

A shock of electric-like current flows through me at the word "prisoner," and I have no clue what the fuck is going on. My eyes flick past Jillian to Connor, who looks worried, and then to Barb, who merely looks curious. It's an improvement over her normal bored facade.

Without another word, Jillian disconnects the call and hands my phone to me. "Come on, let's get back on the road."

I take the phone and reach out to grab her by the shoulder as she turns toward the SUV. "Oh no, you don't. You owe us an explanation."

She looks at me blankly. "Explanation about what?"

"Don't even try to play stupid, sunshine," I snap at her. "Your parents were seconds from calling the police if they couldn't get you on the phone just now. We deserve an explanation on why they didn't know you came on this trip."

"It's none of your business," she says and I note that Connor's jaw drops over the ludicrous statement. She is in group therapy where sharing is the mantra of the day.

How many times had Jillian pushed us to share, and here she was harboring secrets?

My hand slides from her shoulder to her upper arm. It's my half hand, but it still clamps onto her with enough strength to make her eyes flare a tiny bit. I pull her toward me a little and growl, "It's our business because you just put me, and I'm betting Barb, at risk for potential court violations for being out of state. What do you think would have happened to us if your parents had gotten the police involved?"

Jillian gasps, her face crumpling over that possibility, and I tamp down the guilt. I'm being a bit dramatic. I actually have permission to leave the state, and I have no clue about Barb other than I know she's court ordered to attend group as well. I have to assume she has permission like me. But still… I want to make a very clear point to Jillian.

"You put on a really amazing act about how much you care about others, but you were totally selfish by not telling us what was going on with you," I proclaim. "And now that I'm thinking about it, you're the one who suggested this trip under the ruse you wanted to do it for Connor. I'm betting you wanted it just for yourself, right? So you could escape?"

"Ease up, Christopher," Connor chastises me.

"You shut up." I point a finger from my free hand at him over Jillian's shoulder. "You know I'm right."

"You're not right about why she suggested this trip,"

he snarls back at me. "She did it for me, not for herself."

I know he's probably right about that because Jillian's not a selfish person, but I don't admit that to him. Looking back to the source of my disgruntlement, I tell her, "Now it's your turn to share. Why didn't your parents know you came on this trip?"

I'm surprised when Jillian jerks her arm out of my grasp and glares at me. "You wouldn't understand. More than that, you wouldn't care. You don't care about anything, Christopher."

"What about me?" Connor says from behind her, and she turns to face him. "Why didn't you tell me? You know I care."

Jillian nods. Her voice is softly affectionate when she says, "Yeah... I know you do. But like Christopher, you wouldn't understand."

"Why not?" Connor asks.

"Because she thinks her problems pale in comparison to ours, and she's afraid of our derision," Barb says. It's not a guess. It's not a hypothesis. She states it as fact, and I have to say... I believe her.

"Is that true?" I ask Jillian, but she doesn't turn to face me.

Instead, she addresses Barb. "You were raped and abused. You're suicidal. Connor's dying unfairly young. Christopher lost parts of his body, and I'm betting pieces of his soul too. I don't think my problems are something we should waste breath on."

Those words…

It feels like someone punched me in the middle of the stomach, ripped through my skin and muscle, and is pulling my guts back out. I know I've given her no reason to think otherwise, but I don't want Jillian to feel like she's a waste of anything. As much as she confounds me, and as scared as I am of her at times, I know I don't want her feeling badly about herself.

I sure as shit don't want her to feel isolated.

"Your problems are as important as ours," I say, and Jillian turns all the way around to look at me. Her expression is wary and guarded. "Tell us the truth, sunshine… why are you in group with us?"

Her eyes bore into mine. For a moment, I think she's going to remain stubbornly silent but then she whispers, "So I can escape my parents for at least a little bit each week. So I can have friendship and someone to talk to. So I can get out of my house and see a little of the outside world while I still can."

"They're really holding you prisoner?" I ask dubiously.

"Not like in restraints or anything," Jillian says with a roll of her eyes. "But emotionally… I'm as bound to their sides as if I had iron shackles on."

"How?" Connor asks.

Jillian turns, taking two steps back so she can see all of us. Connor and Barb step in closer, and I'm stunned to see a tiny bit of empathy in Barb's eyes. After taking a deep breath, Jillian tells us about her parents.

"Since my diagnosis, their entire world shrank right along with my vision. I became the most important thing in the world to them. Not that I wasn't before, because I so was. I mean, hello... I'm their daughter. Of course, they live, eat, breathe, and sleep for my benefit. But after we lost my sister, I became more than essential to them. I'm the last remaining vestige of their parental identities. Without me, they're just Sandy and Owen Martel, a middle-aged housewife and an ambulance chasing attorney who have a nice 401K plan and play tennis on the weekends."

"So they're what... overbearing? Overprotective?" I ask her.

"As in they won't let me do anything," Jillian says with a nod. "I can't work because I can't drive at night, and they won't let me take public transit. I can't leave the house because I have no transportation. I have no friends because I can't go anywhere. I can't even move out because I don't have any money because they won't let me work."

"But you're an adult," Barb points out. "They can't stop you from doing anything. If you want to work, get a job and take the public transportation. They'll get over it."

Jillian shakes her head. "I'm not explaining it well, but it's emotional blackmail. I've tried to be forceful and tell them I'm going to go out on my own, but then they cry, wail, and beg me not to. They throw Kelly in my face and tell me that they're not prepared to lose me as well. They make me feel so damn bad for causing them worry that I give in and do what they want."

"Sounds like they're the ones who need therapy," Barb mutters.

Jillian lets out a sarcastic snort as she nods. "My parents are simply not emotionally equipped to deal with my diagnosis. They can't process me going blind. They're unable to fathom how I'm a walking heart attack waiting to happen from the cardiomyopathy. They look at me as a fragile egg, and they're terrified I'm going to shatter. They would have never let me come on this trip. I didn't tell them because they would have talked me out of it, and I'm tired of being talked out of things that I want for myself because it causes them worry."

"You didn't forget your wallet at home, did you?" I ask with a cocked eyebrow and a smirk on my face. "You don't have any money."

"I swear I'll pay you back," Jillian says. There's worry in her voice as she begs me with pleading eyes to understand her duplicity. "I've got money in savings from Christmas and birthday gifts. I swear it."

"Relax, sunshine," I tell her with a wave of my hand. "I'm not worried about it."

And I'm not. I'll gladly pay for Jillian's trip. I got a decent amount of money from the government, and it wouldn't dent my bank account.

"I'll cover you too," Connor says. "I've got Dad's credit card, and he told me to go crazy with it."

Jillian gives Connor a shy smile.

"I've got you covered too," Barb says. "Well, I mean... I don't have much money because I spend most of it on drugs, but I'll gladly share those with you."

Letting her head fall back, Jillian gives a hearty laugh. I'm drawn in by the way the sun causes her hair to turn more golden. Her eyes are shining as she looks to Barb, Connor, and then to me. "I'm sorry I didn't tell you. It seemed so stupid. My problem is overprotective parents who I can't break from emotionally. You see why I wanted to keep it to myself?"

I totally get it. Had Jillian told me this story during those first few weeks of group therapy?

Hell... had she told me the day we started this trip, I would have totally mocked her. I would have discounted it completely and tried to make her feel like a moron.

But now, all I can do is nod. Her problems don't match any of ours, but I'm finding that I care about her issues as much as my own.

Chapter 19

THE CAMPFIRE IS getting low so I put another log on. A trail of sparks meanders upward, followed by smoke, and then the log catches fire. Dinner was another easy affair after we made camp. More hot dogs along with beer. No smoking pot out in the open as we are in Wyoming now, even though the campground is practically empty. I expect most people want the experience of actually camping in Yellowstone rather than the Bridger Teton National Forest.

Still, the weed stays hidden, but we do pound a few beers. This site didn't have a picnic table so we had to make do. I had two small folding chairs that only had seats with no backs. I gave one to Jillian and the other to Connor. Barb took a seat on top of my cooler, and I pulled my sleeping bag out of my tent and threw it down on the other side of the fire. I'm now contentedly laying on my side, hand resting in my palm and looking at Jillian in firelight.

Even more beautiful than in sunlight.

"You know what I'm craving?" Connor says out of

the blue.

"What?" Jillian asks with curiosity.

I'm only semi-interested, but Barb is looking at him in question.

"A big brownie sundae... with vanilla ice cream, hot fudge, whip cream, and a cherry on top," he says with a wistful sigh. "Maybe tomorrow night, we can actually eat in a real restaurant."

I laugh, because the hot dogs are getting old and I'd love a mattress. Camping is awesome, but we have the means to stay in hotels if we want. The main reason we're camping right now is because there aren't any hotels near Yellowstone. It's either camp or stay an hour away in Jackson for the night.

"Okay, tomorrow night... hotel and a place for dinner," I tell Connor.

"One that has a brownie sundae," he adds on for good measure. "I haven't had one in years."

"That will make it all the sweeter," Jillian tells him.

"What about you?" Connor asks her. "What's something you haven't had in a long time you're craving?"

Jillian looks upward in contemplation, her eyelids still hanging heavy. A dreamy smile slides over her face as she looks back to him. "I know... I haven't had homemade ice cream in forever. Vanilla. We used to do it at the beach every summer, but since Kelly died... Well, we just haven't done it."

As always, Connor turns sympathetic eyes on Jillian,

his best friend, and nods in understanding. But then he turns to Barb. "What about you? What haven't you had in a long time that you're craving?"

"Sex," Barb says automatically, and all our heads whip her way with shock. She looks around at our collective astonishment and asks, "What? Just because I was sexually abused, you don't think I can have an active and normal sex life?"

"Um... um..." Connor stammers.

"When's the last time you had sex?" Jillian asks, and my head snaps to look at her. Jillian is talking about *sex*? My entire body responds by tightening up all over.

"About two days before we left on this trip," Barb says with a shrug of her shoulders.

"And you already miss it?" Connor blurts out.

Barb gives a laugh that sounds whimsical and so off from her normal demeanor that I have a moment of actual happiness for her. Instead of answering, she asks Connor, "You had sex yet?"

The firelight hides any change in color of his face, but I know without a doubt it's flame red. Connor looks down and shakes his head. "Nope. Not with being sick and all..."

"No excuses," Barb says with another laugh. "Trust me... that has *got to* go on your bucket list."

Had the same thought myself, Barb.

Connor's head stays ducked, but Jillian's tilts, indicating she's still curious. "Soooo... back to the missing it part. Just two days before the trip and you're already missing it?"

"You ever had sex?" Barb directs the question to Jillian this time, and this discussion just got really interesting. I'm all ears now.

My eyes whip over to her. Her shoulders remain straight and proud as she says dryly, "Of course I have."

"Then you know," Barb says with a knowing look.

"Know what?" Jillian asks in confusion.

"If it's really good, you miss it. If it's really bad, you don't. So... do you miss it, Jillian?" Barb taunts her.

My eyes haven't left Jillian's face. She doesn't flinch from the question, only admits, "What I had wasn't all that great, so no, I don't miss it."

"Pity," Barb says smugly.

"Who do you have back home that you miss having sex with?" Jillian continues to pester Barb. I don't think she's so much interested in Barb's sex life as she is in the fact that Barb is freely talking to us.

Barb gives an indifferent shrug. "Just a friend with benefits. Known him since high school. He's a tattoo artist now. But we fuck often and it's good, so I miss it. Answer your question?"

"Completely," Jillian says, but she's still curious. "Are y'all... you know... exclusive?"

"No fucking way," Barb returns with what I can only call a horrified look. "I don't do relationships. It's just sex. A way to get off."

"Sounds lonely," Jillian murmurs.

Barb gives a sad smile back at her. "I've been lonely for most of my life. I don't know anything else, so I can't say the alternative is better."

"I'm sorry," Jillian says quietly. And it's not in a pitying way, but done to let Barb know that while she may not understand fully what Barb has been through and how she feels, she can completely understand being fucked in the head about it.

"Whatever," Barb mutters, but her eyes are soft as she stands from the cooler. "Well, I'm going to head to bed since we have to be up so early."

"Me too," Connor says as he pushes off his little folding chair.

My eyes dart over to Jillian, but she seems content to keep her seat. She looks from Barb to Connor and sweetly wishes them a good night. Connor heads into the large tent he shares with Jillian, while Barb walks over to my Suburban, opens the back door and crawls in, shutting it tightly behind her.

I feel Jillian's eyes on me, so I look across the fire at her. "Not tired?" I ask her.

She shakes her head. "Not really."

We're silent a moment, the only sound the crackling of the fire. Even though we're smack in the middle of summer, the temperature is in the high fifties tonight. I'm appreciating the heat right now, even though I have a heavy flannel shirt on along with a pair of jeans.

"Can I come over there and sit with you?" Jillian asks with a nod toward my sleeping bag.

"Sure," I say casually as I push up from my lying position to make room for her, but my heart starts racing over the fact she wants to come sit near me.

I plant my feet on the dirt and wrap my arms around my knees, the prosthetic joint on the right feeling vastly different than the skin and bone one on the left. Jillian plops down beside me and crosses her legs Indian style, staring into the fire. I want to say something... start a discussion... have discourse... but my mind is blank. It's like I don't even know what to do with a girl sitting beside me.

"Thank you for today," Jillian says quietly.

"For what?" I ask in confusion.

"For not giving me too much crap about keeping that stuff with my parents a secret," she says as she turns her head and looks at me. "I really wasn't thinking that it could have repercussions on you and Barb."

"Water under the bridge," I tell her in a low voice.

Because it is. Jillian opened herself up today and the best thing about it is that she became more human to me. It made me realize she's not as perfect as I thought and that makes her relatable. "But tell me something... this level of sunny optimism you have going on all the time... is that real or bullshit to make your parents and others feel better?"

Jillian chuckles. The firelight dances in her eyes, and

I'm actually relieved when she says, "I hate to tell you this, Christopher, but it's very much real. It's just always the way I've been. My sister was that way too, and I always admired how she could make lemonade from lemons. I guess that rubbed off on me."

I'm relieved that Jillian is exactly as she seems. Sunny, bright, hopeful, and secure in her ability to be that way despite her circumstances. She's more real to me now that I know she has flaws, but I'd never want her to lose that light that attracts me to her. Knowing that's a part of who she truly is makes me feel almost secure in my life right now.

"You know, Christopher," Jillian says as she leans my way and playfully nudges my shoulder with her own, "you chastised me pretty hard today for keeping secrets, and yet... out of the four of us, you're the last one who really hasn't told us anything about your issues."

Normally, I'd shut down tight if someone tried to poke into my business, building the walls around me even thicker so nothing can penetrate. But I surprise myself by offering, "What do you want to know?"

Jillian holds my gaze for a moment, her eyes drilling into mine before she gently tugs on the material of my jeans near the shin rod of my prosthetic. "What happened to you?"

She doesn't look away. Not down at the fire, not down to my legs. She stares right at me. Although my gut is turning slightly at the thought of telling her what she asked, I forge straight ahead. For the first time, I tell someone who is not medical personnel or a shrink my story.

"I was driving a military Humvee and the right front tire ran over a roadside bomb," I say, and Jillian makes a sound of distress low her in throat as her eyes turn sad. "It completely obliterated my buddy sitting in the passenger seat."

To my surprise, Jillian scoots over closer to me and lays her head on my shoulder. She pushes her hand in between my ribs and my arm, curling her fingers over my bicep. It's a show of support. Solidarity. That she's settled in for the long haul of this story, and she wants to hear it all.

"It didn't blow my leg off," I tell her, and I can feel her body jerk slightly in surprise. Her fingers squeeze my bicep. "The fingers yes, the leg no. It just shattered and shredded it badly, but the doctors tried hard to save it."

"Obviously, they couldn't," she whispers the obvious.

"They tried for three months," I tell her, reaching down to grab my phone laying near my left hip. Jillian lifts her head up, watching as I pull up my pictures. I scroll backward, but it doesn't take long to find what I'm looking for because I don't take a lot of photos. I hold the phone out so she can see. "This was taken about a month after my injury."

Jillian makes a strangled sound as she looks at the photo of me in bed. My eyes are half open because I was bombed out on so many heavy-duty pain medications, and I have a grimace on my face. I vaguely remember this picture being taken, and I think it may have been by my brother, Hank, when he came to visit once during that first month. He came a few more times after that, and then he didn't.

Jillian's eyes roam over the photo. My leg is encased in the external fixator with several rods leading from the outside of the cage right into my skin, where it's drilled through and into the bone to hold the pieces together. The wounds on my leg are all open to the air, red and some of them dripping with puss and lined with blisters. I've got IVs in both arms and a PICC line in the right side of my neck to deliver the hordes of antibiotics and pain meds I needed to keep me alive and functioning. I took the maximum dosages they allowed me, preferring to try to be oblivious to what was happening. Yet, the pain was so great it just couldn't be fully erased.

Jillian turns her head to look at me, and I lay the phone back down. "How long were you like that?"

"Three months. But they couldn't get ahead of the infections, which were delaying the bones from knitting. I was in so much pain that I *wanted* them to amputate."

"You had to make that decision?" she whispers.

I nod. "Yup. I mean… the doctors were at the point they felt it was the right way to go, although they were willing to keep trying if I wanted. But I wanted it gone. I was tired of being in the hospital and being in so much pain. I just wanted it gone."

"Do you regret that decision?" she asks me bluntly, but with that still-sweet melody her voice makes. The question doesn't bother me, because even her hard questions sound lovely.

"Yes," I tell her without any shame. "I wonder what would have happened if I held on just a little bit longer. Not long after the leg came off, the pain receded and I became more lucid. Once I'd forgotten how bad the infections smelled, I regretted it."

"Three months is an awful long time to be in pain like that," she points out the obvious.

I shrug. "And the rest of my life is a long time to wonder 'what if.'"

"There's more though," she guesses in a soft voice before laying her head back on my shoulder. "It's not just losing the leg that set you on a course of self-destruction."

I can't help the bitterness in my voice, because it speaks of weakness. I don't want Jillian to think I'm weak, but I tell her truthfully how I feel. "It's everything that leg represented to me. Without it, I wasn't fit enough to stay in the Marine Corps, so my career was taken away. Without it, I wasn't a whole man, so my girlfriend dumped me. My parents shunned me. Society looks at me as abnormal and pathetic. So you're wrong... losing that leg set me on a terrible course."

There are a few moments where I wait for Jillian to

start spouting some Pollyanna shit to me about how I can take these lemons and sweeten them up, but she merely says, "I think you're a whole man."

"You're just saying that," I mumble, completely embarrassed at how much hope just welled up within me.

"I'm not," she says firmly, lifting her head up again. She looks me directly in the eye. "I think you are gorgeous and amazing. I've totally been waiting for you to kiss me again, but you haven't even made a move."

I blink at her several times, stunned by her admission. Other than Jillian, who I'm not sure I even quite believe, I've not had anyone compliment my physical appearance in years. Not since before I was deployed. I'm sure Maria may have said something or other, but coming from Jillian, it flows through me like molten steel, fortifying me and making me feel like a real man.

"So now would be a good time to kiss me," she says with a lazy smile.

"You're weird," I tell her with a smile back, now actually enjoying the pinch of my scar because it indicates I have something to be happy about.

But despite how weird she may be, as well as completely out of her mind to be attracted to man like me, I go ahead and kiss her like she asked.

And it's even better than the previous two times we kissed.

Chapter 20

I MADE EVERYONE get up super early today as I wanted to take Connor fishing at the break of dawn. I'd secured the necessary fishing licenses, put prepackaged sandwiches and lots of water and soda in the cooler, and packed everyone up in my SUV so we could head toward Yellowstone. The dude who sold us the licenses told me about a small stream that feeds off Yellowstone Lake that we'll hit about three miles before the park's entrance. He assured me the fishing would be good, which is what I'm counting on. I want Connor to catch something as there's no sense in knocking off a bucket-list item half-assed.

We locate the stream easily even though it's off the main highway and down a very narrow dirt and gravel road. After I park, Connor and Jillian get out. Barb stays in the vehicle, muttering she wants to sleep some more. At the back of the SUV, I open the tailgate and reach into a gear bag I'd packed before the trip.

Before I knew Connor wanted to learn how to fish.

I packed it for myself since we'd be driving through

areas with good waters, and I intended to do some fun stuff for myself.

Now I pull my fishing vest out of the bag and hand it to Connor. Every pocket and carbine is loaded down with flies, tweezers, clippers, and everything else but the rod needed to catch a trout. I even have my net attached to a hook at the back with a bungee string.

"Put that on," I tell him as he takes the vest.

He does so without question as I retrieve my fly rod. Before closing the door, I grab one of the small folding chairs so Jillian will have something to sit on while she watches us. Connor heads toward the stream, which is across a large ditch and twenty yards on the other side, but I turn back to Jillian.

She smiles at me knowingly, somewhat shyly, and yet there's boldness there too. I don't hesitate. Connor's back is to me, and Barb is probably asleep already. My hands are full, but it doesn't stop me from leaning toward her. Her hands come up to slide around my neck. Our mouths touch, our heads angle, and our mouths connect.

The kiss is sweet and deep, but brief as I'm not ready to share this with the others.

When I pull away, Jillian's eyes are closed. She opens them slowly with a sigh. "That was nice."

Yes, it was.

It lasted all of three seconds, whereas last night, Jillian and I made out for what seemed like hours. We never moved from our sitting positions beside each other, but we did turn face to face and kiss like teenagers discovering each other for the first time. My hands had roamed, but not very far, only skimming her ribs or tracing the skin at her lower back under her t-shirt. Jillian had run her fingers through my hair, gripping and releasing it as our kisses turned urgent and our breathing labored. Her taste and touch excited me beyond reason. I would have loved nothing more than to push her down on that sleeping bag and take things further.

But I didn't.

I kept things tame because ~~I'm scared shitless I'll ultimately disappoint her~~ things are too new between us. I'm in a world I don't understand or recognize, and I'm moving forward with trepidation.

Jillian admitted she's attracted to me, and I sure as hell have been attracted to her from day one. But this isn't a hook up where I can walk away after I get my rocks off. I'm hesitant, solely for the fact I'm a pussy and afraid of getting hurt again. What if they were just words to Jillian? What if she were to look at my leg close up and get grossed out? What if I'm nothing but a social experiment to her?

I don't want a repeat of the rejection I'd faced from Maria. I've lost enough in this life.

Shaking my head, I dispel those thoughts as I smile down at Jillian.

She may be many things, but she's not a people user.

I'm pretty confident about that, but it doesn't make me any less skeptical about where this may all head.

"Come on," I say as I jerk my head toward the stream.

Eyes alight with mischief, Jillian shakes her head. "I'm not coming down there with you. I only wanted to get a kiss from you."

The corners of my mouth pull upward, my scar pinches, and I grin back at her. She sought me out for a kiss. My man card is starting to get some redemption.

"We'll probably be about an hour," I tell her. "What are you going to do?"

"I'm going to call my parents first and talk to them," she says as her brows line with worry. "I want to make sure they're okay."

"Don't let them talk you into flying back," I tell her gruffly, leaning my face down to hers to level a pointed stare at her. "Make sure they know you're safe and we all have your back."

Jillian nods, her eyes shining with gratitude. "I'll tell them. I'm not going to let them guilt me into going back, but I feel bad about hanging up on them yesterday. I just want to reach out."

"That's cool," I assure her.

"Alright," she says with a firm nod of her head. "After I talk to them, I'm probably just going to sit in the Suburban and read for a bit. It's too hard at night by the fire, so I'm going to take advantage of the light."

"Your art book?" I ask.

"Yeah," she says with a bright smile. There's no doubt that art is a passion for her. I wonder if we should go to a museum or something when we get back to Raleigh. I think that's something she'd like, and fuck... I think I'd like it too. Hell, I'd probably enjoy watching mold grow if Jillian was beside me.

"Okay, have fun," I tell her as I head toward the stream. Another thought strikes me and I turn back to her. "You still have a lot of damn eyesight left in you. You got those fucking thick-ass glasses that totally make you look like a professorial-type nerd. Why can't you get a job using your art history degree? Or any job for that matter?"

Jillian tilts her head, her eyes narrowing for just a second as if she were about to deny the possibility of my suggestion, but then her face immediately smooths out as she processes and accepts my suggestion. The blue in her eyes lightens when her entire face breaks into a wondrous smile. "You know... I think you're right. I've broken my hold on my parents... or so it seems... so why not?"

"You can do whatever you want," I assure her.

Her eyes get even larger with awe and a bit of disbelief. "Christopher!" Jillian exclaims with excitement as if she's just learned something very important.

"What?" I ask, almost jerking backward from her enthusiasm.

"You just gave me hope," she says, and my heart

constricts tightly over the pride and elation in her voice. "You just told me I could do something I've been told I couldn't. *You* gave me the recipe for lemonade. *You*."

She's over the moon that I would encourage her that way. It embarrasses the fuck out of me, so I say, "Shut the hell up."

But I say it with a great deal of affection, and she just laughs at me. Nodding toward the stream, she says, "Go catch your fish with Connor."

My steps are light and buoyant, even with the slight gait lurch I have over the uneven ground. The stream sparkles bluish green in the sunlight, there's not a cloud in the sky, and for the first time in ages, I feel almost free. I have no clue what's happened to me in the last three days, but without a doubt, it's all Jillian's fault.

When I reach Connor, I take a few minutes to give him some basic instructions. I teach him how to cast, making sure he locks his wrist as he moves the rod back and forth from the ten o'clock to the two o'clock position over his shoulder, and that he's able to pull line out at the same time to extend the cast.

"We're using dry flies today," I tell him. "That means once you cast, it will float on top of the water. The trout will have to come to the surface to take it."

I take another few minutes to show him false casting—which is the whipping of the line back and forth—so he can dry off the fly to help it float better on the water. When I show him a few sample casts, I make sure he notes how I cast to my left against the current before letting the fly float downstream until I need to reel it back in after it can't go any further.

When I turn the rod over to Connor, I give him one last piece of advice. "Keep your eyes on the fly. You see a trout come out of the water for it, you snap the tip of your rod up so it will get hooked, and then you keep it straight up while you reel. If you don't, the line will go slack and it will be able to jump off."

"Got it," Connor says, stepping up to the edge of the stream with excitement in his eyes. I wish I'd brought waders so he could actually get in the water, but they weren't essential so I left them behind to make room for the camping equipment.

I have to say—the kid is a natural. He'd listened to my instruction well and his technique is damn good for a beginner. He casts out into a riffle, letting his body turn slowly as the current takes the fly downstream. When it reaches the end, he reels it in and false casts to dry the fly before letting it zoom out over the stream again.

"This is so peaceful and relaxing," Connor murmurs as he follows the current with the tip of his rod.

"Until you catch one," I say as I watch. "Then it's all adrenaline."

"Thanks for doing this with me," Connor says as he reels line in. "My dad's a business guy, you know. All suits and ties. He loves me and takes me to all kinds of events, but camping and fishing just aren't his thing."

"Not a problem, kid," I tell him, my face heating a bit under his praise. All my brothers are older than me, and I never had anyone who looked up to me. This is weird, but nice.

"So I'd like to ask you something man to man if that's okay," Connor says, turning to look back at the Suburban to ensure we're alone.

And the minute he says "man to man," I realize I need to stop calling him "kid." He's a man already—almost by age but definitely by circumstance. The mere fact he's had to deal with the inevitable fact he's dying would turn anyone into an adult before their time.

"What's up?" I ask him lightly, having no clue what he's going to lay on me. Whatever it is, I want him to be comfortable because the one thing I've taken to heart in all the chastising I've received from Jillian over my asshole tendencies is that Connor should never bear the brunt of my ire. He's the one who should get a pass on everything.

"So... last night, Barb asked if I'd had sex..." he begins, but then his voice drifts off. His ears turn bright red and he focuses on casting his rod again, perhaps hoping I'll know where he's going.

"You want to knock that off your bucket list?" I venture.

Connor nods quickly, refusing to meet my eyes and keeping his full concentration on his fishing rod. But he adds, "Maybe there's someone you know back home...

or, um… I don't know… a prostitute or something."

My stomach rolls, because yeah… I've had my dick sucked for money a time or two since my injury. I could get him what he wants.

But I don't know if that's the right thing. It could be a terrible experience for him, and wouldn't it be better for him to never achieve that goal than to die believing sex is awful? I mean, not that it would be awful, awful. Pretty much any sex is good for a guy, but still… he's a good guy and deserves better than just okay. He deserves more than anonymous sex with a prostitute.

"Connor," I say hesitantly. "Don't you have any close female friends or anything?"

He shakes his head. "Not really. Once I became the dying kid, I think it was awkward for my friends to be around me. They started gradually pulling away, and I totally get it. Who wants to watch someone you care for die? So really there's just Jillian. She's my best friend, which is gross because she's like my sister. I just thought you might have some connections."

I have no clue if I can find someone who will be good to him and make the experience bucket-list worthy, but that doesn't stop me from promising. "You got it. I'll help you find someone."

He finally turns to look at me. Even though his face is still a bit red, his smile is contagiously big. "Thanks, dude. It means a lot."

"Whatever, dude," I say back gruffly, but he knows

by my return grin that this was a good bonding moment between us.

Connor turns and continues to cast. I let him go for a few more rounds before saying, "Let's walk a little bit further upstream and try again."

After we get to our new place, I point out a large rock in the middle and tell him to aim just below it. He does and immediately gets a strike, but either the trout didn't take the fly completely or Connor pulled up too quickly. So he tries again.

I watch him try over and over again, determination etched on his face. No frustration, no giving up, just pure persistence in trying to catch a damn fish.

"Are you afraid of dying?" I ask him.

Connor's body jolts slightly, and he turns to look at me with eyebrows raised high. I've never pursued such an intimate discussion with him about his ultimate end and how he feels about it.

He reels the line in and doesn't bother recasting it. Instead, he turns to face me completely. "I'm terrified."

"Of what?"

"A lot of things," he says in a matter-of-fact tone. "I'm afraid of being in pain, of dying slowly, of how sad my parents will be after. I'm afraid I won't let go when I should—that I'll linger causing me and my parents to suffer more."

The thought of that punches me in the gut, and I have to hold myself up not to double over. But still, he hasn't really addressed what I want to know. I've thought about dying, and it doesn't make me feel fear. It would be painless if done right, quick, with no one left to really grieve me.

But there's been one doubt that I haven't been able to shake, and I would really love to get Connor's take on it.

"What about after?" I say in a low, hesitant voice.

"After?"

"Yeah… what happens to you after you die?" I clarify. "Are you afraid of that?"

"God no," Connor says swiftly. "I believe I'll go to Heaven. That doesn't concern me at all."

"But how do you know you'll go to Heaven?" I press him.

Connor chuckles and looks at me with amusement. "Clearly, you're not a man of faith."

"My family weren't big churchgoers," I tell him.

"Don't you know anything about Jesus and why he died for us?" Connor asks with his head tilted.

I shake my head. I know nothing of the sort.

Taking a step toward me, Connor gives me a sad look. "You have to have faith. You have to believe in Heaven. You have to know in your soul it's a place where regrets don't matter because Jesus died for our sins and eternal happiness is yours for the taking. With faith, you should have no fear of what happens after."

Well, that fucking sucks. I look out at the river,

foaming and frothing around rocks and releasing a bubbling melody to combine with the sound of birds chirping and the slight wind blowing through the trees.

A thing of beauty.

It gives me no solace.

It's not like I have faith just sitting around that I can tap into. And I have to admit to myself, the big thing that's held me back whenever I've considered ending things on my terms is the fact that I don't know what happens after. I'm afraid that whatever *it* is, it's not good. That it will be worse than what I have right now.

"It's not too late," Connor says softly.

My eyes fly back to his. "For what?"

"To become a believer," he says. "If you want… when we get back to Raleigh, you can come to church with me. I'll help you learn."

I'm not sure how I feel about church and learning stuff, but I do know that Connor offering it to me is the most comforting thing anyone has done for me since I was injured. I'm sure he thinks the offer is nothing, but to me… a doubter and a fearfully driven man at this point, it's more than I've been given in a long, long time.

"I'll think about it," I tell him evasively, not wanting to commit to anything. I've not been a commitment type of guy in forever.

"Cool," Connor says with a smile.

"Okay," I tell him as I nod back at the stream. "Let's try a few more casts here."

Turning to the water, Connor executes three beautiful false casts before he lets the line fly to the water. The nymph lands just at the base of the rock. A millisecond later, I see a trout rise with an open mouth to take it.

"Pull," I yell at Connor. By the time he jerks the tip of his rod up, the trout has its mouth closed around the fly. I can tell he successfully hooked it because his rod immediately arcs from the weight of the fish and the strength of its flight to get away.

"You did it," I yell out in pride.

Connor is triumphant when he shouts back, "I fucking did it."

Another item off his bucket list complete.

Another step closer to his death.

Chapter 21

WHILE THE PINNACLE of what we want to see is Old Faithful, we spend most of the day driving around and checking out the varied scenery. We quickly learn how to find the wildlife in Yellowstone, which is filled with miles and miles of fields, forests, riverbanks, mountains, cliffs, and plains, all home to an amazing and abundant variety of animals. As we drive along, we realize if we see an area of roadway where several cars have pulled off to the side, it means there's an animal somewhere nearby.

The first thing we see is an elk with a rack on its head that seems to stretch out three feet on each side. He's lying in the shade of a tree, just calmly watching us gawk at him from about fifty yards away. Cameras snap and click, and I zoom in with my iPhone and grab a shot for myself. If it were hunting season and I had a rifle in my hand, it'd be a different story right now.

We see a few more elk and lots of deer before we get to the Upper Falls attraction. After we ooh and ahh over the massive waterfall—even Barb joining in—we walk back to the Suburban. I see a park ranger with a group of about thirty people standing around him near the edge of the parking lot where part of the forest starts. I veer off and head his way, hearing Connor, Jillian, and Barb following me.

When we reach the edge of the group, we hear the park ranger say, "Now… if everyone will just stand very still, we should see it soon."

Jillian, who has never met a stranger, asks a woman standing near her. "What are they doing?"

The lady looks at Jillian with excitement. "There's another park ranger in the woods over there, flushing a brown bear this way so we can take pictures."

That is fucking cool.

Jillian apparently doesn't think so as she immediately starts backing up. I reach out, snag her hand, and pull her to my side. "Oh no you don't. You're going to stay here and see a bear."

She shakes her head. "My eyesight isn't that great, so I'll just go back to the—"

"Scaredy cat," I tease her, gripping her hand tighter.

"Christopher," she whispers almost hysterically. "They're flushing a bear this way. Bears eat people."

"It's a brown bear," I tell her with confidence. "They eat berries, not people."

She looks skeptical. I'm pretty sure bears are omnivorous and a hungry one could eat a person, but I don't tell her that. Instead, I add, "And there's no way in hell the rangers would be flushing it our way if it were dangerous."

That seems to calm her down. After about a fifteen-minute wait, a brown bear comes meandering through the edge of the woods, walking parallel to the parking lot. It doesn't seem to care there are dozens of people gawking. Doesn't even look our way. He just ambles past, cuts back inward, and eventually disappears.

"I think that was a trained circus bear," Barb mutters, and I laugh so hard I almost piss my pants.

Getting back in the Suburban, we travel through Hayden Valley on the way to see Old Faithful, stopping again when we see several buffalo grazing in a herd. We walk up a slight hill to get a better look downward into the valley, and as we crest the hill, I come to a dead stop. On the other side of it, just twenty feet away, is a massive bull. Those things are as big as cars. When we entered the park, we were given a yellow flyer stating the bison are extremely dangerous and should not be approached. It even had statistics on it with the number of people killed by buffalo the prior year. They are no fucking joke.

I immediately grab Jillian's hand by pure luck and start backing away. Connor does the same, but Barb doesn't. She halts right there on top of the hill and just stares at the buffalo as it grazes. It seems docile and bored, not bent out of shape by her presence. It even raises its head, mouth chewing grass, and looks at her with indifference. Then it starts to walk toward her, its gait slow and without any seeming purpose.

"Barb," I whisper as I back away, still holding Jillian's hand, my eyes pinned to Barb. I can hear Connor behind me, also moving back down the hill.

Within just a few steps, I lose sight of the buffalo as we make our way down the small incline, but Barb just stands there at the top, not moving.

And then I see something brown come over the top of the hill's horizon and the buffalo comes into view. It is now ten feet from Barb, towering over her as it still slowly chews the grass in its mouth.

"Barb," I whisper again, more harshly so she knows I mean business. "Get the fuck away from that thing. Back slowly down the hill."

But she doesn't. She just stands there and stares at the buffalo. It doesn't come closer to her, just stares right back. I realize in that moment that Barb still very much wants to die. Apparently, she holds no fears about it whatsoever, not the way I do.

Eventually, the buffalo moves on, slowly moving away as it grazes. Barb turns with an almost disappointed look on her face as she comes down the hill. By then, Connor and Jillian are already safe in the Suburban. I stand on the outside, having been ready to call 911 if the buffalo charged and gored Barb like a shish-kabob.

When she reaches me, her eyes are filled with challenge. I ignore it and growl at her. "That was really stupid."

She just shrugs. "Why do you care?"

I take stock of that question and evaluate it very carefully. Do I care if she dies? I'm not absolutely sure how I'd feel about it because while I've developed a fond tolerance of the dour goth chick, I don't know if I actually care about her.

The answer comes to me quickly, though I'm not sure if it's the only reason. "I care because it would have totally crushed Connor and Jillian if something happened to you."

"They don't care either," she mutters as she tries to brush past me.

I grab her arm to halt her, and she at least has the decency to look at me. Behind her, I can see Jillian's face as she looks out of the window with worry. I know she's thinking the same thing I am… Barb's death wish just manifested for all of us to see and take heed.

"They care about you a lot," I tell her firmly. "How can you not see that?"

"That's at their own peril," she snaps back at me, yanking free and getting in the Suburban.

No one approaches what just happened when I get in and drive us out of there. It's getting late in the day, and we're all exhausted. My plan is to leave from the west exit of Yellowstone, which leads into Montana. From there, we'll need to cut south again to pick up the interstate that will take us toward Portland. But we can't leave without checking off the coup de grace of all buckets-lists items when coming to Yellowstone.

Seeing Old Faithful erupt.

The park literature says the geyser goes off around seventeen times per day with intervals ranging from sixty to one-hundred-and-ten-minutes long. There is no way to perfectly time it, but when we arrive, we're lucky. The countdown clock in the general store has predicted eruption in just ten minutes.

We all hurry over to the geyser. The benches along the safety perimeter are already filled with people waiting, and the people standing behind it are four to five deep. I lead our group a bit further away so we don't have people right in front of us. The geyser itself is situated far enough back from everyone that we can still see the entire thing.

It's like the longest ten minutes ever. It's really only a prediction, but it's pretty accurate. I know something's going to happen when I see the base of the geyser start to froth and bubble, spits of steaming water shooting up a few feet. I can hear the rumbling underneath the crusty top layer around the geyser's mouth, and the water gets more animated.

"This is so exciting," Jillian says as she steps into my side. Her arm circles behind my back, and she presses a warm hand to my hip. It's what people in a relationship do... embracing the person they care about. It feels right and good and in no way awkward. While Connor sort of knows there's something there, I have no clue what Barb knows, and I find myself not fucking caring. I let my arm reciprocate, sliding it behind her back. Instead of curling my hand around her hip, I slip my fingers down into her back pocket. It's a bold move for sure, and Jillian looks up at me briefly with amusement. I just give her an innocent look and turn back to the geyser.

Holding each other, Jillian and I watch Old Faithful as it comes to full eruption. The steaming water, which I'd read was over two hundred degrees Fahrenheit, shoots almost a hundred feet into the air.

"Wow," Connor says in amazement as he holds his iPhone out, taking pictures as it goes off. I'd also read that the eruption lasts anywhere from two to five minutes. I bet that kid will take about a thousand pictures in that time period.

"That is amazing," Jillian murmurs.

"You can fucking say that again," Barb says from my other side.

"That is amazing," Jillian repeats at her with a waggle of her eyebrows.

Barb rolls her eyes, muttering, "Har-har."

"Hey, let me get a picture of you two," Connor says, and he can only be talking about Jillian and me. We look over our shoulders at him, and he grins. "Turn around and face me."

Jillian doesn't hesitate, turning her entire body and pulling me around with her as she loops a thumb in a belt loop at my hip. Connor backs up a few paces and holds his phone out to frame us with Old Faithful spouting up high behind us.

"Okay, smile," Connor says goofily.

I don't have to look at Jillian to know her smile will be bright and full of sunshine. My scar pinches as I do my best to match her. I even pull her in a little closer, and we tilt our heads in toward each other.

"Oh, that's going to be an awesome photo," Connor says as he snaps a few frames. "Now, Barb... you get in there."

Barb jolts, spins to look at Connor, and says, "Fuck no. I hate having my picture taken."

"Pl-e-e-e-a-s-e," Connor whines with pitiful eyes. "I'm dying."

Jillian and I snicker, and Barb snaps at him as she stalks to my side. "You little shit... that's not always going to work with me."

Connor smirks as he takes our picture. Barb doesn't do anything but stand next to me stiffly. I think about putting my arm around her waist, but knowing Barb, she'd probably pull out a knife and cut it off, and well, body parts are a precious commodity to me.

"Okay, now we need a selfie with all of us," Connor says cheerily.

"Jesus Christ," Barb mutters as Connor trots up to us.

He hands me his phone. "You have the longest arms, so you take the photo."

I don't hesitate, because damn it… the kid is dying and why shouldn't we take a selfie together to commemorate this trip?

You've come a long way in three days, Christopher, you sappy son of a bitch.

Connor turns his back to me, grabs Barb by the arm, and pulls her to his side. He tugs her until she crouches as he does the same. I turn the camera to selfie-mode and hold it out. Bending a little too, I put my head close to Jillian's. In the camera's frame, Connor's face is just below Jillian's and Barb's is at my chest. Jillian and Connor are both grinning, and Connor's holding his fingers up in a "peace" sign. Barb is scowling while boiling water shoots up behind us.

"For fuck's sake, Barb," I say in exasperation. "Can you at least smile just once?"

Her scowl turns darker.

"Pl-e-e-e-a-s-e," Connor begs without losing his grin or peace sign as he looks at the camera. "I'm d-y-y-y-ing."

Simultaneously, Barb and I both erupt into laughter. I hold down the shutter button to snap multiple pictures while Old Faithful goes off behind us and Barb has a smile on her face.

After I'm done, we turn to continue watching the ecological spectacle, being no less wowed by it as time goes on. When the spout of water finally declines and then disappears, we start walking back to the Suburban.

Connor flips through his pictures as we move along with the crowd.

"This is a great one," he says as he stops in place.

Jillian immediately goes to him, looking over his shoulder. I do the same. Barb just keeps walking.

And it *is* a great picture.

I can't stop staring at Jillian as the late afternoon sun lights her blonde hair up in the photo. Those blue eyes I can only see half of are crystalline... sparkling with joy... real life gemstones. Full lips spread into a wide and natural smile. Her temple rests against mine, our heads tilted together.

My eyes slide over to me in the photo. For a moment, I'm taken aback.

I'm smiling as well.

Big.

Bold.

Full teeth.

Light in my eyes.

Happiness in my expression.

I don't even recognize that guy.

Chapter 22

Seven months ago…

ONE OF MY brothers, Hank, was due for a visit today, and I dreaded it. It would be his third time to see me since I arrived at Walter Reed, but the first time since I'd moved into Fisher House while I completed my rehabilitation. I was on pace to get completely discharged in about two months, which would put my total hospital and rehab time at thirteen months.

The Fisher House was on the Walter Reed National Military Medical Center campus, and it was designed to house military families who had loved ones in the hospital. It also had several rooms that were ADA compliant so those of us who could move from inpatient rehab were able to get a room there as well.

I didn't start to get truly lucid until they took my leg. And with lucidity came knowledge and awareness of my circumstances. I started to understand the meaning of abandonment and hopelessness, and I fantasized about dying. I had fallen into one big cesspool of shit, and my days got darker and darker. I was faced with being a cripple for the rest of my life. My military career was down the drain. I had nightmares about the explosion, reliving every noxious, painful memory of my injuries and recovery. My emotional wounds from Maria breaking up with me caused nightmares of their own… the type that were deep, desperate, and without hope.

I had not one friend I could talk to. The mandatory psych counseling was a waste on me because I refused to engage with the therapists beyond the bare minimum that could get me a pass out of there. I was stuck in an endless cycle of loneliness, pain, humiliation, and anger, and I was just about through with it all. Not even the prospect of getting discharged and having the ability to move on with my life brought me any sense of joy or excitement.

"Barlow," someone shouted from the first floor of the Fisher House. "Visitor."

With a sigh, I laid my *Men's Health* magazine on my bedside table and swung my legs over to the floor. I still had to give a slight rocking motion to propel myself off the bed rather than trust the mechanics of my C-leg, but I was improving every day.

Grabbing my cane for stability, I made my way slowly down the stairs. It was one of the first obstacles that therapy made me conquer as they wanted to get me out of the hospital and over to Fisher House so I could start becoming independent again. They called it part of my "pride healing." It was to teach me that I could be a normal person one day.

What a fucking lie. I'd never bought into it.

At the bottom of the stairs, Hank waited for me. He was five years older than me and was the one I'd always been closest to. He was a coal miner, as was my oldest brother Jody who was thirty-four. My brothers James and Justin, twenty-eight and twenty-nine years old respectively, also worked in the mines. And then there was my sister Sharon, who was a year younger than me and the baby of the family. Her husband was ten years older than her and had been mining since he'd graduated high school.

I was the only one who had escaped a mining fate, and a huge chunk of my bitterness was owning up to the fact that if I'd just stayed in West Virginia where I belonged, none of this terrible shit would have happened to me.

"Look at you movin' around on that thing," Hank said as he smiled up at me. I grunted an acknowledgment back, then concentrated on the last few steps. When I reached the foyer where Hank was standing, he held his hand out to me to shake. We'd never been a hugging type of family. "Good to see you, brother."

I gave him my right hand, wrapping my two fingers and thumb around his palm. The skin was mostly healed but still shiny, red, and angry looking. It was pretty numb and painless, and I was still learning all kinds of fine-motor skills with it, but I could do a good handshake. I watched Hank carefully, but he neither winced, looked disgusted, or put out by my deformity. He just smiled like he was glad to see me.

This actually hurt me... seeing the happiness on his face. It hurt because he was the only one who cared, and this was only the third time he'd been to see me. The lack of familial support I'd received had probably been my most crushing blow, even more than Maria's betrayal. I understood that at least—it had been a relationship that was more tenuous than I'd given it credit for, but my family? We were fucking blood.

When I pulled my hand away from Hank, I gave a nod toward the door. "Want to sit outside?"

"Yeah, buddy," he said enthusiastically and turned to open it. "Nice day."

As I walked out onto the front porch, I noted the balmy summer morning, blue skies, and white fluffy clouds overhead. The large oak trees in the front yard dappled the grass with shadows and flowers lined the sidewalk. Nothing nice about any of it.

The Fisher House was a complex of three buildings done in a beige stucco with white columns. It was surrounded by gorgeous landscaping and dotted with tables and benches for people to sit at. I lumbered my way to the closest bench under a shade tree that was unoccupied and sat down more heavily than I'd wanted. The bench shuddered under my weight for a brief moment. Even though Hank was a roughened coal miner, he settled in far more gracefully beside me.

But, of course, he had two legs and great balance.

"How's rehab going?" he asked, turning to face me and casually throwing his arm over the back of the bench.

"Good," I told him. "Learning all kinds of neat stuff."

"And your leg?" he inquired.

"Still missing," I said in a singsong, happy voice.

His lips turned down in sorrow as his eyes went soft on me. "I know it's hard."

"Do you?" I threw back at him angrily. "Because this is only the third time you've been to see me even though you're only a three-and-a-half-hour drive away. So tell me, how exactly do you know it's hard for me?"

"Christopher," he pleaded with me. "I'd be here every day if I could. You know that. But I got work obligations, a wife, and three kids with another on the way."

"Four fucking brothers... a sister... parents... nieces and nephews... friends... a girlfriend... and this is only my fourth visit from anybody in eleven fucking months," I gritted out as my insides burned with rage.

He reared back from me. From the malice in my voice. Still, his face was awash with sympathy. "I can't speak for anyone else, buddy... but I'm sorry I couldn't be here more."

Hank tried, I knew that. He called me a few times a

week, texted almost every day, and he even sent me care packages. He was the only one who really tried.

And it meant nothing to me. My bitterness stemmed from the overall failure of everyone in my life to protect me. At my government for sending me to a war when I wasn't equipped to understand the risk, and at my family who abandoned me… all of it had completely consumed me with darkness. I was one pissed off son of a bitch.

I hated the world and everyone in it.

I lurched up from the bench and looked down at Hank. My flesh and blood.

A stranger.

"Don't come back to see me," I told him.

"Christopher," he said in shock and shot up off the bench. "You don't mean that—"

But I'd already turned away from him.

"I do mean it," I growled over my shoulder. "Stay the fuck away. Tell everyone to stay the fuck away."

Chapter 23

Present day...

"YOU GOOD?" I call out to Connor as I rake my fingers through my wet hair, scrutinizing myself in the mirror as I wonder if I should shave.

"I'm good," he calls back, then deepens his voice a bit to a serious tone. "Go have fun... but not too much fun."

I grin at myself in the mirror. Just before my shower, I'd told Connor I was going to see if Jillian wanted to go for a walk along the small stream that ran alongside our joined rooms.

We'd made it out of the western side of Yellowstone into Montana and headed south into Idaho, making it to Ashton where there were hotels around seven PM. We were all in agreement we wanted hot showers, mattresses, and TVs, as well as a meal that wasn't hot dogs.

We lucked into a cool motel that sat on a small stream—which was really just a wide ditch with-slow moving water. The motel was clean and had a restaurant attached. Connor knocked off another bucket-list item by ordering Rocky Mountain Oysters, and Jillian gagged the entire time he ate his bull testicles. After dinner, we splurged on two rooms that were duplex-like cabins, with Jillian and Barb taking the left room and Connor and me taking the right.

When I walk out of the bathroom, I find Connor laying on one of the beds, eyes roaming over something on his smartphone. His gaze lifts, and he smirks at me. "Is this like your first date or something?"

"I'm just seeing if she wants to go for a walk," I grumble. The little ditch filled with water had a nice concrete pathway that ran alongside it with decorative light posts every twenty feet or so. The light reflected off the water, the stars hung low in the sky, and… fuck… I guess this would be a date by ordinary definition.

"Be nice," Connor teases with a smile.

I start to say I'm always nice, but I'm not. So I smirk at him and say, "Fuck off."

His eyes narrow at me and turn hard. He's not teasing now. "Seriously… be nice."

"Or what?" I ask, completely amused by his overprotective nature. "Gonna beat me up?"

Connor just shakes his head. "Nah… no way I can beat you up. But I'd poison you or something. I'd be stealthy about it too."

I blink at him several times, wondering if he's serious or not. Regardless, it doesn't really matter because I intend to be nice to Jillian. I have no reason not to be.

On the contrary, she seems to bring out the fucking best in me for some reason.

For a brief moment, I fantasize about what it would have been like had I been with Jillian when I was injured. A woman who hasn't once shied away from my assholery or deformities. Who looks past the broken pieces to see the whole.

She never would have betrayed me.

I bet she would have been by my side the entire time.

A wave of longing and bitterness swells through me. I wonder why I didn't deserve that then, and I sure as hell don't get why I do now.

"I'll be nice," I admit in a low voice, and Connor's eyes lighten. "Be back later."

I pull on my flannel-lined denim jacket as it's a little chilly out. I'll need to remind Jillian to grab hers, although if she forgets, I could be all kinds of chivalrous and offer her mine. Or we could cuddle. Or kiss. Something to warm up.

I'm chuckling to myself by the time I walk out our cabin door, take two paces to the left, and knock on theirs.

Almost immediately, the door swings open. Barb stands there looking wholly unsurprised to see me. She just cocks an eyebrow.

"Thought I'd see if Jillian wanted to go for a walk," I mutter, a little embarrassed to look like a love-struck puppy to this hardened, skeptical woman.

To my surprise, Barb grins at me. "She's just finishing up her shower. You can come in and wait."

I step inside, noting their room looks the same as ours, right down to the same style of bed coverings and wall art—all western themed. I can hear a blow dryer running in the bathroom.

Barb doesn't close the door, but rather reaches down to the floor where her backpack is. She pulls it up, unzips a side pocket, and reaches inside as she steps up to me.

Steps up really, really close to me. I want to take a step backward because I have no clue what she's doing, and I'm even more confused when she pulls a condom from the side pocket. Just as I start an internal freak-out and try to come up with a good excuse to put Barb's advances off, she slaps the condom to my chest and says, "You can stay the night. I'll go bunk in the Suburban or on the other bed in your room."

"What?" I ask as my hand comes up to take the condom. I stare down at it in horror. This was not in my game plan tonight, but fuck if I don't like the possibility of what she's suggesting.

"Fuck her, dude," Barb says as she zips the pocket back up. "You two are making goo-goo eyes at each other, and it's nauseating. Bang her, get it out of your system, or take it to a deeper level, but don't tell me you don't want it."

I lean in toward Barb, jerk my head toward the bathroom, and mutter, "Yeah... but does she want it?"

Barb snorts, steps back, and points a mocking finger at me. "Do you really think I talk to Jillian about shit like that?"

Not really, but I still ask, "Has she said anything?"

Barb smirks at me. "You'll figure it out, champ. See you in the morning."

What a bitch.

Sort of.

She gave me a condom, which is something I do not have nor considered buying. Never thought I'd get an opportunity with Jillian. Not sure either of us is ready.

The bathroom door opens, and I hurriedly shove the condom in the pocket of my jeans. Jillian steps out dressed in what I think are pajamas. The bottoms are loose and flowing with blue and silver stripes, she's wearing a navy-blue V-neck t-shirt, and it's completely obvious to my pervy eyes with just a quick glance... no bra.

She jolts when she sees me, but then immediately relaxes. Tilting her head, she asks, "What are you doing here?"

"Came to see if you wanted to take a walk, but it looks like you're ready for bed," I tell her.

Immediately, I correlate that she's ready for bed and I've got a condom in my pocket, and I suddenly realize I probably should get the hell out of here.

"Where's Barb?" Jillian asks.

"She... um... she... well..." I stammer, the collar of

my long sleeve shirt suddenly feeling tight around my neck.

"What's wrong with you?" Jillian asks as she walks toward me, and my mind races with a million lies that will get me safely out of here without embarrassing myself. But as she comes to stop in front of me, I take in her curious expression and her easy smile as she waits for me to answer. The knowledge that she's one of the nicest people I know prompts me to give into the crazy situation.

"I came over to see if you wanted to go for a walk, but Barb shoved a condom at me and told me to have fun with you. That she was going to bunk in either the Suburban or over in Connor's room so I could stay all night," I blurt out.

I expect some or all of that to offend Jillian, but her eyelids merely droop a little more as her lips curve into a bigger smile. It's sexy amusement at its finest, and the sexy part is confirmed by the husky tone of her voice. "So my choices are to go for a walk or to stay in here with you and a condom?"

Christ.

Be a good guy, be a good guy, be a good guy.

"My only hope was for a walk," I say neutrally. "The condom was all Barb."

"But you didn't refuse it, right?"

I swallow hard. "It's in my back pocket," I tell her in a low tone.

She leans slightly toward me, and I can smell whatever shampoo she used. I can't quite identify it, but it
smells fruity. Sunshiny. It smells like Jillian.

Holding a hand out, palm up, she says, "Let me see
the condom."

Reaching into my back pocket, I hold her gaze as I
grab the foil packet. I place it in her palm and watch as
she looks at it briefly before saying to me, "I think we
should stay in."

"Jillian," I rasp out, completely turned on and ready
to hop in bed, but equally ready to jet out in fear. I don't
know if I'm ready for this, and that sounds like such a
pussy thing to say even inside my head, but I'm freaked
out about her seeing… well, all of me.

"Unless you're not attracted to me," she says as her
smile falters.

I roll my eyes. "I'm totally attracted to you, and you
know that."

"Then what's the problem?" she asks.

Reaching out, I take a lock of her blonde hair and
rub it between my thumb and forefinger. The skin there
was also burned in the explosion, and I only have
nominal feeling. Still, I like being able to touch her
without her flinching or pulling away.

Raising my gaze to hers, I try to protect my man card
and deflect my insecurities at her. "I'm not sure you're
ready for this."

A rich, husky laugh emanates from those beautiful

lips as she places the hand not holding the condom to my chest. "Christopher, just because I've been heavily sheltered by my parents the last few years doesn't mean I'm naive or innocent. I'm a big girl, and I can make my own decisions."

"That's not what I'm—"

"Unless *you're* not ready for this," she guesses... a little too accurately. "In that case, we can wait."

"I'm ready," I snap at her, the words harsh as she's just uncovered my vulnerability. I pull back from her, then immediately close my eyes, take a deep breath, and let it out. When I open my eyes again, I look at her and in a softer voice, I repeat, "I'm ready."

Typical Jillian, her eyes warm with empathy for my struggles. Proving that she's astute as well as intuitive, she murmurs, "Tell me what your true hesitation is, Christopher."

Christ, I'm turning into a woman, I think. "Jillian... we've known each other for five days—"

"No, we've known each other for seven weeks," she counters.

"No," I say with a shake of my head. "You didn't know me and I didn't know you prior to this trip. And truth be told, I'm not sure we really know each other all that well now, or you'd realize we both should be having some reservations about this."

"What reservations?" she asks innocently.

"Jesus," I mutter as I rake both hands through my

hair. I keep them gripped at the top of my head and bore my eyes into her. "You get I'm an asshole, right? I'm broken. I don't care about anyone or anything but myself. If we fuck, that's all it will be... a fuck."

"Now that's a lie, Christopher Barlow," she interrupts, chastising me. "It would not just be a fuck."

"Fine," I say in exasperation as I throw my hands into the air. "It would be more than a fuck, but goddamn it, Jillian... I don't know if I can do that. Open myself up to that."

"Because you're scared," she surmises in a gentle tone.

"Yeah," I admit with a huff of breath, defeated by her constant poking at me. "I'm scared."

"Of what?" Her eyes watch me carefully, perhaps wondering if I'll just bolt the hell out of here.

"Of freaking you out," I mutter, dropping my gaze to my feet. That's fucking embarrassing as hell to admit.

"How would you freak me out?" she asks, and now she sounds genuinely confused.

My eyes snap back up to her, and I scowl. "Come on, Jillian... I have a stump for a leg. It's ugly. Just like my hand." To prove that point, I hold it up before her face, but she's seen it before. She doesn't even give it a glance when she puts her fingers around my wrist and lowers my arm.

"You don't give me enough credit," she whispers, and I can see the hurt in her eyes.

I try hard not to roll my eyes and succeed before I say, "Sure… I know you can look past that and all, and that you're not worried about looks—"

"Christopher," Jillian says with a sharp bite to her voice. "I don't look past that. I look right at it. I see your gorgeous face, I see your scars, and I'd like to see your leg. When I do, I will think it's beautiful because it's what makes you who you are. It's what helped to shape you into the person you are today—"

"An asshole," I blurt out.

"An individual who has been hurt, let down, abandoned, and betrayed. Suffered immense pain and now lives in a world of doubt. But you're also an adventurer and a risk taker. Underneath that gruff exterior, you're kind, thoughtful, and accommodating. Your eyes are angelic, your mouth devilish, and you are without a doubt the best kisser I've ever had the pleasure of trying. Assuming what's down below is in working order and wasn't injured, then I'm going to guess you're probably really damn good in bed even if you do only have one leg."

"Well, truth be told, I have like one and one-third of a leg," I tell her. As expected, she bursts out laughing. I grin at her, feeling a great deal of weight floating off my shoulders. My main concern has been addressed, and I feel better about the prospect of intimacy with this gorgeous creature. She's actually made me feel somewhat safe.

Jillian's eyes go soft, droop a bit more, and her voice is husky again. My entire body tightens when she says, "So… my suggestion is we go lay on the bed and make out for a bit. Let's see where this goes."

"Let's just see where this goes?" I ask, making sure there's no pressure on either one of us for it to go anywhere we don't want it to. I mean, I know where I want it to go. I want a used condom to be in the bottom of the trash can by night's end, but at least I know she can stop if she wants. If I want to stop, I can too, not that I would.

Jillian merely answers me by turning and walking to the bed closest to the bathroom, which I'm guessing is hers. With her back to me, she reaches down to the hem of her t-shirt and pulls it over her head. Her hair disappears for a moment. When the shirt is pulled free, it falls in a glorious golden cascade over her smooth, tanned back.

I walk toward her, more hopeful than I've ever been in my entire life.

Chapter 24

THE ROOM IS dark and I wake up disoriented, confused, and with a full bladder. Not confused about the full bladder, but I am slightly unsure about the soft, naked body pressed up against mine. Or rather, why I'm spooned around a warm, silky skinned, luscious, and clearly female body. Then it comes back to me all at once.

Beautiful images of what we did last night…

Made out forever.

Fondled.

Stripped clothing.

Traced skin.

Struggled out of a prosthetic.

Kissed scars.

Bold touches.

Tongue on tongue.

Awkward handling of a condom.

Making love.

Phenomenal.

Gasps.

Shuddering cries.

Feeling like my heart would explode.

Sleep.

With a glance at the bedside clock, I see it's just past one in the morning. I push my nose into Jillian's hair, listening to her deep, even breaths. The entire front of my body is plastered to her back. We're laying on our right sides, my legs split with my stump cocked back and away from her and my whole leg wrapped up in hers. I didn't do that intentionally; it's just the position I woke up in.

Perhaps it was a subconscious thing—to keep my deformed leg from her—but I don't think so. Jillian spent a great deal of time last night looking at my C-leg, watching how I took it off and asking questions about the liner. When it was bare to her, she ran her hands over my skin from my hipbone to the scar where the flaps of my skin were stapled together after the amputation. She did all of this while I laid on the bed in my boxer briefs, and I was so nervous about it I didn't think there was any way I'd be turned on. Yet, the minute her fingers touched my skin, I got a huge boner that was painfully obvious.

The fear I'd had that she would be turned off or grossed out completely evaporated when she leaned over and kissed me right in the center of what was left of my thigh.

She'd looked up at me. "You know what I hate most about this?" she asked with a hand stroking my stump.

I looked down my body, past my hard dick, and to her eyes, shaking my head.

"I hate to think of the pain you were in," she murmured. "I honestly hate it for you so much."

"It's over," I told her. I suppose, much like childbirth… that my memories of it had dulled somewhat. I could still recall with brutal clarity my wanting to die and how those emotions felt, but the actual memories of the physical pain had definitely diminished.

Her face told me she seriously doubted my claim, but I didn't want her feeling sad for me anymore. She'd seen the worst my body had to offer her, but there was more she hadn't seen. I gave a pointed look down to my erection and then back to her with a lazy smile. "There's more of me to touch if you're up for it. I know I am."

"Hah-hah," she teased with an eye roll, but then her hand was on the part of me that was clearly up for her touch, and my eyes rolled into the back of my head.

Thereafter, I had the most amazing sexual experience of my life. Based on the noises and cries Jillian made, I was pretty sure she felt the same. I imagine, in my case, it was because I hadn't had sex in so long and I'd been rejected for my shortcomings, so when Jillian made it clear that she liked and was attracted to every single inch of me, it gave me the freedom to open up and enjoy the experience without any self-doubts clouding over me.

Right now, I want to wake her up, push her on her back, and start all over again with her. I don't think my mouth had nearly enough time exploring her body, but the pressure on my bladder takes precedence. Carefully extracting myself from Jillian's body, I scoot to the edge of the bed and swing my legs over. Pushing up easily to my left leg, I brace my hand on the wall and take a few short hops to the bathroom. I never bother with my prosthetic for short trips like this. In fact, there was a time early on in my rehab that hopping was just so much easier than using a prosthetic that I considered just hopping around everywhere for the rest of my life.

Stupid as fuck, I know.

I do my business in the bathroom, wash my hands, and then quickly brush my teeth. When I head back into the bedroom, I'm surprised to see the bedside lamp on and Jillian sitting up in bed. She's got the sheet pulled up to her armpits, modestly covering her body, and her hands clasped over her belly.

"You okay?" she asks as I balance myself against the wall on one leg.

"Um, yeah," I say as I take the two most awkward hops in my entire life to the bed, because hopping while butt naked causes things to flop around. Jillian watches me with interest, completely unrepentant in doing so. And when I say she watches me, I mean the bouncing parts.

My ears burning, I play it off by grinning at her as I slide under the covers, turn on my right side, and face her. She places a palm to my cheek, her eyes darkening somberly. "Another nightmare wake you up?"

"Nightmare?"

"You had one about an hour ago," she says. "Sort of jerking around in your sleep and moaning."

I cock at eyebrow at her. "How do you know that wasn't a sex dream?"

I expect her to laugh, roll her eyes, or punch me playfully in the shoulder. Instead, her look turns more worried. "It wasn't a sex dream. You were really scared… distressed. I tried to shake you a bit to wake you up. You never did, but the dream apparently stopped because you went quiet."

"Huh," I say, my eyes drifting past Jillian to look at the far wall. I've certainly had my share of nightmares, but I don't remember one tonight. Or a sex dream for that matter.

"Do you get nightmares?" she asks.

My gaze comes back to hers. I shrug. "Yeah… I guess. I mean, they don't come as frequently now, but…"

With a trailing voice, I turn on my back, put my hands under my head, and stare at the ceiling. What in the fuck was I dreaming about? And worse, I hate that Jillian saw it. It conveys a weakness I don't want her to see. Fuck knows she's seen enough of my shortcomings.

"Tell me about some of your nightmares," Jillian whispers as she scoots over to me and lays her head on my chest. She wiggles her body into me, pressing her leg against my stump and wrapping an arm over my stomach. It's secure and comforting, and my arm immediately goes around her waist to hold her tightly to me.

"They were no big deal," I tell her.

"Then tell me about them," she persists.

"Why?"

"Because I want to know everything about you," she says quietly. "Everything."

I let out a sigh of defeat because Jillian will never be satisfied with just looking at my scars or picking at my scabs. She wants to rip the hurt away, understand it, and then help me try to feel better. I know this because I've watched her do it for weeks with Connor. I've also seen her do it for the past several days with Barb and me.

"I don't get them often anymore. Apparently, I don't remember the ones I do get," I tell her, brushing off the whole thing. "But it's mostly of the explosion and when I got injured. Sometimes I'll have a nightmare where they go in to amputate my leg, but they can't get it off so I'm stuck with the rotting thing."

"Oh, God," Jillian practically whimpers as her hand

slides up my stomach to my chest. She presses her palm over my heart. "I can't even imagine."

I shrug. "Like I said… doesn't happen often. I'm mostly over it."

"Not true," she says, calling me out and then telling me why. "You're not over it and may never be. But I do think you're trying to deal with it for maybe the first time, and I think it's important to talk about it."

"Let me guess," I say dryly. "You have a psychology degree too?"

"Nope. Just an art history degree, but come on, Christopher… you know letting it out is the way to heal. I know you're smart enough to get that. You would never share in group, and you haven't shared much on the trip, but here I am… lying naked beside you, wanting to get naked with you more often in the future, and I want you to know you're safe with me. You can tell me anything, and I don't even have to say anything in return if you don't want me to. You can just talk and vent, and I'll listen. I promise you'll never be judged by me."

I lift my head from the pillow slightly to look down at Jillian as she rests on my chest. She tilts her head to look at me. Her eyes are clear pools of determination, reflecting a promise that she'll do exactly what she just said she'd do.

My head falls back to the pillow and my hand squeezes her waist. "I was just a few short weeks away from returning home when I ran over the explosive device. So fucking close to making it out unscathed. I was there almost a year, saw a thousand different things. Had some good days and some bad ones. Had great friends and a girl back home waiting for me who wrote me sexy letters, but that was all tempered by a constant, nagging anxiety that I could be killed on any given day. And yet, I really don't ever think about that stuff. I don't dream about it. The one thing I keep remembering over and over again, when I'm awake and in my nightmares, was my buddy Jelonek who was in the passenger seat. I mean… I was literally just talking to him. Right in the middle of a conversation. He was there one minute, and then the next… *poof…* he was just gone."

"Oh, my word," Jillian says in a distressed voice.

I give sort of a half laugh, half cry of outrage. "There was this red mist floating in the air, and I thought it was sand, or even something was wrong with my eyes, but when I inhaled in, I tasted copper and knew it was blood. I knew it was the finest of remnants of my buddy Jelonek."

"Christopher," Jillian whispers with sorrow.

"To this day, I can't eat beef unless it's well done. Like almost burnt to a crisp so I can't taste the blood. And if I see blood, real life or on TV, it feels like someone stacked about ten cinder blocks on my chest. It's hard to breathe. And I try to remember… did he scream before he died? Did he have time to do that? I

239

mean… I don't know because the explosion was so loud that I was temporarily deafened. When I think about it, all I can hope is that he didn't feel anything in that split second from when he was alive to when he was dead, because as bad as my leg hurt, I don't think it would have been anything to the comparison of getting reduced to a bloody mist."

Jillian pushes up and rolls until she comes to lay on top of me. Her hands slide to my face as she peers down at me. "Please tell me you talk to someone about this, Christopher."

I shrug. "I'm talking to you right now."

She shakes her head, those blonde locks rippling around her shoulders. "No… a professional. You can't see something like that and not be haunted. And you can't just bury it."

"I had to talk to plenty of shrinks before I got medically discharged. I'm fine."

Jillian narrows her eyes as best she can with her weak muscles. "You are not fine."

"Okay," I say carefully, pushing a hand around the back of her neck and cupping it. "Maybe I'm not fine, but I'm done talking about that tonight."

Jillian gives out a slight huff of exasperation, but then changes tactics on me. "Fine… let's talk about something else—"

My head comes off the pillow, and I crush my mouth against hers. She jerks against me but then her hands go from my face to around my shoulders, and she's kissing me back hard. I keep this in mind for future conversations, filing away that Jillian is way too easy to distract.

But now I'm the one distracted as I feel my body start to tighten under the warm weight of her body, her breasts pressing to my chest and the feeling of her tongue against mine. My hands slip down, skimming her back, and Jillian rocks her body against me, causing me to groan.

I pull back from the kiss and whisper, "No more condoms."

"We can be creative," she pants at me. "Plenty we can do with hands and mouth."

I groan again and kiss her once more. Hell yes… plenty of stuff we can do without a condom.

Chapter 25

I 'VE PULLED THE Suburban up to the side of the cabin duplex, busying myself with pulling everything out so I can reorganize. Over the last few days, we've just been throwing shit in the back and it needs cleaned out.

But this is only a cleaning and reorganizational plan because I need something to keep busy until the others get out here. If they like my brilliant idea, we won't be packing up our bags just yet.

The door to the room I was supposed to share with Connor opens, and he steps out. Last I'd checked, he was in the shower, so I decided to clean up the Suburban until he was done. Barb is back in her room, presumably getting ready, as I'd kicked her out of the backseat about fifteen minutes ago. I'd left Jillian still sleeping soundly when I'd come out here, but I assume Barb will wake her up.

"Morning," Connor says with a cheery grin.

I grunt back an acknowledgment to him before leaning into the back of the SUV and grabbing an empty McDonald's bag to throw away. When I pull back,

Connor is beside me. He asks, "Need any help?"

Again… very cheery. With a wide, goofy smile. His eyes are shining as he rocks back and forth on his feet with his thumbs hooked into his belt loops at his hips. If I didn't know any better, I'd say he was drunk, but he definitely looks like the cat that just ate the canary.

And then it hits me.

My gaze shifts to the door that Barb just walked in, and then back to Connor. I'd found her sleeping in the Suburban, but that didn't mean…

"Did you… and Barb…?" I let the question hang in the air, but it's clear enough what I mean.

Connor's grin gets bigger. Cheesier. "Let's just say I won't need your help on that one bucket-list item we talked about."

I do a quick, critical scan of Connor. His color looks good, he's clearly riding a wave of smug happiness, and whatever Barb did to him or with him last night must have been good. If that's the case, she just scored big time with me in the respect department.

Settling my hip against the back corner of the Suburban, I cross my arms and lean in toward Connor. "How did that happen?"

While I didn't think it possible, Connor's smile gets even bigger. "Dude… she just knocked on the door late last night. I thought she wanted to crash in your bed or something, but, well… she must have had other thoughts because she started getting naked as soon as the door closed."

"You're fucking kidding me?" I ask in amazement. I mean, sure... we learned that Barb likes sex, and she's warmed up to Connor over the last few days. But for her to actively offer to provide him such an intimate bucket-list item is beyond what I thought she was capable of.

Well, because she's not capably of intimacy.

Fuck.

"Connor... you know... Barb doing that with you, that was probably just—"

"—a one-time-only thing," Connor says with a laugh. "Yeah... I understood that all on my own, but regardless... we talked about it after."

"You did?" I'm stunned Barb would bother to have a conversation.

"Yeah," Connor says with a nod and obvious affection in his voice for what Barb gave him. "She was really cool about it. Told me that no one should die without having sex, and that she wanted to give it to me so I didn't have to resort to something seedier. Guess she was talking about a prostitute or something, but she was also clear... it was just that one time. Well, twice. She had two condoms."

"Who had two condoms?" I hear Jillian say from behind me. I turn to see her standing there with a curious look on her face. She's wearing the pajamas she had on last night with her hair a tangled mess, but damn, she couldn't be any more beautiful.

Connor just stares at her, unable or unwilling to answer her question. So Jillian turns to face me, eyebrows raised in question. "Who had two condoms?"

Not my place to tell the story unless Connor wants her to know, so I keep my mouth firmly shut and give a shrug.

Bro code.

Jillian's gaze goes back to Connor, her eyes narrowing imperceptibly. "What's the big secret?"

After a long sigh, Connor says in a low voice that sounds a little ashamed, "I had sex last night."

I make a mental note to disabuse him of that emotion for busting his cherry. He has nothing to be ashamed about.

"With who?" she asks with a stunned expression on her face, never once considering Barb to be an option.

At that same moment, the other room's door opens and Barb comes striding out with her backpack slung over her shoulder. She's clearly had a shower as her short, dark hair is slicked back. Connor's eyes shift her way and his face turns red. Jillian catches it, her head swinging back toward Connor.

"You didn't? Not with her." The slightly horrified tone to her voice is a bit offensive, but not my battle to fight.

"He sure did," Barb says tartly as she walks to the tailgate and slings her pack inside. "Got rid of a pesky bucket-list item. Didn't we, Connor?"

Jillian doesn't even give Barb the time of day. She sidles up closer to Connor and murmurs, "Connor, something like that… it should have been special. And… you're only seventeen for God's sake."

"It was special," Connor says, shutting her down. "And I'll be eighteen in less than a month. Stop being so protective of me. I don't need another mother."

Jillian's face flushes red, but she doesn't argue with Connor. Instead, she turns to Barb and glares at her, but before she can even open her mouth, Barb steps up and gets in her face.

"Save the hypocrisy," Barb tells her firmly. "And don't be a prude. I know you did the nasty last night too."

Barb then pushes past Jillian and walks up to Connor. She leans into him and places her mouth near his ear as if she's going to share a secret, but her words are loud enough for everyone to hear. "You were fantastic last night. All three times."

Connor's face turns a brighter shade of red, but he grins back at Barb. I cover my mouth and duck my head so I don't laugh at the blatant lie. Connor said it was only twice, but Barb is putting on a show for Jillian.

Barb gives Connor a wink and then walks back into the room, shutting the door behind her.

When I raise my head, I see Jillian staring after her with her mouth wide open in astonishment. I lift an arm and place my fingers under her chin, gently pushing up so she closes her mouth.

Jillian focuses in on me and asks, "Did you set that up?"

I hold up both my hands in surrender. "Nope."

Her head turns to Connor. "Are you two like… together now?"

"God no," Connor exclaims loudly, and Jillian's body physically relaxes over his proclamation. "It was only a one-night thing. Just to clear that from the bucket list. She did me a solid, that's all. But she is totally not my type, and besides that… she's way older than me and I'm dying, so—"

"Okay," Jillian interrupts with a chuckle. "I get it. Bucket-list item marked off. I need to get over it. We're moving on."

"Good," Connor says with an impish grin. "Because, no offense to anyone… I mean, egging and camping and fishing have been super fun, but last night was definitely the highlight of my trip."

I snicker, and Jillian gives him an honest to goodness "I'm happy for you" smile before turning to me. She steps right into me and puts her hand on my waist. Her blue eyes give me an intimate look that solidifies the connection we forged last night. When she goes on her tiptoes, my head bends down automatically to accept her lips as they brush against mine.

When she pulls back, she says, "I'm going to take a quick shower, and then I'll be ready to go. I know we have some hard driving to do today to make Portland."

"Actually," I say as I look between Jillian and Connor. "I have another idea."

"What's that?" Jillian tilts her head in curiosity.

"Well, I know Connor wants to do something dangerous and fun like bungee jumping, and while I couldn't find anything like that around here, they have paragliding just across the border over in Jackson, Wyoming."

"Oh, man, that would be awesome," Connor exclaims.

"And they have whitewater rafting," I add. "We could do that too."

"It would add another day to the trip," Jillian muses.

"And on that thought," I forge ahead. "While we're on the West Coast, why don't we see a few things before we head back?"

"Like?" Jillian prods.

I shrug. "Let's head down south after Cannon Beach. We can do San Francisco… maybe L.A., then down to San Diego. Afterward, we can drive back across the bottom part of the United States. Make a big old loop."

Jillian smirks at me. "Who are you and what have you done with the real Christopher Barlow?"

I smile and reach out to take her hand. "Maybe he started having fun on this trip and doesn't want it to end just yet."

I thought I'd seen all the beauty that Jillian had to

offer me, but at my words, her expression morphs. The look she gives me punches straight through the center of my chest to give my heart a warm squeeze.

Jillian takes a step toward me and puts her hand on my chest. "I'm glad you're having fun, and I'm not ready for this to end either."

Pure physical elation rips through the entire length of my body, igniting within me a surge of happiness that I haven't felt since before I was injured. It feels warm, bright, and engaging. It beckons me to step forward and take a risk on life.

Turning to Connor, Jillian says, "You should go call your parents and talk to them. They've been super cool so far, but this will add a few more days onto the trip if we do this. I know they're also anxious to see you, so you need to get their okay to do this."

"Yeah, sure," Connor says. "I'm sure they'll be fine with it, but if not… I can always fly back and y'all can continue on without me."

Jillian and I watch him bound back up the steps and into the room. When the door closes, she turns to face me. Her smile comes off as sweetly sexy but with her eyelids drooping down a bit, she looks adorably shy at the same time.

"Any regrets about last night?" she asks me.

"Not a one," I tell her honestly. Well, except maybe that I didn't have more condoms. I will need to rectify that before the day's end.

"So... um... is this a secret?" she asks hesitantly. "Like do we keep this wrapped up in front of the others?"

"I think they already have a suspicion as to what we did last night." My tone is dry but teasing.

She shakes her head. "No, I mean... how do you feel about spontaneous acts of public affection?"

"Huh?" I ask, completely confused.

"Well, what would you think if I just decided to lean over while you're driving the car and kiss your neck? Or maybe hold your hand while we're walking somewhere. Or even a spontaneous hug."

I just blink at Jillian, stunned she even has to ask such a question. She's never stopped before when she's had the urge to grab my hand. And she has never been one to hold back on her feelings. I'm assuming she must feel the need to ask because while she may be sure about the way she feels, she's really has no clue what's going on in my mind. Let's face it... we haven't had a ton of serious discussions.

Leaning down, I brush my lips against Jillian's temple as I wrap my left hand around the back of her neck. Pressing my cheek to the top of her head, I tell her, "Jillian... you can kiss me, hug me, hold my hand, or jump my bones whenever you feel like it. Sound good?"

"Sounds good," she murmurs.

Pulling back, I take her by the shoulders and turn her toward her room. "Good... now go in there and convince Barb she wants to extend the trip. Then we're off to go paragliding."

"On it," Jillian says as she hurries up the steps.

I wonder if she'll call her parents and tell them, or if she'll just send them a text. She hasn't said anything more about them since she called them yesterday morning while I was fishing with Connor, and I didn't think to ask. But I should ask, right? I mean… I think we're in a relationship. We're definitely friends. We've definitely exercised benefits. I like her, and she likes me. She still fascinates me, and she makes me want to learn and experience more about this new life that's unfolding before me.

Yeah… I should ask her. Should ask a lot more about her if this is going to be something that grows between us. I remember enough about my time with Maria to know that relationships take work. They require communication. It's a give and take.

Suddenly, a wave of sadness overcomes me as my mind goes to my family in West Virginia. The parents and siblings who couldn't handle what happened to me and the one brother I had who at least tried to support me. And I turned him away and haven't talked to him since, other than an occasional text exchange.

Filled with an almost painful need to assuage the feeling of guilt that's now pulsing within me, I pull my phone out and dial Hank's number.

He answers on the second ring, sounding both elated

and cautious at the same time. "Christopher… is that you?"

I give a small cough to clear the emotion from my throat. "Yeah… it's me."

"How are you, bro?" he asks, and I have to smile. I've missed his voice.

Fuck… I've missed him.

"I'm doing good," I tell him as I lean back against my vehicle. "I'm in Idaho actually."

"No kidding. What are you doing out there?"

"I'm on a trip with some friends," I tell him, and that makes me smile too. They weren't my friends just a few short days ago. My how fast things can change.

"Cool," he says. I can hear the relief in his voice that he's talking to me and that I haven't been an asshole yet. "So what made you decide to take a trip?"

I brush my fingertips over the stubble on my chin and wince internally when I tell him, "I sort of got in some trouble with the law. Got ordered into group therapy to avoid jail. Not sure how it happened, but I got talked into taking this trip with the people in the group, and well… it's actually not what I expected it would be."

There's a scant second of silence before Hank says, "You sound happy, Christopher."

"Listen," I say as my voice cracks a little, because I'm not ready to admit that happiness is real or genuine for the long term. "The reason I'm calling is… well, I just wanted to say I'm sorry for the way I treated you. For telling you to leave and not come back."

"Hey, man," he says in a soothing voice. "You had some messed-up shit you were dealing with. I never begrudged you your anger or the way you tried to handle it."

"We're good?" I ask hesitantly.

"Yeah, we're more than good," he says, and I can feel a weight lift from my shoulders and evaporate around me.

He continues. "Now, tell me about this trip. Who are the people with you?"

Smiling, I remember Jillian underneath me last night and her total acceptance of the incomplete me. I know Hank would really like Jillian if they ever met.

"Well, there's this girl…" I start off, and then I tell him everything.

Chapter 26

JACKSON, WYOMING IS a popular destination in the short summer months. There's an abundance of outdoor activities, each one providing a three-hundred-and-sixty-degree panoramic view of some of the most stunning scenery I've ever seen. The crown jewel of the area is the Teton Mountain range that runs north/south on the eastern edge of Wyoming, just across the Idaho state line.

I'm not a well-traveled man. I went from West Virginia to Parris Island, South Carolina for boot camp, and then to Camp Lejeune, North Carolina where I was stationed. From there, I've been to the Helmand River Valley in Afghanistan, a brief but entirely unconscious trip to Landstuhl to get stabilized, then back to the States where I spent months trying to recover from my injuries. Outside of that, I've seen the states we've driven through to get here. While my experiences may be minimal, I'm pretty positive I'll never see anything as beautiful as the Teton mountains in Wyoming.

It takes us only about an hour and a half to get there

from Ashton, Idaho. Along the way, Jillian was able to get noon reservations so we could go paragliding. We lucked out and got reservations for three of us due to a last-minute cancellation. I have to think it's providence of some sort that's allowing Connor to have another bucket-list item checked off.

Of course, there's four of us and only three slots, but Jillian quickly and gladly gave up a spot. She said she had no desire to go paragliding. Connor and I teased her mercilessly about it, but then she set me way fucking back on my heels.

"Tease all you want," she'd said back to us primly. "But I'm more likely than not to have a heart attack if I run off that mountain with the shape my heart is in."

I wasn't prepared for the feeling of dread and unease that statement provoked within me. I sometimes get so focused on Jillian's impending blindness that I forget she has a serious heart condition too. She could actually die without warning, and I had to choke back the nausea that welled within me.

I wasn't ready to let her go.

Another horrifying thought had slammed into me, and I'd whipped my head toward her. I muttered low, but I know the others heard me, "Is it safe for you to have sex?"

Jillian busted out laughing. After I let her get through it, tears and all, she was finally able to say, "Christopher... my heart is weaker than an ordinary person's, but it's not really in danger of giving out right now. It could get worse later, but maybe not. But to reassure you, I'm good to have sex. And I'm using the heart excuse because I'm just too terrified to jump off a mountain."

I was so relieved I didn't care that the others were listening in. But if I had any question as to whether my feelings for Jillian are real or merely a product of so desperately wanting something good for once, it was dispelled by the terrible roiling of fear that went through me when she teased she could have a heart attack if she jumped off the mountain. Whether that would happen or not, I realized... having someone like Jillian in my life is as complicated as her having someone like me. Sometimes, I get so dazzled by her brilliance and spirit I forget she's as physically broken as I am.

Needless to say, Connor and I didn't tease her about her clear fear of paragliding again.

Rendezvous Mountain is what we'll be jumping off. It's at the southern end of the Teton range with a peak of over ten-thousand feet. Connor wanted adventure. We'll be strapping ourselves to a paraglide pilot, who will sit in a harness underneath a baffled chute, and we're going to run off the edge of the mountain and fly down to the ground.

After we park at the Teton Village, which sits at the base of Rendezvous Mountain, Jillian and Connor scramble out of the vehicle. Their little hamster bladders are at the point of bursting since we were on a time crunch to get here and I wouldn't stop. They take off running to the large crop of buildings at the base of the mountain, while Barb and I take our time. She rummages in her backpack for her earbuds, and I'm betting she's going to have some crazy jams cranked as she flies through the air.

After she puts her pack in the rear cargo area and I lock up the SUV, we start walking in the direction that Jillian and Connor took off in. I'm glad for the moment alone with her because we need to have a serious conversation, although I intend to keep it short.

"Tonight... I'm going to sleep with Jillian," I tell her.

She turns her head and shoots me a look that says, *No shit, Sherlock.*

I forge ahead, because I know what I just said wasn't a surprise. It also isn't the reason we needed to talk. "Do you want to get a separate room?"

"Nah," she says without looking at me. "I'll just take your bed or sleep in the Suburban again."

I know I should tread carefully and handle this with some sensitivity, but honestly, our walk isn't going to last very long until we run into Jillian and Connor, so I get to the point. "Are things cool with you and Connor?"

Barb stops so abruptly that I take two more paces before I can stop myself. I turn to face her, and she looks pissed.

"What's that supposed to mean?" she grits out.

"It means I'm worried that he's seventeen years old and you just provided him with his first and only sexual experience last night, and I'm not sure what expectations he'll have tonight if you stay in the room with him," I tell her candidly.

Connor's parents were not all that crazy about him extending this trip, and it wasn't only because they missed him and were anxious to have him back in the fold. The clock was counting down for them too. Although they very much wanted him to have this trip, they are missing out on precious time with him. Connor's dad asked to speak to me, wanting some details on where we intended to go and a time frame for being home. I think he really wanted some assurances that everything was truly okay and that we weren't leading his son off on an adventure he'd never want to quit. I assured him everything was fine and laid out my plans going forward. I also assured him Connor was doing great and having the time of his life.

I obviously didn't tell him that the highlight was losing his virginity, because I'm pretty sure his dad would not like that, but for whatever reason, he trusts me with his son and I had to make sure things were really cool with Barb.

I expect her to lash out at me for questioning her at all, because... well... she's an angry woman ninety-nine percent of the time. Instead, her face sort of crumbles

THE HARD TRUTH ABOUT SUNSHINE

before she hides it away from me with a downward tilt of her head. Her shoulders slump and her voice is small... the smallest I've ever heard it. "I would never hurt Connor."

"I know you wouldn't," I automatically say, but up until that very moment when I heard the angst in her voice, I didn't know that for sure. But I believe her now. It's the only time I've ever seen Barb feel for another person in a deep way.

"We talked last night," she says as she raises her gaze to mine, and I can tell by her expression she's bothered by his impending death. "A lot. Not only about what happened with us, but about life and death. We talked for hours after. Trust me when I say that Connor is probably the most mature out of all four of us in this group. He has a better handle on what happened between us than I do."

My chest constricts inward as I realize that Barb has actually opened herself up and let someone inside her narrow little world. Who would have ever thought a pimply faced teenager with a death sentence would do it?

"Alright," I say as I turn toward the buildings where I can see Jillian and Connor waiting for us. "It's all cool then."

Barb doesn't respond, just follows me across the parking lot.

◆

AND HOLY FUCK, it's cold up here. The temperature was in the low seventies at the base of the mountain when we arrived, but by the time the tram got us to the top, it had dropped almost thirty degrees. We were told to expect this by the paragliding company, but none of us had planned for this type of cold while driving across the United States in late July.

Jillian's heaviest coat is a light windbreaker and she's shivering, even as she stares around in awe. As I look out over the valley, which is rich with horse pastures, swaying grasses, and fragrant sagebrush, I realize it's weird sitting at the top of a cold mountain with patches of snow still all around while doing so. It's like standing in one world while looking at another.

I offer Jillian my heavy denim jacket but she refuses, telling me it's going to be a lot colder for me than it will be for her as she's taking the tram back to the bottom of the mountain after we launch.

Poor Barb… I don't think the girl owns a pair of jeans without rips in them, but at least she has a thick leather jacket on.

Connor is next to me, getting strapped into the harness with his pilot. We'd spent almost half an hour getting instruction as a group—there was a total of seven of us taking these flights—and now it was almost go time.

"You okay?" I ask him, because his face is a little pale and I can see sweat glistening just above his brow. His bald head is covered with a knit cap I loaned him.

"I'm fine," he says as an assistant helps to buckle him in the harness in front of his pilot.

"You're pale," I point out.

"I'm one month past my last chemotherapy, I'm dying, and I'm getting ready to jump off a mountain," Connor says dryly. "I've got reasons to be pale."

I laugh as his instructor's head pops up at this news, and Connor grins back at me. I thought my own pilot's eyes would bug out of his head when he asked me if I had any physical restrictions that he needed to be aware of before we launched. I'd pulled the bottom of my jeans up so he could see my C-leg and told him that while I could run, I couldn't run as fast as he could. After he got over the shock, he assured me we really didn't need to run hardly at all. Once the chute above us filled with air, it would practically lift us off the mountain when we were ready to go.

As my pilot helps to get me secured into the harness, I take another look at Jillian. She's watching me with hooded eyes, so I jerk my head in an indication I want her to come closer. She walks up to me, arms wrapped around her middle for warmth and her head tilted to one side.

I ask her the same question I just asked Connor. "You okay?"

"Yeah," she says with a small smile. "Just worried."

"You're the eternal optimist," I point out with a grin.

"You can't be worried."

"You're getting ready to run off the side of a mountain," she returns dryly. "My optimism has limits."

"This is perfectly safe," the instructor behind me says, but Jillian and I ignore him.

I crook my finger at her, beckoning her closer. She does... close enough I can put my hand behind her neck and pull her in for a brief kiss. Our intimate relationship is so fucking new, and yet, casually kissing her right now seems so damn natural. Not a single awkward moment for me, and I can't fathom how I can be so open to this. How I could have been so jaded just days ago, and now it feels right that Jillian should be the last thing I see before I jump off the mountain, and that her kiss inspires within me the knowledge that my life is going to be just fine.

When I pull back, I tell her something I'd been thinking about last night just before I fell asleep. "You're a cup-half-full kind of girl."

She nods with a smirk. "True."

"I'm a cup-half-empty kind of guy," I add.

"Also true."

"Both of our cups are still missing something." My thumb rubs along the side of her neck, and it doesn't matter that it's scarred and missing compatriot fingers.

"About four ounces each," she quips, but I can tell she knows where I'm going with this.

"You put us both together and we're full," I tell her

tenderly.

The pilot I'm strapped to shifts uncomfortably behind me, I'm sure feeling completely awkward to be witnessing this.

"Okay, you're freaking me out," Jillian says with a playful push on my chest. "You can't go from asshole to romantic in just a few days."

The pilot gives a slight cough.

I grin at Jillian as she backs away. "See you down at the bottom."

"Hopefully in one piece," she calls back to me.

The aide who was checking Connor's harness comes over to me and does a lot of pulling and checking of straps. He gives me a thumbs-up and moves down the line.

"You ready?" the pilot behind me asks, and a surge of adrenaline leaves my skin tingling in its wake.

I nod my answer but turn my head to the left to look at Connor. "You ready?"

He nods back at me, face still pale, but there's excitement sparkling in his eyes. I look past him to Barb on his other side. "You ready?"

She gives me the smallest hint of a smile and nods back. "Ready."

And out of the three of us, I'm sure she is because she probably doesn't care if she lives or dies. In fact, she might even be hoping for a rip in one of the baffles that will help to keep her airborne.

"All clear," I hear shouted from the end of the line of seven people strapped to seven pilots, prepared to hurtle ourselves off the side of a ten-thousand-foot mountain.

I look back to Connor. "You scared?"

I'm asking about this moment as we prepare to experience a thrill of a lifetime, but I could be asking about life in general.

He nods. "Scared shitless."

That answer could be about us leaping off a mountain or about the fact he'll probably die before the year ends. It could be about so many things, least of which is what we're about to do.

"Okay," my pilot says behind me as he gives a last pull on my harness. "We're ready."

"How about you?" Connor asks as I watch him and his pilot get prepared to run for the edge. "You scared?"

I look over my shoulder at Jillian and she gives me a thumbs-up signal, her smile encouraging. Her belief in me is contagious.

Looking back at Connor, I tell him the truth. "I'm scared shitless too. But there's no reward without the risk, right?"

"Right," he says with a firm nod of his head.

"Then let's do this," I say as I turn my gaze to look over the valley spread wide before me. It's fine… because I know Jillian and my future wait below, and my future is nothing like I thought it would be just a few short days ago.

Chapter 27

Eight weeks ago…

M Y FINGERTIPS PUSHED against the large stack of mail on the tiny, wobbly kitchen table. I hadn't been through it in days, and I really didn't want to go through it at all, but the voice mail I'd just listened to from a woman named Mags had motivated me slightly.

Either I went through that mail and laid my hands— or well, hand and a half—on the letter addressed to me from the Wake County Clerk of Courts office, or I would go to jail.

This Mags woman had left me a friendly reminder that tomorrow was the first group therapy session I'd been ordered to attend in exchange for commuting my jail sentence for assault. Apparently, I should have received a letter giving me the details on where we would meet and the program itself.

I located the letter and pulled it from the pile. I didn't bother looking at anything else as I'd put all my living expenses on auto draft so I wouldn't miss anything. I wasn't the best about paying bills, mainly because I didn't give a shit. But this crappy little apartment kept a roof over my head and the meager disability payments from the government were enough to at least keep me in beer, weed, and pills. So I used auto draft so I wouldn't fuck up my pitiful existence.

Draining the bottle of beer in my left hand, I tossed it in the garbage can, heard the glass break, and pulled another one from the fridge. The only thing in there was beer, a half-empty bottle of vodka, and a pizza box with two slices left over. I should have put something in my stomach but that would take effort, so I closed the refrigerator door and twisted the cap off. I carried the letter and bottle of brew to the couch and sat down heavily. My stump was aching because when I put on my prosthesis that morning, I didn't bother with a sock liner. I'd be well served to take the damn thing off and let it breathe a bit, but I knew as soon as I popped a few of the pills in the little clear baggy on the table beside the couch, I wouldn't be feeling anything.

I took a long swig of beer and looked around my apartment. It only had two rooms with the main portion consisting of a tiny kitchen where on any given day I'd find a cockroach in the sink, a living area that was basically a worn couch and a battered side table, and a twin bed up against one wall. The other room held a small bathroom that had a toilet, sink, and shower, also home to cockroaches. I'd been living here about three months, and only because the dude I'd been living with back in Jacksonville had kicked me out.

I supposed he had reason. Rich was a buddy I'd served with in Afghanistan. He was three vehicles back when my Humvee rolled over the IED. We'd kept in periodic contact and when I was officially released from rehab and was just awaiting my final medical board discharge, he told me I could crash at his place for a while. He had a small duplex out in town rather than on base, and it was sort of a party central type of place. Which was cool and all, but even Rich had limitations when it came to partying.

First, he only did so on the weekends, and only with beer. He couldn't afford to pop on a random piss test that the Marine Corps was so keen on throwing at us. Eventually, Rich just got a little tired of the fact I was constantly drunk and a permanent haze of pot sort of hovered just under my bedroom ceiling. He told me I had to go.

So I did. Westward to Raleigh, North Carolina where I only went because the dude I got pot from in Jacksonville had a cousin there who was looking to sublease this shithole of an apartment. I figured what the fuck... I could afford it so why not?

When the government processed me out of the military, they looked at my injuries and they rated them to determine how much money they'd pay me for the rest of my life for my sacrifices.

Turns out, the loss of two fingers was worth twenty

percent. My amputation, since it was from mid-to-lower thigh down, was sixty percent. I found out it would have been ninety percent if it would have been from the hip down, but whatever. I still made a hundred-percent total by the time they put in my shredded forearm and PTSD. There some talk about a complicated diagnosis of Traumatic Brain Injury, but honestly... I wasn't sure what the fuck was wrong with me really. I just knew it was enough to pay me about three thousand bucks a month.

I was afraid and pissed and I hated the world so passionately that I really didn't want to live in it anymore. This made me not only an asshole, but also violent, particularly when I was wasted. I had absolutely no recollection of the douchebag I'd beaten the shit out of in a dive bar, but I was sure he had it coming to him.

And now I was going to be forced to start hanging out with a group of losers and expected to share my pain with these strangers.

Fat fucking chance of that.

I tossed the letter on the couch beside me, not wanting to open it up. I was in a mood.

A terrible mood.

Deep in my heart, I knew I should take advantage of some of the counseling programs the VA offered, but the thought of opening myself up to scrutiny was too scary. I took the easy way out and decided wallowing in my misery was just easier. With enough alcohol and drugs, I could keep things numbed somewhat.

Leaning forward, I gripped my bottle tighter so I wouldn't spill any precious alcohol and reached under the couch. My mechanical knee bent but not as far as my real knee did, so I had to sort of lean to the side to get what I was reaching for.

My Smith & Wesson .44 magnum revolver.

When I sat back up straight, I took another long pull of beer before laying it on the table. Then I opened the cylinder to confirm what I already knew. It was filled with bullets.

I had bought the gun about a year after I'd entered the Marine Corps from a buddy of mine who wanted to propose to his girlfriend. He had no money to buy a ring so he sold me his gun. She got a small diamond, and I got a pretty cool revolver.

I'd always been into guns. You couldn't live in rural West Virginia and not own one, especially for hunting, nor could you join the military and not learn how to deftly handle firearms.

The gun had sat in a shoebox in my closet for years, ignored and unused. The Marine Corps had given me a TOW missile and that was a way cooler gun.

It hadn't been looked at until I came to Raleigh, where I had put it under my couch. I didn't do that for safety reasons, but rather because I was contemplating what that gun could actually do for me.

I slapped the cylinder shut and laid the gun on my

lap. It felt warm, heavy, and reassuring. Reaching over to the baggy, I pulled out a ten-milligram oxy and popped it in my mouth. I chewed it quickly, ignoring the bitter taste, and washed it down with swig of beer.

It didn't take long for the high to hit me, which was why I chewed rather than swallowed, but what I had left in that baggy had to last me until next payday. Depending on how I would feel in fifteen minutes or so, I might or might not chew another.

My gaze dropped to the gun, and I lifted it in my hands. Leaning back, I rested my head on the back of the couch and held the gun up to inspect it. That moment, before the true oxy buzz hit me, would have been the best moment to put it to my head. I was just starting to feel the effects, and my courage was bolstered. It would have been so easy to put the muzzle up against my temple and pull the trigger.

No pain.

No more misery.

No more deformed body, phantom leg pain, hideous scars, or pitiful stares from strangers. No more loneliness. No more memories of a heartless girlfriend and a family that couldn't help me. No more memories of Jelonek getting vaporized, and certainly no more memories of the insidious pain I endured for months.

No more anything.

I wondered what my family would think when they got the news I'd killed myself. Would they be relieved?

Would they be guilt-ridden? Or would they just ignore it the way they'd ignored me?

I'd used legal services through the Marine Corps to make a small will to distribute my estate should anything have happened to me while I was deployed. Because I was smitten with Maria and was pretty sure we'd be married quickly when I came back, I'd left it all to her. I hadn't even bothered to fucking change it, so if I put that gun to my head and pulled the trigger, she'd get all my money.

I wondered if she'd get my prosthetic leg too.

I snorted at the thought, and then started laughing. It lasted only a second, dulled into chuckles, and then left nothing but a placid smile on my face. The oxy had kicked in, and I was feeling pleasantly mellow.

Dropping the gun to the cushion beside me, I closed my eyes and floated.

I wouldn't be killing myself today.

Chapter 28

W^{OW.}
                  Not feeling any pain and that's oh so nice. Whatever gas they're pumping into me via this mask on my face is working well. My head lolls to the left, and the anesthesiologist gives me an encouraging smile. I only know this because his eyes crinkle up, and I can see his jaw moving beneath the paper mask he's wearing.

My head lolls right, and the nurse gives me a wink. She's cute. I think. Nice eyes.

"Okay, we're ready to begin, Christopher," the doctor says, and I have to lift my head slightly to look down my body at the doctor. My torso, hips, and left leg are covered in a blue sheet. But my right leg is exposed, swollen, and bruised with open wounds running the length. Knobby protrusions indicate broken bone trying to poke through skin. I try to wiggle my toes, but they won't move. Then again, I'm not feeling any pain right now so maybe I can't control my leg.

The doctor reaches over to a tray and picks up a butter

knife. I can see an etched pattern on the handle, and I think my mom used to have a set of flatware like that. He holds it up and the operating room light glints off it, hitting me right in the eye. I wince slightly. But then the doctor moves the knife toward my thigh, and I focus in on it.

"Um... Doc... are you sure that's sharp enough?" I ask hesitantly.

"Of course it is," he says indignantly. "Your leg is barely hanging on. It should come off quite easily, and then we can butter our bread."

No, wait... that sounded ominous. He drops the knife and presses the edge into my skin, right near the opening of a large wound. I feel nothing, even when he starts sawing. I watch in morbid fascination as the doctor puts all his muscle into the effort of trying to saw through my skin with a butter knife, but he isn't making any progress. Sweat pops out on his brow, and he has to repetitively wipe it dry with his sleeve in between cutting attempts.

"Hold up," I cry out in frustration. "It's not working. You need something sharper."

"We don't have anything sharper," the doctor says as his movement halts. He looks at me with guilt, but it is the women he turns to who surprises me.

Jillian is standing in the corner of the room with Maria, and they are both looking at me with concern.

"I'm sorry," the doctor tells them quietly. "I can't get it off."

Jillian and Maria's eyes fill with tears as they nod their

understanding and grasp hands in solidarity. They look across the room at me with pity.

"I'm sorry, Christopher," Maria says in a pained voice.

"But we can't stay with you unless that leg comes off," Jillian adds.

My head whips toward the doctor. "Take it off," I shriek at him. "Take the fucking thing off."

"I can't," he says in defeat, holding up the butter knife.

"Take it off," I shriek again.

My eyes pop open and I let out a tentative gust of air, terrified that I actually cried out in my sleep. That nightmare was real, vivid, and is still hanging around me.

But Jillian is sleeping soundly beside me. I had apparently rolled onto my back at some point after we had fallen asleep all wrapped around each other. She's on her side with her face pressed up against my shoulder and a hand curled around my bicep. It feels warm and secure, but my racing heart feels anything but.

I've never had a nightmare like that before. Maria's never entered one that I can remember, and to have Jillian there with her freaks me out. And I totally don't understand why them wanting to be with me hinged on my leg coming off. I would have thought they'd want me as whole as possible.

It's so fucking weird and disturbing all at the same time.

I'm wide awake now, my body actually tingling from

the thought of my leg getting cut off with a butter knife and my hands shaking from the terror of it. I know there's no way in hell I'm getting back to sleep without a little bit of help, so I slowly slide away from Jillian and out of the bed. It takes me no time at all to get my leg on and throw on a minimum of clothes.

Gym shorts.

Sweatshirt.

The matching tennis shoe to the one that's on the prosthesis.

Reaching into my duffle bag, I grab the baggie of joints I'd rolled back in Colorado and a lighter from the side pocket. I head out the door as quietly as I can, gazing at Jillian's form still soundly sleeping on the bed just before I close the door.

When I turn around, I almost trip right over someone sitting on the bottom step of the room-duplex we're staying in. I can't see who it is, but I immediately recognize the smell of marijuana and know it's Barb. We'd split the total haul of joints between us, and she had her own little baggie.

"What are you doing?" I whisper.

"Getting high," she says, and I watch as she inhales deeply on a joint. When she pulls it away from her mouth, she reaches her hand up to offer it to me. I take it and sit down on the steps next to her before I take a hit.

When I hand it back to her, I ask, "Connor okay?"

"Yeah," she mutters softly. "He was fucking whipped

after today. Fell right asleep."

I would imagine so. He jumped off a mountain and rode a raft down a foaming and frothing Snake River, his cries of joy echoing out as the raft dipped and plunged through the rapids. Jillian came on that adventure with us, and while it wasn't as thrilling as jumping off a mountain, it was better because she was sitting next to me.

We smoke the rest of her joint in silence, but I light one of mine up next and we continue to share. The air is crisp and as the drug swims through my system, I start to mellow out and forget about my dream.

"Did you think Connor looked okay today?" I ask, knowing he is the safest subject to talk about. I'd learned today that she has a soft spot for the kid.

"You noticed it too?" she counters.

"He looks paler, right?"

"I noticed," she agrees. "And he was sweating a lot on the ride back here this evening. I asked him if he was feeling okay and he said he was, but I don't know. I noticed he took some Tylenol when he got out of the shower tonight."

"Today was exhausting," I theorize. "Maybe it was just a little too much for him."

"Maybe," is all she says, and we once again lapse into silence.

When we finish the joint, I expect Barb to go back inside, because she's not a social creature. I'm not normally either, but I'm finding myself with a lot of patience for my newfound friends as well as curiosities, particularly about Barb since she's the most reserved of us. But she just sits there, staring out into the dark beside me.

Since I'm floating on a good buzz, I tell her, "I'm going to ask you something really personal."

"Go for it," she says, challenge in her tone. "Doesn't mean I'll answer."

"You've tried to kill yourself since that first time in your parents' kitchen," I surmise. It's not really a question, but more of a statement. I've seen the additional scars on her wrists.

Her head turns slowly to me, but there's enough glow from a nearly full moon that I see the surprise on her face. I'm equally surprised when she chooses to answer me. "Three more times. Two more attempts on my wrist. The third time I tried to OD."

"How come you didn't succeed?" I ask curiously. I mean… I know why I didn't succeed when I'd held a gun to my temple. Ultimately, I didn't have the fucking balls to do it. But I'm curious if all suicidal thoughts are the same.

She shrugs and turns her face away from me. "I guess I'm not really dedicated to the mission."

"You want to live more than you want to die?"

"I don't know if that's it," she says carefully. "I actually think more about dying than I do about living."

"Why?" I press her.

She turns back to me, crossing her arms and resting them on her thighs as she huddles against the cool air. "Let me ask you something... what did you see when we were paragliding today?"

"What do you mean?" I ask in confusion.

"What did you see?" she repeats. "Describe the scenery."

My mind filters back through those few minutes of soaring among the mountains and the clouds. "Green valley with darker green trees dotting it. Mountains that looked silvery-green with white peaks. The sky had a cloudy haze to it, but there were pockets of clear blue."

She nods and says, "Green, silver, white, blue."

"Huh?"

"You used colors to describe what you saw," she says quietly. "Want to know what I saw?"

"What?"

"Gray," she says. "Dark gray, light gray, medium gray. Nothing but gray."

Fuck, that's depressing, but I guess maybe that's what depression looks like if described in colors. I've personally never seen the world like that. I know I've been depressed, but I've also come to learn that our problems are all apples and oranges. Our issues are varied and the ways our minds process them are unique.

"Do you ever see color?" I ask her, needing to hear her say something hopeful. Because Jillian taught me the value of hope, and I don't really want Barb reminding me that it's possible to live a life without good possibilities.

Barb pushes up from the steps and turns to face me. She shoves her hands down into her jeans pockets. "Yes, I see color sometimes. Not often, but it seems to come at odd moments, like when I'm at my lowest. At the times when I feel so utterly hopeless that I know death is the only cure for my problems. It's tempting, Christopher. When it's gray and dark, it's oh-so-fucking tempting to end it."

"Maybe you need to find ways to get more color in your life," I suggest, which is my way of saying she needs counseling or medication or both to help her heal. I know this trip alone won't do anything for her… urine-soaked gravesites notwithstanding.

Barb gives a sharp laugh and leans toward me. In a soft voice, she says, "I actually envy you sometimes."

This takes me aback. How could someone look at me and be jealous?

"I envy your ability to come on this trip, look past all the darkness, and learn how to laugh. I watch you laugh with Jillian and Connor, and I'm envious of all three of you. What you three have is genuine. It's real."

"I've seen you laugh," I point out, desperate for her to realize she's got some normality going. Needing her to see that she has friends now. I need her to see it; otherwise, I might not believe it's real.

But she doesn't answer me, just moves past me up the steps with a curt, "I'm tired. See you in the morning."

I'm left sitting out there to wonder... did Barb refuse to answer me because she knew I'd be crushed to learn that her laughs are actually joyless acts to make people think she's going to be okay? Or did she refuse to answer me because it would crush her to admit that she can't be helped?

Chapter 29

I T'S BEEN A hard day of driving, especially having just battled Portland rush-hour traffic to make it to the western side of the city on our journey to Cannon Beach. Even with the hour gained because of the time-zone change, it's close to nine PM when we make it to the campground because we had to stop at a grocery store to get some food and drink.

When we pile out of the Suburban, Connor immediately heads toward the bathroom. He's not having a good day, and we're all worried about him.

This morning, he came out of the room he shared with Barb looking even paler than before with dark circles under his eyes. Jillian immediately played "mom" and felt his forehead, declaring him to be hot to the touch. This prompted a stop to a drug store on the way out of Ashton to buy a thermometer, but it showed his temperature was very low grade at 99.1.

Connor insisted he must have a bug, but given his only symptoms were being pale and running a low fever, along with the fact he said he felt a bit tired, I was doubting that. Regardless, he shunned off our concerns, including a surprise suggestion by Barb that we stop at an urgent care to get him checked out. Instead, he directed us to haul ass to Cannon Beach and he slept most of the time, curled up in the corner of the backseat, covered with Barb's leather jacket she'd draped over him. We made stops only to gas up, use the restroom, and grab food to eat in the car. Each time, Barb gently shook him awake, and he was all smiles for us. He'd go to the bathroom, eat a little bit of food, and then go back to sleep. Jillian must have felt his forehead a million times. I know she was worried, but she didn't say a thing. Barb was worried too. She shared a few concerned looks in the rearview mirror with me when I'd periodically look back there to check on Connor.

Jillian meets me at the back of the Suburban, followed by Barb. With Connor well out of earshot, she tells me, "I'm going to sleep in the big tent with Connor tonight."

This doesn't surprise me at all, as Jillian is a hoverer.

What does surprise me is Barb saying, "If you want... I'll sleep in there with him. That way you and Christopher can have privacy."

Jillian narrows her eyes at Barb and snaps, "I don't need privacy with Christopher. I want to make sure Connor is okay."

Barb narrows her eyes right back at Jillian and leans into her. "I want to make sure Connor's okay too. You're not the only one who cares about him."

I really wish Connor were here to see this. Two women fighting over him. I bet it's a bucket-list item.

"I have an idea," I say smoothly as I pull the large tent out of the back. "Why don't we all sleep in this behemoth thing? It could fit ten people. That way we can all be assured Connor is okay throughout the night."

Jillian blinks at me, and Barb's shoulders relax as she says, "Good plan."

I turn to look at Jillian. "Cool with you?"

She doesn't say anything for a moment, but then she smiles at me. "Yeah… that's cool. Big ol' slumber party."

"I'm not painting anyone's toenails," I tell her seriously.

Barb snorts and pulls her pack out of the back of the SUV. Jillian giggles.

I smile to myself, hauling the tent to a good spot and dropping it there. As I unzip the bag to remove everything, Jillian squats down beside me. "You think Connor's okay?"

"I don't know," I tell her honestly. "I have no clue what it means to die from cancer. I don't know if his symptoms are a sign of that or if he's got a freaking cold. But he says he's fine. That's really all we can go on."

"Maybe I should call his mom," Jillian frets.

"Maybe you should let me be an adult," Connor says from behind her.

She stands up and turns to face him. I know she

283

wants to retort with "but you're not an adult," but she wisely holds her tongue. She knows damn good and well that Connor, at the least, should be treated like an adult if for nothing more than the grace with which he's handled his diagnosis.

"I'm just worried about you," Jillian says apologetically. Barb walks up behind Connor, but she doesn't say a word.

"I get that," Connor says, but his voice is firmly nonnegotiable. "But I cannot have you treating me like a baby. It makes me feel bad about myself, and I pride myself on my strength. It's what's gotten me through so far."

Barb steps around to Connor's side, and he turns to look at her. She puts a hand on his shoulder and says, "I don't think Jillian quite knows how to alleviate her fears with you, and I think that's because we don't understand what the fuck is wrong with you. We only know you're going to die from cancer. So maybe if you told us what is going to happen to you, and when, maybe she'll settle down."

I read her entire little speech to mean, *I'm wigged out too but I'm too tough to say that, so I'll put this all on Jillian being a silly worrier.*

I'm glad she said it though, because I've found fear of the unknown is one of the worst kinds of fears, and as of this moment, none of us know if Connor will drop dead on us. I mean... I doubt it. He's mentioned he probably has months, but still... I think he needs to share the details with us so we can all relax.

"What do you want to know?" Connor asks Jillian, completely buying Barb's cock-and-bull story that Jillian is the worrier. He doesn't notice as Barb sidles a bit closer to him so she doesn't miss a thing he might say.

Jillian's eyes cut to Barb. I see a flash of annoyance before they come back to Connor. "Fever... being tired... pale... in my mind, that makes me think it's the cancer doing this to you."

"Don't forget about the diarrhea I've had all day," Connor says with a grimace. "It could simply be food poisoning from those breakfast burritos we ate this morning."

"What's your prognosis?" I ask Connor, cutting to the chase.

"You mean—when will I die?" Connor asks me, and I can tell he's getting angry. For a kid who has been completely open, he's bowing his back up big time now that we're pressing for more details. I'm smart enough to understand that he doesn't like us worrying, and that's what's pissing him off.

"When... how..." I say with a shrug. "You know... details."

"You're a morbid son of a bitch," Connor mutters, but he casually pushes his hands down into his pockets and looks around at us. Finally, he says, "My original diagnosis was stage four alveolar rhabdomyosarcoma.

That was when I was fifteen after I noticed a lump in my hand. They cut it out, did a CT scan and PET scan, and found that it had metastasized into some of my lymph nodes. I was started on aggressive chemotherapy and some radiation. The lymph nodes shrunk, and I was hesitantly placed into remission. But then four months ago, on a follow-up PET scan, it was found that the cancer had spread to my liver and lungs. They tried more chemo but it had no effect, so they stopped all forms of treatment."

I imagined what Connor felt like when the doctor told him he was terminal. That there was no hope. That his life would be over soon.

Was it the same feeling I had when I first regained consciousness and understood I'd lost part of my hand and might lose my leg? Or maybe when they told me they couldn't save my leg, and I knew I was going to permanently lose a major part of myself?

I search back, trying to recall exactly how bad I felt upon hearing those words, but for the life of me, I can't recall it. I don't know if I was shocked or angry. Sullen or withdrawn. Bitter or accepting. I don't remember anything about how I felt in those moments when such terrible news was dropped in my lap. Yet, I can't really imagine it was anything like what Connor probably felt.

All those weeks in group therapy when I was so angry for being there, refusing to believe that these people's problems could outweigh my own, seem trite now. I realize now that out of all of us, Connor has the shittiest rap. He's a young, vibrant, smart, and funny kid. He's someone who deserves to live.

I feel the heavy weight of despondency press down upon me—purely for Connor's benefit—and I have to admit to myself—to the very selfish asshole these people first came to know—that I have no clue what real hopelessness is like. I'm ashamed I never gave that kid credit for his trials until now.

Barb clears her throat and asks, "And I assume that the cancer will continue to spread and that's what makes you terminal?"

Connor nods. "It will keep growing. My liver won't be able to clean out toxins, my lungs will be impaired. Cancer can affect appetite and nutrition. Eventually, my body will just shut down on me."

Jillian gives a small cry, and I turn to see tears streaming down her face. I immediately reach out and pull her to me, and she buries her face in my chest. She takes in a ragged breath and lifts her face to look back at Connor. "Will you be in pain?"

It happens so fast that I'm not sure anyone caught it, but I saw the flash of deception in his eyes. He gives Jillian a smile and shakes his head. "No way. It will come on fast, and pain meds will control everything."

Total damn lie.

"How soon will all this happen?" Barb asks, and I'm taken aback by the desolation I see in her eyes. She really has become fond of Connor. From what little I can tell, he may be the only person in the world she cares for.

After taking in a deep breath, Connor lets it out in exaggerated fashion through a forced smile and says, "Well, I'm positive it won't be tonight or for many nights. I can assure you that I'm fine."

"How long?" Barb presses him, and Connor's smile slides.

"Probably a few months," he admits in a soft voice, and Jillian's face goes back into the middle of my chest where I can feel her tears soaking through the cotton of my t-shirt.

Barb suddenly turns from our group and mutters, "I'm going to go take a shower."

But she doesn't turn fast enough that I miss the light film of moisture covering her eyes. Asshole Christopher would have called her out on it, but newly reformed and smitten Christopher lets her go with without a harsh word.

Absolutely no harsh words for any of them for showing a weakness such as sorrow or empathy, because fuck if I don't feel like I want to cry myself right now.

Chapter 30

"**I**S IT TOO weird to ask if you'll come over and meet my parents after we get back?" Jillian asks as we walk north up the beach back to where we left Barb and Connor.

Her right hand is in my whole left hand. While I'm not ashamed to hold her with the half hand, I can feel every detail of her skin against mine this way. I give a slight squeeze that in no way lets her know the enormous impact her request makes upon me. Jillian and I haven't talked about what will happen when we get back to Raleigh. I think we've both been under the assumption that we'd continue to see each other, but I'll be the first to admit that I had some doubts.

How could I not after having had so many loved ones turn their backs on me?

"Think they'll totally blame me for inducing you to run off behind their backs?" I ask her.

"No, they completely blame me for that," she says with a laugh.

"Then count me in," I tell her as we walk along the

shoreline. It's getting very close to sunset, and we want to get back to share that with Connor.

We'd been on Cannon Beach almost all day. After a quick breakfast of Pop-Tarts and orange juice at our campsite, we'd donned bathing suits covered with layers since the morning was chilly. As the day heated, the layers came off, but only Connor ventured into the chilly water. He seemed fine this morning, although he said his stomach still hurt a little, but at least Jillian and Barb didn't hover over him.

We pitched our blankets and hunkered down on the beach about a hundred yards from Haystack Rock with a cooler full of food, sodas, and beer. We people watched, played Frisbee, went for walks, and poked around in tidal pools. We napped after lunch, and then Connor had braved the cold water for a bit. I made out with Jillian when Connor and Barb went for a walk down the beach, and then we napped some more in the afternoon. Dinner was sandwiches of bologna and cheese along with potato chips right out of the bag. Barb and I drank a few beers while Jillian and Connor drank bottled water.

It was a great day.

Connor got to see the Pacific Ocean. Very soon, he's going to watch the sun sink into that same ocean.

The beach starts to get heavy with people coming out to see the sunset. Jillian and I plop down on our blankets next to Barb and Connor, the four of us sitting in a row facing the horizon. I'm worn out and beat from spending all day on a windy beach, but I also feel loose and relaxed as we take a moment to appreciate nature's beauty with our hands held up over our eyes to shield us from the brightness.

We watch in silence as the swollen, golden sun starts to drop lower and lower in the sky, until it's just hovering right over the edge of the world. It turns the blue waters orange with pink-tinged waves, and it starts to dull a little the lower it falls, allowing us to drop our hands from over our brows.

"There's not anyone in the world I'd want to see this with other than the three of you," Connor says softly, but his words carry true over the waves and wind to hit our ears. All three of us turn our heads to the right to look at him. He knows we're staring at him, so he turns to level us with an impish grin. "What? Can't I get sentimental?"

None of us say anything, and I can't speak for Jillian and Barb, but I've got a fucking lump in my throat so I can't say anything. Connor grins bigger, knowing he just punched us all in the feels, and turns his head to look back at the approaching sunset. I can feel Jillian turn her head back from my left, but I watch as Barb just stares at Connor for a long moment. Then she slowly raises her arm and drapes it around his shoulders. Leaning over, she places her head on his shoulder and mutters, "You're okay, kid."

Connor brings his hand across his chest and pats

Barb on top of the head. "I know."

Jillian scoots closer to me. I wrap my arm around her in turn, pulling her tight. Looking down at her, I see her face is happy and sad all at once from the poignant moment we're sharing right now. It's the culmination of our journey, the end to what we started. While we all agreed to keep going on this trip, this is really what we came for. The big bucket-list item that Connor wanted to knock off.

The bottom of the sun seems to rest for just a moment on the horizon. While it feels like it's taken forever for it to get to this moment, now it starts to sink swiftly from our view. The waters turn darker until the orange and pink bleed together and turn red. The skyline above the sun is still light blue but tinged with dark purple as the night starts to come.

Within just a few minutes, the sun seemingly drops off the face of the earth until it's completely gone from our sight and nothing's left but a slight golden glow along the horizon.

I can't help but compare this to a boy named Connor, who will one day soon fade away from this world, but because he's become so influential to our group, I'm sure his glow will remain behind within us. I smile internally at myself over the fucked-up, mushy stuff I'm feeling right now, but it's like when Jillian opened the doors on my emotions, they started to run rampant.

Eventually, the sky darkens completely, turning from

purple to black, and it's one of those amazing nights when the stars seem to hang so low you can reach out and touch them. I pull Jillian with me as I lay down on the blanket and look up at them. Barb and Connor also lay back, and we silently stare up at the night sky.

Lost in thoughts about life and death and the frailty of it all.

"Timon," Connor says in a raspy, nasally voice. "Ever wonder what those sparkly dots are up there?"

I have no clue what the fuck he's talking about, so I raise my head a little to look over at him. He's just lying on his back, hands tucked behind his head with a silent grin on his face. I see Barb grinning too.

"Pumbaa… I don't wonder, I know," Jillian says in what sounds like a Brooklyn wise-guy accent. "They're um… fireflies… that got stuck up in that big, bluish-black thing."

Huh?

Barb snickers and Connor snorts, but he replies, "Oh, I always thought they were balls of gas burning billions of miles away."

"Pumbaa, with you, everything's gas," Jillian says in the same accent.

Connor, using his regular voice, adds, "That was totally true with those stomach issues I was having yesterday."

Jillian's entire body jerks up as she starts to laugh, and Connor joins in. I look at Barb and she's laughing too, but more silently than the other two.

"What the hell are you guys talking about?" I ask in confusion, and that makes Jillian laugh harder until she rolls on her side and brings her knees to her chest.

Connor is laughing so hard that he farts, proving his stomach isn't quite settled down yet, and Barb laughs even louder.

"What?" I ask in frustration.

Barb sits up and tilts her head to look down at me. "It's like only a famous quote from one of the best movies ever."

"Can't be that famous," I retort.

Jillian sits up, pulling on my hand so I sit up too. "It's from *The Lion King*. You've never seen that movie?"

"Nope," I tell her, but I readily admit. "I've heard of it, obviously."

"How can you have not seen that movie?" Connor asks as he joins the rest of us in sitting up. "I thought every living being on the earth had seen that movie."

"Sorry, buddy," I say, disabusing him of that notion. "I didn't grow up in a household where Disney movies were a normal occurrence."

"That sucks ass," Connor says. "When we get back, we're going to have movie night at my house. We have a home theater and a real movie popcorn maker. It will be awesome."

"I'm in," Jillian says with a laugh as she settles in close to me again, winding her arm through mine.

"That means Christopher's in," Connor says with delight. He gives Barb a playful push on her shoulder. "You up for a *Lion King* movie extravaganza?"

Barb shakes her head and grimaces. "Sorry, kid, but do I look like someone who would watch a Disney movie?"

"Well, you clearly did at some point in your life because you recognized the line from the movie," Connor retorts.

"So I saw it when I was kid," Barb says with a smirk. "That was back when I still believed in Santa and thought the boogeyman was just a made-up thing."

I think Barb is teasing Connor, because her tone is light and she's got a mischievous look on her face, and trust me... that's a look that's so at odds with her nature that it stands out. But her words point out a scary truth about Barb. She was a young girl that had her innocence brutally destroyed. She went from Disney to Steven King in a nanosecond.

I glance at Connor, seeing he's horrified by what she said, and more importantly, at how he made her go there with his own teasing about Disney.

"Barb," he croaks, his voice heavily laden with guilt. "I didn't mean—"

"Relax, kiddo," Barb says as she pats him on his knee a few times. "But while I appreciate the offer, sitting around watching Disney movies just isn't my thing, you know?"

Connor nods, but I can see he's uncertain as to whether he's offended Barb or flayed open some raw wounds.

Barb pushes off the blanket, stands, and brushes a bit of sand from her pants. "I'm going to head back to the campground."

"I'll come with—" Connor says as he starts to stand up, but she holds a palm out to stop him.

"No offense," she says in a clipped voice even though she graces us with a small smile. "But I'm all kumbayah'ed out. Need some alone time."

She turns and marches across the sand toward the main road that runs parallel to the beach. Our campground is on the other side, about a quarter mile north of where we are now.

Connor slouches back down and lets out a sigh.

"Hey, don't worry about her," I tell him good-naturedly. "Remember, she's more bitch than human. She'll come around though."

Connor tries to put on a brave face, but Jillian manages to knock it right back off again. "No, she won't."

"Pardon?" I ask as I turn to look at her.

"She won't come around," Jillian says in a sad voice. "It's too much for her."

"What do you mean?" Connor asks with some trepidation.

"She cares for you," Jillian tells him pointedly. "But she's fragile. She can't continue to build a friendship with you knowing you're going to die. She doesn't have it in her."

Connor's head snaps toward the western part of the beach where Barb had headed. "But... she's the toughest one out of all of us."

"No, she's really not," I say, agreeing with Jillian's assessment.

While Jillian and I are down with movie nights at the McCann household so we can spend time with Connor before he dies, Barb isn't going to get on board with that. She's protecting herself because she doesn't want the pain that his death will cause her. I guarantee when we get back to Raleigh, Barb will be in the wind. We'll never see her again.

Chapter 31

MY EYES POP open, and I'm instantly alert and awake. I've always been an early riser and that was only reinforced into me when I was in the Marine Corps. The pressure on my bladder spurs me into action, and I extricate myself from my sleeping bag and get my prosthetic on. In the pre-dawn light, I see Jillian and Connor are dead asleep in their respective sleeping bags. We'd stayed up late last night on the beach, gazing at stars and talking.

It was that easy type of conversation you have with friends who know all your weaknesses and forgives you for them without a second thought. I've never had friends like Jillian and Connor before. Soon, it will only be Jillian.

Outside of the tent, the cool air causes me to shiver and I rub my arms briskly. It had dropped down into the fifties last night, but our sleeping bags kept us nice and toasty. I'm not sure how Barb fared in the SUV as she only has a blanket in there, but she seemed fine when we walked into the campsite last night. She was on her side with the blanket pulled up to her chin, fast asleep, when I'd peered in the window last night.

After walking to the community bathrooms, I take a long piss, my bladder sighing with contentment as it empties. I growl at myself for not grabbing my toiletry kit as I could have knocked out a thorough scrubbing of my teeth at least. I run my tongue over them, thinking they feel vaguely furry. Still, even a morning-breath kiss with Jillian is better than any other kiss. I smile at myself in the mirror and head out of the restrooms.

I think I'll go ahead and get everyone up so we can get an early start to the day. We're going to head straight to San Francisco. Last night as we sat on the beach, we'd thrown about the possibility of staying a day in Portland, but ultimately decided against it because seeing the San Diego Zoo is high on our agendas. Given the fact that Connor's parents are anxious to have him back, we decided to hit San Francisco for a day and then head to San Diego for a day at the zoo. From there, Connor decided Vegas needed to be on his bucket list, and Jillian and I laughingly agreed to it.

So Portland was out and Vegas was in, then we'd head home.

Now we have to inform Barb of our plans and hope to God she's on board with it. I think she will be. As much as she made clear that she needs to distance herself from Connor when we get back home, I know deep down she isn't going to begrudge him this trip. She might put on a cold, hard outward appearance to keep people at arm's length, but I know Connor has wormed his way into her heart, just as he has mine.

Little fucker. He's going to cause me a world of hurt when it's all said and done, but I've accepted that burden.

I approach the SUV, deciding to go ahead and get Barb up. She's the crankiest and slowest in the morning. When I open the back door, I'm surprised to find it empty with the blanket that had been covering her last night tossed to the floorboard.

Looking around the campsite, I don't see her, but I suppose it's possible she got up and went to the bathroom while I was in there doing my thing.

Shrugging, I shut the door and walk back to the tent. Opening the flap, I call out to Jillian and Connor. "Okay lazy butts, get up. We need to hit the road."

Jillian's head pops up, her eyes heavy with sleep as she tries to focus in on me. "What time is it?"

"About 6:30," I tell her, having looked at my watch just a bit ago.

She nods, yawns, and then nudges Connor in the sleeping bag beside her. "Time to get up, Connor."

He groans, burrows down deeper into his sleeping bag, and mumbles, "Five more minutes, Mom."

"Get up now," I say in an authoritarian voice. To my surprise, Connor's head pops up. He looks at me with wide eyes, and I grin back at him. "Come on... I'm starving. I want pancakes."

Jillian shakes her head with a smile, completely enjoying the new and improved Christopher Barlow, and I must say, I'm enjoying her enjoying me. With a smile at her, I back out of the tent and wait for them to emerge. When she does moments later, Jillian gives me a kiss on the corner of my mouth and a breathy, "Morning, handsome," before she and Connor walk off toward the restrooms.

Yes, pride swells through me that she called me "handsome," and I hope I never get used to this feeling of euphoria that she produces inside of me. I don't know why I trust it so much, but I do and I'm running with it. Now that I've committed to seeing where Jillian can take me, and I've opened to the possibility that I can have an amazing life just as I am, I'm riding this bitch as far as it will take me, even if at the end, more hurt is waiting. I have to take this chance.

I pull the sleeping bags out of the tent and efficiently roll them up. I'm about halfway done dismantling the tent when Jillian and Connor come strolling back into camp.

"Hey, did you tell Barb we're heading out and going to get pancakes?" I ask Jillian.

She frowns at me. "She wasn't in the bathroom."

"Huh," I say with confusion, wondering where in the hell she is. I drop the poles in my hand that I'd just pulled free from their trappings and walk back over to the Suburban. Opening the passenger door again, I look for her backpack. I see nothing but the blanket and her pillow, so I check the rear of the SUV. No backpack.

"What's wrong?" Connor asks as I swing the tailgate shut.

"Barb's gone," I say as I scratch my head. I turn back to Jillian. "Are you sure she wasn't in the bathrooms?"

Jillian's brows furrow as she shakes her head. "I'll go check again."

"I'll go check the beach," Connor says helpfully with a confident smile. "I bet she's just on the beach."

"Yeah, you're probably right," I agree, shaking off the feeling of unrest within me.

He takes off trotting down the small trail that cuts through to the beach, and I make my way back to the tent to finish packing it up. My eyes sweep around the campground and the unsettled feeling increases, causing the hair at the back of my neck to stand on edge.

There's the thick row of trees bordering one side with the opening to the trail that Connor just took to the beach. A double row of campsites, almost all of them filled with tents, but there's no people milling around because it's so early. A gravel drive for vehicles, then the community buildings, and then a small field with waist-high brown grass. There's a large shade tree with huge branches that stretch out like arms with a tire swing. I hadn't seen it last night when we pulled in, but I imagine plenty of kids in the campground have played on that tire. My eyes move past the tree, finishing their three-hundred-and-sixty-degree perusal as they reach the forest edge, but something stops me.

My gaze swings back to the tree, and I peer harder. The eastern sun is coming up on the other side, and it's bathed the meadow and the tree in golden light. On the side opposite the tire swing, I see something near the base of the tree. It looks like Barb's backpack.

I start walking that way, tilting my head to the side as I get closer, not knowing what I'll find. Her backpack comes fully into view, followed by a pair of jean-clad legs stretched out with her recognizable combat boots on the end. My lips curve into a smile, knowing I've found her and that she's probably getting high before we hit the road.

I sneak up, still only able to see her backpack and legs, but it's clear she's sitting with her back up against the tree trunk. With a slight hop around the side of the tree, I yell, "Caught ya," as I come to a rest beside her, hoping to scare the shit out of her. I even start laughing, knowing she'll cuss me out big time.

Instead, she doesn't move.

Her hands rest on her lap with her fingers curled slightly inward, and her head is lolling on her shoulder. I walk around further, looking at her slack face with her eyes closed and her lips slightly parted.

"Barb," I say hesitantly, nudging the tip of her boot with my shoe.

She doesn't move, and I'm thinking she must be trashed.

"Barb," I say a bit louder as I squat down in front of her.

Still nothing, and that's when it hits me... her chest isn't moving.

"Barb," I yell at her as my hand shoots out to palm her face. Even through my roughened, scarred skin, I can feel how cold she is and I jerk my hand back involuntarily.

"Barb," I whisper, bringing my hand back to her and placing my index and ring finger against her carotid.

I get nothing but icy skin and utter stillness.

My entire body goes numb and my good leg turns to jelly. I collapse backward on my ass, and I just stare at Barb in disbelief. I look around, but I don't see anyone. I swivel my head and look at the area around Barb, and that's when I see it.

An empty baggy next to her.

I have no clue what was in it, but whatever it was, it was lethal. It's empty, and now Barb is no more.

My guts twist, feeling like a wet dishrag being violently wrung out, and nausea overwhelms me. I take in a deep breath through my nose and exhale it through my mouth, willing the bile to stay down. Moisture leaks from my eyes, and I hastily rub the back of my hand over them.

"Goddamn you, Barb," I whisper hatefully toward

her. "Goddamn you for this."

Goddamn her for being so complex and broken and yet completely real to me. Fuck her for being just like me. In this moment where her truest weakness is exposed, it shines a light as bright as the sun on my own weaknesses. Fuck her to hell for that peaceful look on her face that says she's escaped this hard world and left us behind. And fuck it all as I wonder what we could have done to prevent this.

And mostly screw her goddamned tortured soul all the way to hell because while Jillian's actions alone have given me unfettered hope, I'd given part of the credit for my transformation to Barb—the woman who pissed on graves and defaced headstones—thinking that she truly was the strongest out of all of us. She was the one who raced to rescue Connor from a furious homeowner whose house we egged. And she was the one who, oh so sweetly and with great care, gave Connor a very special experience before he died. She was strong for a whole host of reasons that she probably never even recognized, but mainly because she had many times chosen to live when she wanted to die. She'd faced suicide down before and walked away from it. That should have been her destiny.

To live.

If I had miscalculated Barb and her ability to pull herself back from the edge of darkness so poorly, what else am I wrong about?

I think back to when I questioned Jillian about her strength and courage while facing impending blindness and how she gave me the hard truth about sunshine. She said she wouldn't miss it when she could no longer see it, because it wasn't going anywhere. It would always be there for her to feel in other ways. The only thing that would change was her ability to perceive it in a certain way and she said she'd accommodate that.

She made it sound so easy.

She made that optimism seem attainable to me, and I jumped at it like a starving man handed a ribeye steak.

I bought it hook, line, and sinker, and I was gullible enough to think that Barb would be able to understand that hard truth about sunshine too. I thought with enough support, her gray world would brighten and she'd find her way out of the darkness the way I was.

But she hadn't, even though she was so strong, and now I have to question my own strength and whether I can actually accept the truth about sunshine.

Chapter 32

I STEP OUT onto the hotel balcony and shut the door behind me. Digging in my pocket, I grab onto the pack of cigarettes and my lighter. I don't give a second thought about pulling one out and lighting it. It's not my first since I found Barb, and it won't be my last. Since smoking a joint, drinking a fifth of liquor, or popping some pills isn't an option, this is the only thing keeping me semi-sane. At the very least, my hands don't shake as much while I'm smoking.

Taking a deep drag, I pull the smoke down into my lungs, hold it for just a moment, then let it out on a forceful sigh. Resting my arms on the balcony railing, I drop my head down and stare at the street five floors below us. Would I die if I jumped from here?

Probably not. My body would just be mangled, and I've already been there and done that.

Besides, I couldn't do that to Jillian and Connor. Not after what they've gone through today.

They are in the hotel room. Jillian's dead asleep, exhausted from the myriad of emotions that she's been having. Obviously, she was distraught and cried hard for almost an hour. I was afraid she wouldn't be able to stop. But then she squared her shoulders and became the one to comfort because she knew that Connor was taking Barb's death really hard. She spent most of the day blowing sunshine up his ass about "God's plan" and "circumstances beyond our control." I know it was mentally draining for her to keep up that façade, and she's been sleeping hard for a few hours. Connor is just sitting on the other bed, his back up against the headboard. When I came out onto the balcony, I left him staring at the wall.

When my fingers touched Barb's cold skin and I knew she was dead, something inside me shifted. I felt like I was dangling from a precipice. I was so angry with her—still am for that matter—and I knew it wouldn't take much more for me to let go and fall from that cliff. I could fall right back into misery and self-loathing, because Barb's suicide gave me tacit permission to continue to feel crappy about my life because she damaged the hope I'd been building up.

But then Jillian came walking down the gravel drive from the bathrooms, and I knew I had something more important to do than to give in to the darkness. I had people I needed to protect other than myself.

I'd scrambled up from the ground, wiped my eyes again, and hurried over to Jillian before she got too close to the tree. She took one look at my face, and she knew.

She just fucking knew.

Her face crumbled as tears started streaming down her face. She shook her head forcefully in denial. "She didn't. Please tell me she didn't."

"I'm sorry," I said gruffly as I jerked her into my arms and held her tight against me. Jillian let it all go, immediately pouring out her sorrow and despair in racking sobs that carried throughout the campground. Some people came out of their tents and looked at us with worry, yet I did nothing to try to calm her down. She needed to get it out. The more she cried in my arms, the stronger my backbone felt.

Good thing too, because Connor appeared from the trailhead and he immediately locked eyes on us. And even though he was a good fifty yards away, I could see on his face that he knew too.

In hindsight, it was no surprise to us.

It made me realize how foolish I'd been to think that just because Jillian managed to point out a different, more optimistic view of the world, it didn't mean everyone would subscribe to it. I'd also been foolish to underestimate the depth of Barb's despair, and I feel guilty that perhaps I didn't do enough to help pull her back. That fucking conversation I'd had with her about suicide replays, and I can't believe I didn't do anything to help her.

Connor's gaze had swept around the campground, and he spotted Barb's backpack with an eagle eye. He

took off running for it—for her—and I had to let go of
Jillian to intercept him. But the little fucker was fast.
Faster than me on a prosthetic leg, and he breezed by me,
coming to a skidding halt by the tree.

"Connor... don't," I called out to him.

He ignored me and knelt on the ground beside
Barb's body. He just stared at her blankly.

Jillian brushed past me and I lunged to grab her
hand, missing it totally. She ran to Connor and knelt
beside him, her arm coming protectively around his
shoulders. Her sobs continued, and I'd never felt more
helpless in my life.

Not even when the pain was so unbearable that I
wanted to rip my own leg off.

By this time, the people who had come out of their
tents started to realize something was wrong, a few
moving closer to get a look at what Connor and Jillian
were looking at on the other side of the big tree. While I
very much wanted to go pull them away, I knew I had
other things to do.

So I pulled my phone out of my pocket and dialed
911.

Taking another drag off my cigarette, I look out over
downtown Portland as the sun starts to set. I glance
down at my watch, noting that Connor's parents should
be here in a few hours. They were able to get a flight out
of Raleigh today.

Immediately after I called 911, I called Connor's dad

and quietly told him what happened. I asked him to please come to Portland, because I just didn't know what to do or how to handle things with his son. I also didn't know how to handle anything with Jillian either, but figured I could take some cues from the McCanns. His father didn't hesitate and jumped into action.

After that, I'd called Mags, who for the first time since I've known her was stunned speechless. But she recovered and went into counselor mode. I let her do this because she needed to, and I promised I'd have Jillian and Connor call her later.

While I dealt with the police and the rescue workers who didn't even bother trying to resuscitate Barb, and finally the coroner, Connor and Jillian sat in the Suburban. I know Connor talked to his parents, and Jillian talked to hers. I had no fucking clue what was going to happen, but I was grateful that Mr. McCann got us into a Portland hotel and told us to wait for them there.

So that's what we're doing. I'm smoking, Jillian's comatose, and Connor is staring blankly at a wall.

Fun times.

I finish my cigarette and because I don't want to go back inside the room, I light another.

I smoke that down, and then I light another.

I smoke that down, but this time, I find my pack empty.

With a sigh, I turn and open the sliding door, quietly

slipping into the room through the heavy blackout curtains. Jillian is still asleep on one bed, and Connor is still staring at the wall from the other. The room is dark, gloomy, and depressing as fuck.

"I'm going to go get some smokes," I say in a low voice to Connor as I grab my wallet and keys off the small desk in the corner.

He doesn't respond, and I'll admit I'm a bit worried about him. He hasn't said much since this morning.

Regardless, I head for the door because I need some fucking cigarettes. I'm sure they'll be fine without me for a few minutes.

But just as I put my hand on the door to open it, Connor's voice reaches out to me from the depressing gloom where he's sitting. "Why do you think she did it? Why now?"

My shoulders sag as I let out a sigh. I'd like to ignore this hard-as-fuck question, but I know I can't. He needs answers, even if mine are wrong.

Turning around, I walk over to his bed and sit down on the end to face him, cocking my left leg up on the bed and stretching my C-leg to plant on the floor. His eyes are red but currently dry. He's been crying in spells, and it hits me hard… this is the first time I've really seen this dude shaken up. For living under a death sentence, he's been so stoic about everything that I sometimes forget he's probably still just a frightened boy.

"Did we do this?" he asks. "Did I do this?"

I shake my head, place a palm on the mattress, and lean closer to him. "No, Connor. She did it all herself. It had nothing to do with you, Jillian, or me."

"How do you know that?" he asks... no, he *pleads* almost, sounding as if he's asking me to take away whatever this guilt is he's feeling.

"Because I've had my share of mental health professionals poking around in my head," I tell him honestly. "Because I've had those thoughts run through my head, and it's difficult to ask for help with it."

"I thought she was happier," he mumbles as he looks down at his hands clenched in his lap. "She seemed like she was opening up and was having a good time with us."

"I know. I think she probably had some of her best days this last week. There are ups and downs with depression. Sometimes, it's not obvious a person is feeling bad because they can hide it."

"It makes no sense to me," he says with frustration. He lifts his face, and his eyes are blazing with fury. "I'm really pissed at her for doing this."

"Me too," I tell him. "And I think that's probably natural."

"It was a selfish move," Connor grits out, his hands bunching in anger.

"No, it wasn't," Jillian's voice rings out from the other bed. Connor and I turn to look at her. She's on her stomach, both arms crossed with her head resting on them, her face pointing our way. Her eyes are red and puffy. "Barb was trying to deal with her demons the best way she knew how. It wasn't the best way for us, but if she made the choice to go through with it, she thought it was the only way for her."

"I just wish we could have recognized some sign," Connor says. "Something that would have alerted us... gave us the chance to do something."

I want to tell him there was no sign—that her decision to do this was imminent.

No obvious signs anyway.

It's in this moment I have a new appreciation for Keith when I sneered at him for having "survivor's guilt." I know Connor's feeling it, and I've got a prickle of it making me uneasy.

I do think she was opening up, and that she was carefully watching the group come together as a unit. She had some fun times this week, and I think some of her wounds were cut open again. But mostly, I think she developed as close of a bond as someone like her could with Connor. Whether it was his youthful enthusiasm to want to do something as silly as egging houses, or the intimate moment she shared with him, Barb had let him in and she cared for him.

Last night... when Connor invited us to his house to watch movies... I think that's when she made her decision. I think Barb knew she would never survive Connor dying. That she didn't want to be around and watch him wither away. She didn't want to have her soul shredded from watching him suffer. I think last night, she chose to go out of this world on a high note, or as high of a note as someone like Barb can achieve in her dark world.

In my mind, she wanted her last memories to be of Connor watching the sunset over the Pacific, knowing he achieved his ultimate goal on this trip and that she was a part of that.

There is no way in hell, however, that I will ever tell Connor that. He'd take it personally, and it would overwhelm him with guilt. I'd much prefer him to think that Barb was being selfish so he doesn't have any more burdens on his plate.

"I'm sure we'll talk about this when we get back with Mags," I suggest. She's a professional. She'll be able to help him make more sense of it.

"But we don't have any more sessions with her," Connor points out. "She said she'd let us all out of them if we went on this trip."

"No," I correct with a smile. "She said she'd let *me* out if I went on this trip. But I think it would be good for us to get together with her when we get back. This is hard to process."

And I cannot even believe I'm actually volunteering for therapy. Man, the changes in my life in the last eight days are making my head spin.

Connor nods in understanding, dropping his gaze

briefly before raising it again. "I'm sorry I'm not driving back with you two."

I glance over at Jillian, seeing the tears well up in her eyes again. I think she's worried this is the beginning of the end for Connor. That maybe his soul has taken such a blow by what happened today that his body is going to feel the effects of it. When he talked to his dad earlier, he was so upset that all he wanted to do was go home and be with them. All three of them are flying to Raleigh tomorrow.

"Hey," I say as I turn back to him. "We had a blast. This trip was momentous. Who cares if we're cutting it short?"

Jillian nods in agreement, sucks in a breath, and adds in a cheery voice, "Yeah. You accomplished a lot on this trip, and we have so many more things we'll do together when we get back."

Jillian and I haven't even discussed it yet, but I assume we'll be heading straight back across the country. I know I'm personally not up for continuing with the trip. Without Barb and Connor, it's just not right, and I bet Jillian feels the same way.

"You promise?" Connor asks hesitantly, his eyes flicking back and forth between Jillian and me.

"Promise what?" she asks.

"That we'll do stuff together when you two get back?" His voice is small and afraid. I think he knows this is the beginning of the end too, and that he might suspect Barb took the easy way out to avoid watching him die. He probably thinks we won't tough it out with him either.

I grin at him to lighten the mood. "Fuck yes. First on the agenda is movie night at your house for *The Lion King*. Tell your dad to have lots of beer for us, okay?"

Connor's mouth curves into a smile as his gaze drops almost shyly before coming back up again. He turns to Jillian, but he's addressing both of us with a clear warning. "It's not going to be pleasant. Watching me die."

"And yet we'll watch you and be with you all the same," she promises him.

Swallowing a hard lump in my throat, I nod my agreement. In my mind, there is no other choice for me. I have to see it through with him.

Just eight days ago, Connor was nothing but "Dead Kid" to me. But I know the end is coming soon, it's going to be bad, and I allow myself a brief moment to envy Barb for the out she took.

Chapter 33

Two days later…

WHEN THE AUTOMATIC pump clicks off, I pull the nozzle out of the gas tank and return it to its holder. Fishing my wallet out of the back of my shorts, I open the driver's door to the Suburban and ask Jillian, "You want anything from inside?"

She's got her thick glasses on and her head bent over her art book, but she doesn't even bother looking at me. Just a slight shake of her head and a soft, "No thanks."

With a sigh, I shut the door and head in to grab me a coffee. I'm tired as fuck, but Jillian and I are anxious to get home. We know Connor's there and we don't want him to feel abandoned, so we're racing to get there. The first day we left Portland, I drove almost eleven hours to Salt Lake City. Jillian and I had collapsed into bed, utterly exhausted from the weight of our emotions.

The next day, I went even further, spending fifteen hours on the road and making it to the eastern side of Kansas City. We were still over fifteen hours from home, but one more day of hard driving isn't going to kill me.

Besides, I want to get Jillian back in her environment. She's been so fucking quiet since Barb died that it's wigging me out. I've tried to engage her, and she'll talk in short sentences. She's sleeping a lot in the car and not eating very much.

Last night, I tried to snap her out of it when we got into the hotel room. I realized tiptoeing around her wasn't going to work, so I told her point blank, "I need you to talk to me and tell me what's wrong."

It pissed her off. With flashing eyes and red cheeks, she said, "Well, I'm fucking sorry I'm being so quiet, Christopher. A friend of mine just committed suicide."

That pissed me off, and I—admittedly wrongly— told her, "Barb was no friend of yours. You two barely tolerated each other."

That was the wrong thing to fucking say for sure. Jillian's blue eyes filled with tears and her bottom lip quivered. "You're an asshole," she said quietly.

God, I was a total asshole. But I rectified it immediately by pulling her into my arms and laying down on the bed with her. I told her how sorry I was and whispered words of comfort, assuring her Barb was indeed our friend and that I was as confused and lost as she was. These words were all the truth, and she accepted them.

And then she admitted something to me that set me on my heels. "Seeing Barb there… dead and knowing she felt so alone that it was her only option… that was the darkest day of my life, Christopher. Even worse than when Kelly died, and way worse than when I got my diagnosis."

"How's that?" I asked in a raspy voice as my hands rubbed up and down her spine to soothe her. That was a pretty strong statement to make.

"Kelly dying was awful. She was my sister. My other half. But she was happy and had a fulfilled life. I think her calling was greater than what she served here on earth, and I know she's in a happier place. But Barb… she was so lonely, so afraid, and I was just starting to see her open up to us. I let my own goddamn optimism convince me that she'd be okay. That she would look at the bright side the way I always stupidly tell everyone to do. I spouted crazy shit to you about the hard truth about sunshine… that it's always there, you just have to see it in other ways, and I realize now that I couldn't have been more naive. I've learned that I really don't know anything at all about life, and I feel like such an idiot."

"You are not an idiot," I scolded her. Pulling back my face, I made sure she could look me in the eye. "It's your hopefulness… your belief that a good life is what we're handed but a great life is what we make of it… that made me open myself up to the possibility that I deserved more."

She shook her head, so mired in her own pity that she refused to accept acknowledgment of the gift she'd given me. "No... you had that within you already."

"Exactly," I tell her. "But I couldn't pull it out without you. Barb didn't have it in her. There are some people who can't be helped, baby."

Jillian didn't respond to me, but she did snuggle in closer. I continued to hold her and stroke her back until she fell asleep. I had hoped that maybe my words would penetrate, but she's as closed off as ever this morning. Now I'm getting worried. I'm not sure I can handle it if the woman who made me believe loses belief in herself.

Inside the gas station, I quickly grab a large cup of coffee and take it to the counter. I consider buying a pack of smokes, but I resist. I never did go out and get another pack after our talk with Connor in Portland, but I sure as hell wanted one. To say the last few days have been stressful is an understatement.

As the cashier rings me up and I hand over a five-dollar bill, I notice some colored tri-fold brochures. I pick one up out of the holder and examine it.

"Those tours are a lot of fun," the cashier says. "And the history is cool too... you know, if you're into that sort of thing."

I look up to him. "Oh yeah? Is it far away?"

"Nah... about half an hour northeast of here," he says, unknowingly giving me my chance.

I shove the brochure in my back pocket. "Maybe we'll give it a try. Thanks."

♦

"I DON'T UNDERSTAND why we're stopping here," Jillian practically whines.

"Because I've always wanted to do a cave tour," I lie. "It was too close to pass up."

Truth is, touring caves would probably be the last thing on my agenda. I'm slightly claustrophobic, and I sure as fuck don't like bats. But we need a break. A change of scenery. The long miles on the road coupled with grieving have left us in a very weird place. There's hardly any conversation, and I can't tell if we're running toward something or away from something, but whichever direction we're going, I'm feeling alone in my travels right now. We need to reconnect.

So we're going to take a little break on this hellacious drive home, and we're going to do something different. It might not be on either of our bucket lists, but we can have bragging rights after that we toured the historically significant Mark Twain Caves.

Jillian is either sulking or just doesn't have it in her to talk to me because she's completely quiet the entire time I sign us up for a tour. We congregate to watch an informational video first, then our tour guide brings us into the cave.

Interestingly enough, I actually kind of dig the tour. The passages are wider than I'd imagined and the place is well lit, so I don't even have a moment where I felt claustrophobic. I'll admit, I'm a little wigged out to learn that a mad doctor in the 1840s used the cave as a mausoleum for his deceased daughter, but past that, it was interesting to learn how Mark Twain wrote about the cave in *The Adventures of Tom Sawyer,* one of the few books I liked reading when I was in school.

Jillian listens to the guide intently and because the cave is dank and chilly, she presses up against me often. Our hands remain clasped the entire time. This I like very much, and I'm glad I decided to take this detour. We needed a bit of a stress reliever.

As the tour winds down, the guide—a young female, probably a college student working for the summer—stops and says, "Now, before I open this up for questions and answers, we have something a little fun we like to do."

With dramatic flourish, she points out that the cave has been outfitted with electricity to make walking through safe, but she asks us to imagine the days when Mark Twain would run through here as a little boy with only a fire torch to light the way.

"And imagine... being deep in the caves and your light goes out," she says ominously. And, with perfect timing, the overhead lights go out and we are plunged into absolute and complete darkness.

Several people gasp as it's disorienting, but Jillian actually lets out a pained cry that sounds like it ripped her chest open. As the tour guide drones on about finding the way out of a cave in the dark, Jillian's hand squeezes mine so hard I'm positive she's breaking bones. Her voice is nothing but pure panic when she whispers, "Christopher... I can't... I need out of here. Where's your lighter? I need light."

I can hear the tears in her voice, the hysteria vibrating off her. Jesus fucking Christ, Jillian is experiencing total blindness and for someone who will one day be blind, I bet it's completely freaking her the fuck out.

I slap at my pocket and realize I don't have my lighter because I'm not smoking anymore. Instead, I reach out and blindly wrap my arms around her, somehow managing to put my lips near her ears. I keep my voice low and reassuring, "Jillian... you're fine. This is just temporary. I'm right here, and I'm not going to let you go. Just close your eyes, take a deep breath in, and—"

The lights pop back on. I know we couldn't have been in the darkness any more than ten seconds, but it was about nine seconds longer than what Jillian could tolerate. My eyes squint against the sudden light, but they immediately adjust since we weren't in the dark that long. I can't stand the look of terror in Jillian's eyes when I look at her.

Taking her by the hand, I push my way through the group of tourists and walk out a door on the left side of the cave that's marked with a lit exit sign. We practically burst out into the Missouri summer sunshine, and I immediately turn to Jillian and place my hands on her shoulders.

"Are you okay?" I ask her with worry.

She nods but has to take a couple of deep breaths. "I'm sorry. That was just... really intense and scary as hell. I wasn't prepared for it."

I can imagine. Jillian and I had talked a lot about her medical condition that day on Cannon Beach so I could understand it. I was heartened to learn her blindness wouldn't be a complete blackout type of inability to see, but more of a blurred distortion that will make it impossible for her to see much other than large shapes or moving shadows. She would be legally blind one day, but it won't be blackness. And though she may not be able to see the actual shape and color of the sun, some of its miraculous light will be able to get through.

But still, there's no doubt that having her sight ripped away when she wasn't prepared for it, knowing it's her permanent destiny one day, shook her up and with good reason. I'm surprised Jillian's still standing on her feet.

"I'm sorry," I say as an afterthought. "I didn't even think they would do something like that."

"No, it's okay," she says, still a little breathless. Something that sounds like it may be a laugh comes from her, but then her face crumples and tears fill her eyes.

"Hey, hey... what's wrong, baby?" I say in a soothing tone as I bring my hands to her face. Other people are now walking out of the cave past us, but I pay them no mind.

"I'm an absolute mess," she says with a quavering voice. "I talk such a good game of being brave and optimistic that I almost believed my own hype."

"Jillian," I start to say consolingly, but she shakes her head.

"A few seconds of darkness and I freaked out," she says quietly, dropping her gaze from mine. "And do you know what was running through my mind?"

I shake my head, but she doesn't see me because she's looking at the ground, so I clear my throat and say, "What was running through your mind?"

"That I couldn't do this," she says with utter desolation. "That I cannot handle being blind. I don't want to lose my sight. It's not fair."

I use my palms to tilt her face back up, leaning down so we're staring eye to eye. "That's bullshit, Jillian. You can handle anything."

"No, I don't—"

"I said it's bullshit." This comes out forcefully and with firm resolve. She blinks at me in surprise. "Listen… it's okay if you want to sunshine your way through life and look on the bright side of things. And it's also okay if you get scared and think the world is falling in on you. You can have both. You can have moments of great confidence in yourself, and then moments where you're so low you don't think you can make it another day. But the one thing you can never do is give up the belief that it will all be okay. And you'll know it will all be okay because regardless if you're up or down, I'll be with you through it all."

Jillian's mouth falls open, her eyes filling with surprise. "You will?"

I don't answer her directly. Instead, I follow my heart because it is now completely wide open with all the amazing possibilities that could be my life if I have the courage to face it. "One day in the future, a long time from now when we're old and gray, someone will look at me and they'll note the way I look at you. You may not be able to see me, but they will. And they'll see that look on my face, and they'll be compelled to ask me, 'Christopher, do you remember the day you started to fall in love with Jillian?'."

"And what will you say?" Jillian asks on a whisper.

Leaning down, her face still held in my hand and a half, I brush my lips against hers. "I'll tell them the truth. That the process started for me on the very first day I met you. I'll never forget the radiance that you emanated from your sunshiny blonde hair, to your sweet, tender voice, to the way in which you clearly had room in your heart for everyone in that room."

"Even assholes like you?" she asks with a smile.

"Even assholes like me," I tell her and then I continue. "And I'll tell them that I kept falling in love with you during an amazing seven-day trip across the country where not even death could mar the perfectness of our time together."

"Wow," Jillian says in breathless wonder. "I did not know you had such poetic words in you."

"Neither did I," I tell her truthfully with a grin. "But I mean them. You've taught me so much in such a little bit of time, and I am so fucking lucky that you can see past the broken parts of me. You made me see that hope is a wonderful thing, and I want to work hard to turn those dreams into reality. Jillian, *you* were my bucket list and I didn't even know it."

"Christopher," Jillian says as she steps into me, breaking my hold on her face. She places her cheek on my chest and wraps her arms around my waist. "I know there was a time you didn't believe it, but I think you can accept it now. You're an easy man to love."

We stand like that for God knows how long. Her arms around my waist, mine tightly wound around her back. Her cheek on my chest, feeling my heart beat, and mine on the top of her head that was warmed by the summer sun.

I have no delusions that my life will now be all unicorns and rainbows. In fact, I anticipate Jillian and I will have tough times ahead as life continues to throw its curveballs at us. But my heart has been softened and my mind has been opened, and I've learned some important truths about myself.

A great gift has been bestowed upon me, and that is

the gift of life. What I choose to make of it is all on me, but I can lean on my friends when I need to. I also know not everyone can reap the rewards of the life that's been handed to them, and some will lose it along the way, intentional or not. Those losses will forever be etched upon my soul.

I choose to live.

I choose to love.

I choose to forge my path.

Life is my choice.

Epilogue

Four months later...

DEATH ISN'T PRETTY and because we loved Connor so much, it was uglier than normal. He held on for far longer than he should have, despite his parents begging and pleading his heavily drugged mind to just give up the fight and let go. Toward the end, he wasn't conscious. I'm not sure if he even knew we were there, but I'll never have a single fucking regret about Connor McCann being my friend, even though his loss was the most painful thing I've ever endured in my life.

Jillian and I spent every bit of our free time with him, and I think we've officially been adopted by Mr. and Mrs. McCann. We had movie sleepovers at Connor's house, and when he was well enough, we'd take weekend trips to the beach or the mountains. Day by day, his cancer grew, spread, and started to deteriorate the healthy parts of him. His body became skeletal because he had no appetite, and his skin turned an ashy gray. Before he started getting hardcore pain medications that kept him almost coma-like, he'd be so tired he'd fall asleep in the middle of a conversation.

But through it all, he always had that smile and his mischievous sense of humor that made it bearable.

As we stand in the cemetery under gray skies and a misting rain that makes the tip of my nose feel like ice, I suppress a spinal shiver that has everything to do with the frigid December weather and nothing to do with the fact I find death to be an abysmally ugly condition.

But this isn't our first rodeo—standing before a gravestone, I mean.

Grieving.

The McCanns generously buried Barb in the same cemetery, one plot over from Connor's so they can rest side by side. She had no family or friends. To prevent her from being buried a pauper by the state, well… I guess you can say the McCanns adopted her too.

I'll never forget the day I last spoke to Connor before he went under the deep sleep before death. He'd told me that he was confident Barb would be waiting for him on the other side, so I wasn't to worry about it.

I hope that's true.

As the minister talks about the afterlife over Connor's casket, my eyes cut to the left to look at Barb's headstone. While the McCanns paid for her burial, I paid for the headstone. I wanted to do something nice for Barb, and I hope she appreciates it. Otherwise, if anyone ever had the ability to come back and haunt me from the grave, it would be her.

Let's pray for the sun to shine its warmth upon us always,

So we never forget the hard truth of it.

Jillian came up with the epitaph for Barb's grave marker. It's followed simply by the words "Barbara H. Stiles. Our Friend."

Nothing more needed to be said. We chose not to put the years she lived beneath her name. Frankly, we think she stopped living the night her uncle first abused her.

Jillian squeezes my hand, and I look down at her.

"What are you thinking?" she asks softly.

"Whether Barb will haunt me at some point," I say.

Jillian gives a quiet laugh. "I think Connor will keep her under control."

God, I hope so. Standing here, among this plot of earth collecting souls and dried bones—my heart hurts for me, for her, for them—and I know I should feel some guilt because I'm the one who got a silver lining.

All thanks to the girl with the glass perpetually half full.

No… wait.

That's not right.

Jillian doesn't do half full. She's a brimming-to-capacity kind of woman.

My kind of woman.

I look back to Barb's headstone one more time and

read the beautiful words Jillian chose. They're poignant and mean so much to me. When she said them aloud all those months ago as we watched the sun come out after a dark rainstorm, I never thought they meant anything more than a basic tenet of Jillian Martel's philosophy on life. I never realized they would have a profound effect on me. To others, they would fall on deaf ears.

Still, there is no denying it.

Whether we all understood the importance of the truth she imparted, the words still hang around to haunt us.

Comfort us.

Lead us.

Whatever.

I try to focus in on what the minister is saying as we stand at Connor's graveside, but I really can't accept the peaceful words being offered. I've made my peace with him dying, just as I made my peace with Barb's suicide. They're both in a better place, as am I. In the end, I have to believe that all of us are happy now.

"Are you about ready?" Jillian asks as she squeezes my hand. I blink, noting that the casket is being lowered and people are coming up to say their final goodbyes. The McCanns are devastated as they accept condolences. Jillian and I will probably stay the night with them tonight so they won't be alone, but for now, she has to get to work.

Jillian started working at a pharmaceutical company,

doing customer service calls. It certainly doesn't have anything to do her degree, and it isn't what she wants to do with her life, but she's thrilled to actually have a real job that pays money and makes her independent. It was a tough process, but her parents finally loosened their claws and fearfully let Jillian spread her wings. That really means she flew to my apartment to live with me, although we'll get out of my dump as soon as the sublease is up. I also just started a job at a local CrossFit gym that specializes in people with disabilities. I started out there as a member, but I made such amazing strides getting my body in shape that the owner offered me a job as a trainer and a motivational coach.

Crazy, right?

But as I look down to the best thing that has ever happened to me, I know I can't doubt my abilities to pass on the same lessons that she taught me.

"Sure, let's get going," I tell her as I bring her hand up to rest in the crook of my arm. But before we leave and because I note the wetness on her cheeks, I lift my half hand to wipe the tears away with my scarred fingers. I give her a smile, and she returns it.

Just as we start to turn away from the grave, a warmth settles over the top of my head, almost like a comforting palm pressing down in reassurance. It only takes me a moment to realize that it's gotten incrementally brighter, and I raise my face up to see a parting of clouds in the overcast sky.

A sliver of Carolina blue sky struggles to expand outward, and then a blast of sunshine surges forth, hitting me so hard in the face I have to close my eyes against it.

It burns against my skin, and I can't help but smile.

This.

This right here.

It's the hard truth.

Acknowledgments

If you've read any of my books before this one, you know that *The Hard Truth About Sunshine* is a complete departure from the sexy romances I write. It's been over two years in the making, but I *had* to write this book.

You see... there was this thing that happened to me in the Orlando airport a few years ago that rattled the shit out of me. There was a young marine veteran sitting across from me that was waiting to board the same flight I was on. He'd lost a leg and part of a hand. He was heavily scarred. I noticed people staring at him and the seats to his left and right were empty.

Now, I am no stranger to military veterans. My dad is a Vietnam vet and was wounded in action. I was raised in a Marine Corps community. I've had dozens of friends serve and some who were wounded. I am also no stranger to people that have had catastrophic injuries. During my sixteen years of practicing law, I've represented more than my share of victims that have been maimed.

I am a deeply patriotic woman, and I never miss an opportunity to thank a veteran or an active duty soldier for their service to our country. It's almost an ingrained habit with me.

This marine veteran in the Orlando airport (and I

know he was a marine because he wore a scarlet t-shirt with the letters U.S.M.C. in gold) had been severely wounded. He still wore his hair in a "high and tight" so I had to assume he hadn't been medically discharged yet. Since he was flying to North Carolina, same as me, perhaps he was going back to his home base at Camp Lejeune. As I contemplated his service to our country and what he lost and what his back story may be, he stood up from his chair and walked around a little, perhaps just to stretch.

Perhaps to remove himself from the people staring.

I have no clue but he didn't go far.

I used that opportunity to get out of my seat and walk up to him, because I wanted to thank him for his sacrifice. He watched me approach warily but that didn't stop me from reaching my right hand out to offer a shake to his wounded one that was heavily scarred and missing some fingers. With a sincere smile I told him, "I just wanted to thank you for your service to our country" or something along those lines.

The young marine didn't take my hand. The first thing he offered me in return was a glare. The next was pure hostility when he snapped at me, "I don't need your thanks."

He turned around and walked away from me.

I was so stunned, I couldn't even move for a moment. I was embarrassed, because how many people just saw that? And admittedly, I was angry that he was so rude to me.

I thought about that marine over the next few weeks, trying to come to grips with his absolute right to not accept my thanks.

To be bitter, perhaps.

Angry over his circumstances.

Potentially suffering from severe PTSD. Or a whole slew of problems he may have been suffering that I couldn't see.

The conclusion I came to was the problem was with me, not the young veteran. I think I had fallen into this mindset where I tended to glorify military veterans. We see them walking through airports to cheers from strangers as they walk by. We read about heroic tales performed. We look up to them as inspiration and as role models for courage and bravery. We want to believe they do their job and are honored to make a sacrifice. Let's face it... they're almost like gods in our minds.

But I don't think I was even remotely close to understanding what really happens when a soldier returns home from war. I'm not naïve. I know about PTSD and the terrible rate of suicide among veterans. But those were just numbers to me. I hadn't thought really past that, and I had this belief that they needed to know they were appreciated.

In that airport, I encountered a man that wasn't just angry at me. I think he was angry at the world.

He didn't want my thanks or appreciation, and as I

researched more about wounded veterans and amputees and those that suffer from PTSD, I started to understand how significant the emotional trauma is.

I no longer think that veteran was rude to me, but only that he was not able to accept what I was offering at that moment. He was being true to himself.

I knew I had to write a story based on this experience to help me to continue to make sense of what our veterans go through.

I want to give special thanks to my beta readers, Lisa, Darlene, Janett, Beth and Karen for encouraging me on this book. Sorry I made you cry.

To my dad, for his service. Semper Fi, marine!

And to all those that serve with bravery, courage and honor, I truly do thank you for your sacrifices. It's important you know that an entire country relies on you and our safe existence is only possible with you protecting us.

If you enjoyed *The Hard Truth About Sunshine* as much as I enjoyed writing it, it would mean a lot for you to give me a review on your favorite retailer's website.

Connect with Sawyer online:

Website: www.sawyerbennett.com

Twitter: www.twitter.com/bennettbooks

Facebook: www.facebook.com/bennettbooks

To see Other Works by Sawyer Bennett, please visit her Book Page on her website.

About the Author

Since the release of her debut contemporary romance novel, Off Sides, in January 2013, Sawyer Bennett has released more than 30 books and has been featured on both the USA Today and New York Times bestseller lists on multiple occasions.

A reformed trial lawyer from North Carolina, Sawyer uses real life experience to create relatable, sexy stories that appeal to a wide array of readers. From new adult to erotic contemporary romance, Sawyer writes something for just about everyone.

Sawyer likes her Bloody Marys strong, her martinis dirty, and her heroes a combination of the two. When not bringing fictional romance to life, Sawyer is a chauffeur, stylist, chef, maid, and personal assistant to a very active toddler, as well as full-time servant to two adorably naughty dogs. She believes in the good of others, and that a bad day can be cured with a great work-out, cake, or a combination of the two.

73222974R00209